# GOLDIE

A **MAGIC+CITY WONDERS** NOVEL

## TAYLOR THOMAS SMYTHE

LAMPLIGHT
UNIVERSE

WEST PALM BEACH, FLORIDA

Cover design and interior layout by Taylor Thomas Smythe

Published by Lamplight Universe
ISBN: 978-1-959345-08-4

Lamplight Universe
West Palm Beach, FL

www.lamplightuniverse.com

In memory of
Grandma Nancy.

# MAGIC✦CITY WONDERS

## TIMELINE

**1980**

# GOLDIE

**1981**

COMING 2023

ALSO BY TAYLOR THOMAS SMYTHE


KINGDOM OF FLORIDA SERIES:
I. *The Golden Alligator*
II. *The Lamplight Society*
III. *The Place Beyond the Sea*
IV. *The Fountain of Youth*
V. *The Curse of Coronado*
VI. *Coral and the Treasure Hunters*
VII. *Guardians of the Willow*


MAGIC CITY WONDERS SERIES:
*Goldie*
*The Dream Team (Coming 2023)*


*More stories coming soon!*
*Visit* lamplightuniverse.com *for more.*

# Table of Contents

(continued)

(continued)

# GOLDIE

A

**MAGIC·CITY WONDERS**

NOVEL

# CHAPTER 1

*South Beach. Miami, Florida. Spring 1980.*

"Turn that racket down! I can't stand Michael Jackson."

Donna Locke nearly spilled the glass of fizzing Coke in her hand as she whipped around to glance across the counter at the woman who had made the disgruntled remark: an old, Jewish retiree who fanned herself with a menu and wore sunglasses the size of her face—though the shades did little to hide her annoyance.

Donna steadied herself and carefully set the cold, over-filled glass on the counter along with a straw fished out of her apron. She slid them toward the woman. "Who doesn't like *Michael Jackson?*"

"*I* don't," the old woman puffed over the music while she tore the straw from its paper sheath. "He's a heathen—and he's *too* loud!" She accentuated her words by jabbing the straw through a hollow ice cube. An ocean breeze through the diner's slatted windows ruffled her wispy white hair.

"What makes you think he's a, er, *heathen*, exactly?" Donna leaned on the counter impatiently and grabbed a menu-fan of her own while she waited for her bespectacled customer to finish a long, dramatic sip.

The lady set the soda aside and tipped her sunglasses up so Donna could finally gaze upon her drooping eyes. "The drums and the hips," she answered matter-of-factly. "Can't stand 'em!"

The weary waitress sighed, lowered the volume slightly on the nearby radio, and inspected a clock on the wall. It was late afternoon—nearing the end of Donna's shift.

Just then, the kitchen door swung open and a short woman with a graying, messy bun emerged. The smell of cigarette smoke hovered around her, an invisible cloud. "Afternoon, Miss Doris," she nodded to the old woman sipping soda. Then, without waiting for the retiree to answer, she shifted her attention to Donna. "Can you make sure the counter gets wiped down before you clock out?"

"Sure thing, Mary," replied the waitress. *Mary: somehow the name didn't seem to fit the woman's hardened appearance.*

"Thanks, hun." With a finger, Mary beckoned Donna to move closer to her—away from their contented customer—then muttered somewhat loudly: "Sorry to say it, but I'm going to have Louie open next week."

Donna ruffled her brow: "*Just* Louie?"

Mary sighed and nodded.

"But I've been on that shift for years!"

"'Fraid business just isn't as bustling as it used to be," the owner said apologetically. "You can keep the opening shift through this weekend."

Donna was about to raise her voice, then remembered Miss Doris was nearby. "I was counting on those hours," she said as calmly as she could muster. "I can barely make rent as it is—"

Mary held up a hand to cut her off. "If things get busy, I'll call." The woman turned and started for the kitchen again.

"And if anyone can't make a shift or calls out sick?" Donna called after her.

"You'll be the first to know." The weary diner owner flashed an empathetic smile and paused near the kitchen door. "You and Sondra... when your sister worked for me, she was the same way—always trying to take on every extra shift she could."

"I need the money," Donna stated, trying to sidestep the comparison to her older sibling.

Mary nodded. "I know, kid. Keep your chin up." The woman offered another faint but genuine smile before disappearing behind the swinging door.

Donna sighed and rested her back against the bar. After another quick wave of a menu, Donna set her makeshift fan aside and wiped a bead of sweat from her sun-freckled forehead with a deep sigh: "Are you eating anything today, Miss Doris?"

Doris rifled through a bag and slid a one-dollar bill across the counter. "That's all, Miss Locke. Keep the change."

The old woman returned to contentedly sipping her

ice-cold Coca-Cola. Donna rang up the order in the nearby register and exchanged the crinkled bill for thirty cents in change, which she double-counted before stuffing carefully into her apron pocket.

When she looked up a moment later, Donna thought she heard the faintest, high-pitched sound. *A siren?* She hurried to peer through the jalousie window and glanced down Ocean Drive, her wavy blonde mass of hair bouncing as she moved. Sure enough, the tell-tale red and blue lights were just barely visible at the end of the street. The siren grew louder.

"That your man?" Doris shouted from the counter.

Donna, surprised the old woman could hear the siren from so far away, strained to see if she could identify the driver of the invisible cop car. "Marcus is *not* my man," she replied definitively. "I mean, we've been on a break. But..." The vehicle came into view, close enough for Donna to just barely make out the distinctive Metro-Dade Police emblem on its side. "I think you might be right." Ahead of the car, though, was another vehicle—a dilapidated conversion van that weaved through the thickening seaside traffic, clearly doing its best to evade the diminutive Dodge and its blaring siren. The chase was on.

Donna hurried out the door and stood at the edge of the sidewalk curb, using her hand to shield her eyes from the fading golden sun rays. The oncoming vehicles zoomed in her direction, headed up South Beach's main drag. First, the van lumbered past with a violent honk, but it slowed as traffic halted ahead of it to make way for a group of elderly pedestrians inching their way across the narrow road. When Donna turned to look back down the street, she could finally see the driver of the cop car through its tinted window: it was Marcus.

"Marcus!" The young woman shouted and waved frantically to get his attention, while her wispy, wavy locks danced in a breezy mess around her face.

The police cruiser slowed—it had no choice at the moment—and its driver rolled the half-open window all the way down. The man inside wore a pair of Ray-Bans, a weary smile, and a loose-fitting linen shirt patterned with palm fronds.

"Oh, pardon me," Donna hollered in a sing-songy manner. "I thought you were a man in uniform."

"Undercover, ma'am," Marcus grinned. He stole a quick glance ahead to ensure the van hadn't yet got away.

"Then don't stop on account of me, officer," Donna pointed up the street. "Your man's getting away!"

The young officer nodded in the direction of the van, revving but trapped between stopped vehicles. "It's nearly rush hour. I think I can spare five seconds."

Donna held up five fingers. "Better make 'em count."

Marcus revved the engine as Donna folded her thumb.

"Four seconds."

"Dinner tonight?"

"Where?" Donna replied. She lowered another finger. "Three seconds."

"Frankie's?"

"Too far. Two seconds."

"Th-the Floridian?" Marcus stammered. The pedestrians were nearly across the crosswalk. The van started honking furiously to urge the car ahead of it to move.

"You bet!" Donna smiled and held up a single finger. "One second."

"See you at seven, Goldielocks!"

With a wink, Marcus pushed the gas pedal and sped off, leaving Donna in a gust of exhaust and wind. The woman shook her head and smiled.

A voice spoke from behind her: "Goldielocks?" It was Miss Doris. "You said he's not your man but you've got *nick*names for each other? Gimme a break."

Donna sighed and put her hands on her hips in a playful reprimand of the amusing old woman. "It's my stage name, Miss Doris."

Doris raised an eyebrow. "Stage! What stage?"

Donna's eyes grew wide. "Oh, gosh! The gig. I almost forgot!" Donna nearly stumbled back into the diner and Doris trailed her inside.

"Gig?"

Donna hurried behind the bar, untied her apron, and removed the change and cash she'd collected as tips. She briefly disappeared through a kitchen door then reappeared holding a small duffel bag with a zipper pocket, into which the frazzled woman placed her meager earnings. "I've got a gig at The Jade Lion." Donna shot a glance at the clock. "If

I'm not there in ten minutes that old weasel will dock my pay by half."

Miss Doris yanked off her sunglasses, revealing wide eyes. "And how on earth do you expect to make it to The Jade Lion in *ten* minutes? That's halfway across town!"

The blonde waitress unzipped the duffel and reached into it. Donna beamed and pulled out a pair of clunky inline skates, their neon wheels well-worn. Before Doris could reply, Donna scampered to the door, stepped outside, and crouched to strap on the skates. As she stood up, Donna had to take a moment to adjust. With her balance regained, the determined young woman slung the duffel over her arm and turned to Doris once more: "Wish me luck!"

The two exchanged hasty nods. Donna turned and began to roll toward the crosswalk. Ahead she could see Marcus' sirens. Over her shoulder, she heard Miss Doris shout one last exclamation: "Go get 'em, Goldielocks!"

"Myles, what's your twenty?" The voice crackled over the car's intercom.

Marcus Myles kept his eyes on the van ahead of him and wiped a splotch of sweat from his forehead. The air conditioning was broken and the waning South Florida summer sun beat oppressively on the outdated police car. "Tailing the suspect, moving north—just passed 8th Street."

"Roger," the voice replied. "Sending backup to try and cut him off."

A slow-moving sedan turned off a side road and placed itself squarely between Marcus and his quarry. With an impatient honk, the young cop swerved into the other lane then revved the engine to get past the sedan. Marcus narrowly avoided an oncoming rusted pickup as he settled back into the proper lane, now once more on the tail of the recklessly-driven van.

The van careened around a car that had stopped to pick up a sandy beachgoer, nicking the driver-side door as it cleared the vehicle. Marcus followed closely, managing to avoid the same cosmetic damage to his government-issued car. In the rearview mirror, he caught a look at the confounded expressions of the other car's owner inspecting the damage. In seconds, the civilians were long gone; the van accelerated as the way cleared before it.

They were nearing the end of South Beach's primary thoroughfare. Marcus pressed his foot to the gas, knowing he'd miss his shot to apprehend the van's driver if he didn't catch him soon. The old engine sputtered and struggled. The young officer placed a comforting hand on the dashboard as if to coax the poor old car into persistence.

The distance between Marcus and the old van was growing. Soon the suspect would be gone. With one last push, Marcus steered the car to sidestep a pedestrian and felt the car accelerate ever so slightly. Then, to his delight, he saw a glimmer of hope: at the end of the street, a half-dozen red and blue lights materialized from every direction. Backup had arrived. The van had nowhere to go.

No *roads*, anyway.

As quickly as his spirits had lifted, they drooped once more. Marcus watched in what seemed like slow motion as the grungy van took a hard right turn, jolting as it jumped over the curb and the sidewalk and zoomed across the serene lawn that separated the street from the beach.

"Myles—stay on him!"

Marcus scrambled for his walkie. "He's got nowhere to go, sir!"

"Do it, Myles!"

With a huff, Marcus dropped the intercom and sharply yanked the steering wheel. For a moment, it seemed that the car was floating as it bounced over the curb. Then—with an alarming *crash!*—the weathered vehicle planted all four of its wheels on the soft grass.

A group of sunbathers hurried out of the way. The van burst through the low coquina shell wall that served as a buffer between lawn and beach. As it was already moving so quickly, the impact of the wall seemed to do little to slow the van's forward trajectory. The tire treads dug into the sand and ascended the low dunes, crashing through a swath of infant mangroves.

"I don't believe it," Marcus muttered to himself as he dodged the stone rubble of the damaged wall. "This guy's crazy." The young officer cleared the top of the dune and realized his suspicions were correct: the van was headed directly toward the water.

The wheels of the van now began to sink into the wet

sand at the water's edge while the foamy tide reached toward the oncoming vehicle. A large wave rolled onto the beach, resulting in a massive splash as the suspect drove headlong into the sea. The van came to a stop, bobbing halfway under a few feet of the cloudy surf. The engine sputtered then turned off, drowned in saltwater.

Marcus brought his ride to a stop at the top of the dunes, swung open the driver-side door, then sprinted toward the van. He reached a hand toward the pistol at his side, casting a glance at the throng of curious citizens convening just a few meters away—no doubt waiting to witness the action that was sure to end up on Channel 4's six-o-clock news report.

Cautiously, Marcus sloshed up to his ankles in the luke-warm saltwater, keeping his back against the side of the van as he pulled his handgun from its holster. He glanced ahead at the driver-side mirror to study the suspect, but the heavi-ly-tinted windows obscured his view. *Drat.*

The waves lapped around his thighs. Marcus shouted: "Metro-Dade PD! Slowly exit the vehicle with your hands up!" No response. He couldn't tell what the suspect was doing—or if he was even moving. Officer Myles took a deep breath and reached for the door handle. *Locked!*

"Last chance!"

The gun clicked. Marcus aimed toward the door handle, then quickly raised the pistol to the corner of the window. A frantic shuffle inside affirmed that the suspect had seen him in the mirror. *Good.* The young officer turned his face away as he pulled the trigger. The window cracked and shattered into a million pieces. Marcus whipped around, smashed the remaining large fragments with his elbow, then thrust the pistol at the cowering man inside. With his other hand, he unlocked the door.

One of the man's hands was behind his back. Marcus' pulse fluttered. "Hands where I can see them," the young officer instructed as he moved the barrel of his handgun closer to the man's chest.

The suspect said nothing. His eyes were slightly blood-shot. *Coke?* Marcus caught a glistening on his cheek. *No. Tears. Or, maybe both: he's afraid to get caught.*

"I said, hands where I can see—"

Marcus heard the *click* of a gun in the man's hand. Instinc-tively, the officer withdrew his arm from the broken window and rolled against the side of the van—just in time! The gun fired. Marcus inhaled the mixture of gunpowder smoke and the salty mist that splashed at his legs. The next thing Marcus saw was a gun-wielding arm extending through the window, pointing toward him.

Thinking quickly, Marcus reached for the handle of the door and flung it wide open. The door caught the man's arm while loose crystals of broken glass dug into his flesh. The suspect's gun tumbled into the ocean water with a *plop*. Marcus fished it out then once again rose and confronted the man.

"Let's try this again, shall we?" Now, both of the man's hands were visible and he was unarmed. "Step out of the vehicle."

Cautiously, the suspect inched his way out of the van and stepped into the shallows. The man winced as he felt the sting of saltwater spray on his open wounds.

Marcus kept his weapon locked on the man: "What's in the van?"

No reply.

"I said," Marcus repeated, moving closer, "what do you have in the van?"

Before the officer could prod the man any further, both turned as they heard the shouts of a cadre of officers descending the beach. *Backup. About time.*

"You gonna tell me what's in the van or what?" Marcus was getting impatient with the man.

One of the other officers stepped into the shallows and opened the back doors of the van. With much effort, he managed to swing it open wide.

The officer seemed taken aback: "Uh, Myles, you see this?"

"I've been a little busy," quipped Marcus, his handgun still locked on the runaway.

"You're gonna wanna see this."

Marcus nodded for the suspect to walk toward the back of the van. With some hesitation, the man followed these unspoken orders and the two rounded the vehicle. Finally, they could view the cargo compartment: inside the van were stacks upon stacks of small plastic-wrapped packages—each a little smaller than a shoebox. One of the officers picked up a package and held it so all could see; on its top was a black marking—the symbol of a scorpion.

With a raised eyebrow, Marcus turned to the smuggler and asked him, "Who hired you?"

"No English! No English!" The man waved his hands frantically.

Impatient, Marcus holstered his gun and produced a pair of handcuffs then slapped them over the man's wrists. "You're under arrest, amigo."

# CHAPTER 2

Donna was unaccustomed to moving this fast on skates. All those years in the roller rink as a kid were surely worth something, however, for the woman miraculously maintained her balance as she dodged fire hydrants and café tables strewn across the too-narrow sidewalk. At one point, she nearly sailed into a couple walking hand-in-hand, but quickly reached for a stop sign to pull herself off the precarious trajectory.

Soon she reached a corner with a three-way signal and came to a stop. Waiting for her chance to cross, Donna glanced eastward across the street, where she saw deep, dirty trenches in the grass that had clearly been formed by the skidding tires of two vehicles. *Yikes. Marcus?* A flurry of police cars formed a makeshift barrier between the street and the grassy beachfront lawn. *He's probably fine. Right?*

The walk sign lit up and snapped Donna back to the

task at hand. She took off, moving one foot over the next as she picked up speed. She could feel the grit of beach sand sticking between the plastic wheels, but she had no time to stop for a cleaning. Still, the young and determined woman had enough forward momentum to propel her despite the granular resistance.

The sun was waning—and with it the oppressive heat. One by one the neon signs and Art Deco patterns lit up down the row, each hoping to draw in the weary beachgoers for an end-of-day drink or bite. Donna squinted and scanned the block ahead, recalling that the lights of The Jade Lion were on a faulty timer that would illuminate at precisely 5:44 p.m.—one minute before the deadline for her arrival. Her eyes zeroed in on a distant point down the street. *Still off—good.*

By now, the streets were filling with cars and pedestrians eager to get out on the town—those desiring to see and be seen. Occasionally, one might encounter a famous celebrity—like Burt Reynolds or Daliah Lavi, the latest to be glimpsed by the tabloids—or, if one was less fortunate, an infamous ringleader of a smuggling gang (though, the average civilian wouldn't know it, of course). Donna took a few quick breaths between the pumping of her legs and once again looked for the lights of The Jade Lion.

Then she saw it: the sign flickered on—first the rudimentary symbol that barely resembled the King of Beasts, then the name of the club in both English and Chinese characters.

*One minute!*

Donna hustled past a convenience store and a club, both of which were pumping out the latest hit from Pat Benatar, though the two tracks were out of sync just enough to make Donna wince at the sound as she wheeled by.

*One block to go. Forty seconds? Thirty?* Donna had lost count.

Quickly, Donna rolled into the alley as she reached the building and made a beeline for the side entrance. She pounded on the door three times then frantically began to unsnap the blades from her feet while she waited for a bouncer to answer. A moment later, the door creaked open, allowing a muffled, synthesized drum loop to escape. In the doorway stood a large man dressed in black.

"Can I help you?" His voice was gravelly and he barely moved his facial muscles.

Donna stood as she slipped the second skate from her foot. "I'm here for my gig," she said, still gasping to catch her breath. "I'm the singer—I'm on at six."

The imposing man produced a clipboard that appeared minuscule in his huge hands and studied it closely in the dim light. "Goldielocks?"

"That's me," Donna smiled. "This isn't my first time singing at The Jade Lion—"

The bouncer looked at his wristwatch. "It's 5:47—"

"And I don't go on 'til six," the woman chimed with haste, forcing a half-smile. "Good thing I got here early, huh?"

"Call time's 5:45," the man in black said with the straightest face imaginable. "You're late. Boss says to dock your pay by half."

"Half? Listen, buddy, my rent ain't gonna pay itself—"

"Get inside before he cuts you from the program." The huge man moved about an inch closer to the woman and whispered: "*No* one calls me 'buddy.'"

Without another word, Donna puffed, tied the laces of her skates together, then threw them and the duffel over her shoulder as she passed through the dim portal, which closed quietly behind her.

Though Donna knew her way to the dressing room, she followed the hulking bouncer down a narrow hallway. One wall was covered in square, glass bricks—the tell-tale sign of its 1930s construction date—which, during the daytime hours, would let in ample light while preserving an air of privacy. The pair rounded a corner and the man ushered Donna into the small room, where a fluorescent light flickered precariously on the brink of burnout.

"You'll have two thirty-minute sets with a fifteen-minute break between. No originals. Band's all ready." The man started to walk away, then added: "Be backstage at 5:58."

"That's awfully specific," Donna retorted, moving to close the door.

"Boss is awfully specific."

Without another word, the bouncer disappeared and Donna closed the dressing room door. With the utmost haste, she unzipped her duffel and began to change.

Marcus strongly disliked elevator music; it was far too subdued for his tastes. *Not enough drums.* Fancy restaurants always played elevator music—or something near enough to it. This was the main reason he had suggested the pizza place first—that and its casual, easygoing atmosphere—but he knew Donna would appreciate the gesture of an invitation to an establishment at the level of The Floridian—the latest in a string of new, hip restaurants that had sprouted up overlooking the beach. *And what better way to win back a woman's heart than with fine dining?*

"Will anyone be joining you, sir?" The maitre d' materialized, his stoic tone breaking Marcus' thoughts.

"Um," the young man checked his watch. *Ten after seven. Maybe she's just hit some traffic?* He had hurried over after wrapping some intake paperwork at the office and made a quick stop to freshen up at his place, but the traffic had *seemed* light enough, even taking into account the fact that Donna primarily utilized public transportation or her skates to get around. Marcus tapped a finger on the table before replying: "Let's give her five more minutes?"

The head waiter vanished to another table and Marcus leaned back in his chair with a sigh, taking another sip of his glass full of water and melting ice. From his vantage point, the young officer could see the door and the bustling nightlife on the beachwalk beyond it. There was no sign of Donna Locke.


"Ladies and gentlemen, wasn't she wonderful? Please give a round of applause for our very own Goldielocks!" The crowd erupted in cheers and the announcer glanced over his shoulder at Donna, adding disingenuously, "Voice of an angel, sweetheart." He was the sort of man where only half of his face smiled.

The beaming woman twirled in a short, sequined dress and took a half-bow. Though her set had consisted entirely of covers of popular hits, Donna reveled in the affirmation from the faceless crowd. The thrill of it! If *her* voice had moved them in some way, what more could she ask for? *And then there was the hope of fame and fortune—*

The half-smiling man gestured toward the side of the stage and followed Donna into the shadowy area out of view from the club's guests. Immediately, he opened one side of his jacket and removed an envelope from a large pocket. Inside was a wad of cash—five and ten dollar bills, mostly—which he quickly thumbed through before thrusting a few toward Donna. She received the cash and was about to count it when the man spoke.

"Twenty-five bucks," he said without making eye contact. The man folded the remaining bills and returned them to the envelope, which he promptly tucked into his coat.

Donna raised an eyebrow and crossed her arms. "That's it?"

The man replied, again without looking her in the eyes: "My associate tells me you were late."

The hulking bouncer from earlier appeared behind him, stepping into the dim light without a word.

"It was only a minute—!"

"*Two* minutes, boss," the bouncer corrected.

Finally, the boss met Donna's gaze and said with all

sincerity, "I have a *thing* with people being late." He took a step closer. Donna tried not to wince as she caught a whiff of some spiced meat on his breath. "I don't like it when people are late," he whispered hoarsely.

"B-but—"

The boss held up his pointer finger to interrupt her. "It's in the contract," he said with another half-faced smile. Slowly, he moved his raised hand toward Donna's shoulder. The woman tensed and her breaths became short. She was about to protest when he made a sudden *pluck* and moved his hand in front of their faces. Between his thumb and forefinger, the boss held a loose thread.

"Try to be a little more presentable, Goldielocks," he hissed. "The Jade Lion is a high-class establishment." With that, he pivoted and skulked into the darkness with his large friend.

*Maybe I could afford a new dress or two if you weren't such a cheapskate,* the defeated young singer wanted to shout as he walked away. But, realizing it would do her no good, Donna kept her thoughts to herself and slumped back to the green room to gather her things; she didn't bother to change out of the shimmering cocktail dress as she placed her newly-earned cash into the duffel's zipper pocket then began to strap her skates to her feet.

Donna rolled down the hall, where her eye caught a neon clock, and nearly tripped as she realized the time: it was already almost seven-thirty.

*Marcus!* Donna scrambled out the alleyway door into the

darkness. *If I hurry I can make it before...*

The woman had little time to finish her thought, for she now frantically pumped her way to the sidewalk and looked both directions before rolling across the street between two slow-moving cabs. It was a strange sight to be sure (what with the sequined dress and the chunky skates), but nothing out of the ordinary for Miami. The streets were full of revelers clad in the latest colorful ensembles—night owls just beginning to preen themselves and stretch their tired wings to the beats of disc jockeys and car horns alike—but Donna had little time to partake in such enjoyments as she hurtled herself between the passersby.

The Floridian was only a block away now, and Donna could see its vibrant glowing letters casting a pinkish glow on the sidewalk before it. For a moment, she rolled and swiveled to avoid a turning car, then hustled across the mouth of the side road. Glancing up to verify she was at the right establishment, Donna pressed her face up against the crystal-clear glass of the restaurant's front window to see inside. Through her slightly-squished vision, she scanned the large room. Even in the darkness, she could tell that none of the individuals inside was Marcus Myles.

Donna peeled her cheek from the window with a surprising amount of resistance on account of the humidity. The sticky feeling only made her more upset as she tightened a fist, bit down on her lip, and rolled slightly backward on her skates. Finally, with a deep breath, Donna lowered her head and began the long trek back home.

# CHAPTER 3

The next morning, the sun crept over the silent dunes as Donna punched in at the diner and slipped on her apron. A string of the usual customers—and a few disheveled clubgoers who had been out all night—kept her occupied and on her feet for the first couple hours of the day; by ten, her legs were aching and sore. *All that rollerblading...*

Around the time that the diner cleared out between breakfast and lunch, two peppy, sunkissed women with big hair waltzed through the door and scanned the small room. Donna caught a brief glimpse of the duo as she set a plate down for her only other present customers.

"Donna!" Both shouted in semi-unison, clearly excited to see her.

The young waitress finished with her table then gave each of the women a hug and a smile as she made her way behind the bar counter.

"You guys having anything today?" Donna asked.

"Two coffees?" said one of the pair—a redhead—checking with her counterpart.

The other woman nodded, her massive, permed dark hair bouncing as she bobbed her head: "Lots of cream and sugar with mine—it's the closest I'll get to café con leche at the Seaside Diner."

Donna pivoted and grabbed two heavy mugs from a shelf, which she promptly filled from an industrial-size coffee pot that had just finished brewing. She carefully slid the mugs toward the pair then leaned on the counter with her chin resting lazily on her hand.

"Girl, you look terrible," said the redhead as she took a hesitant sip from the steaming mug.

"Lisa!" Her companion chided playfully. "Is that any way to talk to our best friend?"

"What? Shouldn't a friend be upfront and honest?" Lisa retorted.

Donna chortled. "Sue has a point, Leese."

Sue, the dark-haired woman, tore the foil lid from a small packet of cream and dumped the contents into her coffee while she shook her head. "Right? I'm just saying, most people prefer a *compliment*."

"Sorry, Don." Lisa took another sip of coffee.

Donna grinned again and stood upright. "No, you're right—I had a crazy night."

The ladies gasped and nearly slammed their mugs down.

"With Officer Myles?" Sue asked.

"Sort of—"

"He invited you on another date after all those months on a break?" Lisa interrupted, continuing the interrogation.

"Well, yes, but—"

"Yes?" Both women clapped excitedly.

Sue leaned in: "*Do tell!*"

Donna rolled her eyes. "Yes, Marcus asked me on a date. But—"

"But!" Both echoed Donna loudly in unison, per their habit.

"I stood him up," Donna finished softly.

"Donna!" Lisa gasped. "Why on earth would you do something like that? Marcus is *totally* your soulmate."

Reaching for a damp cloth, Donna stepped to the side and began to wipe the counter, avoiding eye contact with the inquisitive pair of women. "It's embarrassing, actually."

"Spill it, Donna," Sue demanded.

The weary waitress heaved a deep breath and turned back to Sue and Lisa. "I was late," she explained reluctantly. "He asked me so quickly—in the middle of a high-speed chase, mind you. I forgot I had a gig at The Jade Lion, which I was late to—the dweeb at the club conned me out of half my pay, but that's another story—and I hurried as fast as I could but I was late *again* and—" Donna paused, took a breath, then added under her breath: "He probably thinks I hate him now."

Sue placed a gentle hand on Donna's and their eyes met. "You gotta stop working so much, hun—you're gonna miss out on more than just dates with hot cops."

"Believe me," Donna answered, "I wish I could just 'stop working,' but I'm barely scraping by as it is."

"What about your sister," Sue offered. "She's still in the area, right? Have you asked her for help?"

Donna shook her head vehemently. "I don't want her charity—and besides, Sondra and I aren't on good terms."

"Still? I thought you were working through that." Lisa gave a sympathetic tilt of her head.

"There's no 'working through' it because there's no communication. It's been years—I told you she had a kid, right?"

"That was ages ago, wasn't it?"

"Seven years!" Donna threw her hands up and raised her voice just a smidge louder than her employer preferred. She took a glance over her shoulder to make sure she hadn't ruffled any feathers, then added after a deep breath, "She refuses to let me see her—her daughter, I mean. Never even met the girl."

Neither Sue nor Lisa knew what to say but silently sipped on their drinks as Donna grabbed the coffee pot once more.

"Can I top you off?"

Both women nodded and Donna added a splash to each of their mugs before groggily returning to the lone table of customers in the corner.

When the blonde waitress rejoined her girlfriends, Sue seemed ready to burst.

"You alright, Sue?" Donna raised a skeptical eyebrow.

"I've got it!" The woman said, her eyes wide with a spark. "You could be a guinea pig!"

"A *what?*"

"A guinea pig," Sue said again. "You know, a *lab rat?*"

Donna rolled her eyes.

Lisa patted a hand on the counter: "She's serious, Donna. Pelican Innovations has those advertisements everywhere—I hear they pay well, too!"

Donna sighed slowly. "Pelican has advertisements *everywhere* because of that story that broke last month."

Sue perked up. "You mean the one about the lady who grew a third arm?"

All three laughed.

"You're right; I forgot—there was that rumor going around, too," Donna answered. "But I was referring to the one about the man that's missing."

Sue's jaw dropped. "Wait, I thought they found the body!"

Lisa gasped. "They *didn't?*" Both turned to Donna.

Someone outside the diner blared their car horn and held it for far too long.

When the commotion was finished, Donna leaned in close to the ladies. "All I'm saying is that I'm not desperate enough to farm out my organs for some psycho *experiment.*"

Lisa tilted her head toward Sue. "Well, can't say we didn't try." The woman rifled through a small handbag and fished out a couple of bills, which she slid across the bar.

"Leese, come on," Donna said. "It's on the house."

"I insist!" The red-haired woman placed the cash in Donna's hand. "It's the least we can do."

Donna gave a grateful nod while a diner patron raised a hand and began waving it to get her attention. Donna acknowledge the customer, then quickly turned back to the ladies. "Thank you," she mouthed, reaching out her hands affectionately. "Gotta get back to work. See you 'round?"

"For sure!" Sue flashed a scrunch-nosed smile and blew a kiss with a "mwah!"

Donna moved toward the table as the two friends departed, allowing a burst of salty air to drift through the door just enough to ruffle the young waitress' wispy blonde bangs. For a moment, she paused to glance at the little vignette of paradise framed by the slatted windows—palm trees, big hair, neon pink swimsuits, and all. Then, with a deep breath, Donna returned her attention to the mundane task at hand.

The boardroom was stark and modern, an award-winning design with a coveted, million-dollar view of both the bay and the Atlantic Ocean—cerulean waves undulating pleasantly in what looked like slow-motion from so many stories up. Angela Hyde couldn't help but allow her gaze to drift toward the idyllic scene, though its serene appearance couldn't have been farther from the knotted feeling inside her gut.

"What do you think, Angie?" A man's voice interrupted impatiently. It was the same voice that had been droning on for several minutes about quarterly deficits and a recent PR disaster. Angela turned to him, caught off guard, for it was rare for her to be called upon in such a meeting.

"Earth to Angie," the uninspired man chided when she didn't respond immediately. The rest of the men around the table chuckled to themselves—all of them dressed in expensive suits.

*It's Angela,* she wanted to say; but now was not the time or place. "I think," Angela said instead, drawing a deep breath, "that we can do better."

"Do better?" The director raised a skeptical eyebrow. "How so?"

"Well, all of this bad press focuses on what Pelican's doing *wrong,* right?" The men nodded hesitantly, as it was a question with an obvious answer. Angela continued: "I'm no public relations expert, but perhaps if we highlight all the *good* we're doing, we could shift the public's perception."

The director rolled his eyes and paced along one of the floor-to-ceiling windows. "That would be a simple solution if your department had something to show for all of the investor dollars that have been poured into it, Angie."

Angela's jaw dropped as she scanned the room, hoping someone would come to her department's defense. Or bring up the fact that nearly *every* division at Pelican Innovations had suffered losses in the last quarter. All of the men shifted uneasily in their seats, a few literally twiddling their thumbs to avoid eye contact. *So I—the lone woman in the room—get to be the scapegoat? Unbelievable.* Angela took a deep breath. "Innovation takes time... *and* money," was all she could think to say.

"Too much time," replied the director. He ceased his pacing and sauntered back to his tall swivel chair, where he placed his hands on the back and leaned forward slightly. "And too much money. Expect some significant cuts in budget and personnel in the coming days." He said it so matter-of-factly that Angela wasn't sure she knew the full gravity of the statement's implications.

The woman, frustrated, fumbled over her words: "R&D is understaffed as it is—"

The director interrupted. "We've all got to make sacrifices to keep this company afloat."

"We're on the verge of something *great* and—"

"I'll give you a week," he interjected again. "I don't *want* to hand Mr. Ducane a recommendation to restructure R&D under one of the more experienced department heads—" Here he gestured at the others around the table. "—but I will do what I have to in order to keep us from going under."

*Usually, the threats are more thickly-veiled,* Angela thought but said nothing. The woman took short breaths as the director continued.

"Well, I think that's enough for today." These words cued a frantic shuffling of papers and folders, a noisy soundtrack under the director's continued speech. "If anyone has any other brilliant suggestions, leave them with my secretary. See you next week."

Angela rose and made a beeline for the door; traffic bottlenecked as a few men stepped ahead of her without a word. One rubbed shoulders with her and muttered under his breath: "Good luck, Angie."

She gritted her teeth and allowed him to pass before issuing into the hallway.

*It's Angela.*

# CHAPTER 4

It was late when Donna rolled up to the apartment building, its half-illuminated sign buzzing with tiny moths. The whir of a struggling window-mounted air conditioner filled her ears as she skidded to a stop on her skates. The woman clomped the rest of the way up to the stairs, where she carefully ascended the steps with surprising balance. Finally, she coasted the remaining few feet down the open-air, second-floor walkway until she reached her door.

Donna flicked on the overhead lights as she entered the apartment. One of the fluorescent bulbs was burnt out, leaving a conspicuous shadow over the woman's faded blush-pink sofa. Donna ignored this—as she had for weeks—and took a seat, unstrapped the clunky blades from her feet, then stretched out her toes. She was about to lie down on the threadbare couch when her eye caught a blinking red light on the kitchen counter: the answering machine.

*That's odd.* It was a rare occasion for someone to take the time to leave *her* a message.

Slowly, Donna moved over to the counter and placed a finger on the large button. She pressed it down and a loud *click* prompted the playback of the message:

"Hello?" The voice was garbled and crackling, but Donna's heart leaped when she recognized it: "Morning, Donna. It's me, Marcus—Marcus Myles. You know, the same Marcus who somehow managed to get a table at The Floridian with*out* a dinner reservation?"

"Sorry!" Donna winced under her breath.

"I waited for you for half an hour," the voice of Marcus continued, "but, uh, they said I'd have to leave if I wasn't going to order anything, so I did."

The listener shook her head. *Ugh. How did I forget I had the gig?*

"Anyway, I just wanted to call and say that I was really looking forward to dinner, uh, with you." Donna could hear his smile. The man paused for a moment and became more somber. "But look, Donna: if you're not into this anymore, would you just tell me? I know we've both got a lot going on and if you've got, er, more important things—someone else, maybe—just say the word and we can call it quits—for good this time."

Donna hardly realized she was doing it, but she'd leaned closer to the answering machine as she listened.

"So I guess if I don't hear from you I'll know what that means." The voice became softer as he said these words then followed them with his phone number. At one point, she had it memorized, but the past few months apart had allowed his number to drift from her mind. Donna scribbled it down on the back of an old convenience store receipt—the only paper within arm's reach—and finished just as the machine beeped to signal the message's end.

Leaning against the laminate cabinets, Donna stared wistfully at the number in her hand. She took a deep breath and moved toward the phone. Just as her finger was about to type the first number in the sequence, the phone rang. The sound startled Donna, but her pulse quickened and she grabbed the receiver.

"Marcus, I'm sorry, I—"

A voice cut her off. "Is this Donna Locke?" It was a woman's voice.

Surprised and caught off guard, Donna replied, "Y-yes, this is she. And... who am I speaking to?"

"My name's Dierdre," the woman on the other end of the line replied. Donna couldn't recall having any friends or acquaintances by that name. As Donna thumbed through her mental list of connections, the voice continued. "I'm with Saint Mary's."

"The hospital?" Donna's eyebrows narrowed. "But I don't—"

"There's been an, um, accident," Dierdre shared, clearly searching for the most tactful way to relay the news.

*Could something have happened to Marcus? Or the girls?*

Donna's speculation ended with the words that came

next: "It's your sister."

"Sondra?" Donna asked, though she had only one sister.

"Yes," the nurse verified.

"I think there must be some sort of mistake; we haven't spoken in years and I—"

Once again, Dierdre interrupted, an urgency in her voice: "You were listed as her emergency contact. You need to get over here as soon as possible."

*Emergency... Sondra... an accident...* Donna's focus narrowed as the nurse's words echoed in her mind. Then her thoughts shifted. "Sondra has a daughter," Donna stuttered. "Is she...?"

"The staff will fill you in when you arrive."

It was not the answer she was looking for, but Donna nodded and slowly replaced the receiver on its base as if she was in some sort of trance.

*Fill me in?* She had so many questions. The most pressing was: *What's the fastest way to get to the hospital?* Donna checked the clock. She could catch a bus, but she'd have to hurry. With only a small handbag, Donna scurried out the door, wondering what was in store.


Saint Mary's General Hospital was about a fifteen-minute drive by car, but public transit multiplied the commute. It was nearly midnight when Donna entered through the sliding glass doors and scrambled to the check-in counter. The waiting room, decorated with strips of fading nautical wallpaper pulled from a watercolor assembly line, emanated a surprisingly calm atmosphere—but Donna's heart hadn't stopped racing since she had picked up the phone.

A tired nurse in wrinkled scrubs lifted her eyes just enough to signal her awareness of Donna's presence. "Name?" The beginning of the usual script—she'd probably said it four hundred times that day.

"Locke," Donna replied quickly.

The nurse scanned a clipboard then looked up. "No one by that name here, hun," she said.

"Oh, *my* name's Locke" Donna clarified. "Donna Locke. I'm here to see my, er, sister: Sondra Gordon."

Immediately, the nurse's disposition changed. "Ah, I'm sorry, Miss Locke. Miss Gordon's in room 108—just through those double doors." She handed an ID badge across the desk with a sympathetic half-smile and pointed around the corner. "You can go right in."

Donna nodded politely and slinked down the brightly-lit hallway. She inspected the numbered door plaques to confirm that she was indeed headed the right way, glancing at weary patients through the open doors, until she finally arrived at room 108. The door was open just a crack and Donna heard voices inside. She gave a light knock as she pushed on the heavy door.

"Hello?" Donna peered inside and the voices stopped.

The bed was situated on the far wall, so Donna could see her sister's weathered face as soon as she rounded the corner. Sondra appeared to be sleeping and was surrounded by a mess of tubes and cords that ran to large, gray machines all around her. Next to the bed, a tiny child was curled up in a mint-green, faux-leather armchair, her wavy reddish hair covering her face. Two other women stood at the foot of the bed.

One of the pair whispered and they both turned toward Donna.

The first woman, who wore glasses and a white coat, extended her hand and spoke in hushed tones: "You must be Donna. I'm Dr. Morena." Donna shook her hand somewhat limply and glanced at the other woman, who was clad in a gray blazer. "And this is Elizabeth from Social Services."

Donna acknowledged her with a quizzical look but quickly returned her focus to the doctor. "What happened to her?"

"Well, we don't quite have the full picture yet," the doctor began hesitantly. "We likely won't until she wakes from the coma. For now, her vitals are stable and—"

*Did she say "coma?"* Donna began to drift again, her eyes turning to Sondra's expression—pale, devoid of emotion, cold. They were the sorts of descriptors Sondra had taken on in Donna's mind since they'd last spoken, but now they had become all too literal.

"—we aren't sure how long she'll be under," the doctor continued with Donna only half-listening, "which is why we'll need to discuss options for custody in the meantime—"

Donna snapped out of her thoughts: "Custody?"

Elizabeth from Social Services nodded slowly, sensitive to the recent arrival's tone of concern. "Sondra was her sole caretaker." She gestured toward the slumbering girl.

*Caretaker? Coma? Custody?* It was so much all at once. Donna turned to the sleeping child on the green chair. "I think there's been some sort of misunderstanding here," the blonde woman said as tears began to well up in the corners of her eyes. She waved her hands in front of her. "Sondra and I—my *sister* and I were *not* close. And I don't think this is something she would want if she could talk to us right now—she never let me near the kid."

The social worker nodded. "It's a tough situation for everyone involved," she affirmed. "But *legally* she's supposed to go to you, Miss Locke."

"*Legally,*" Donna repeated, her mouth agape. "I can't do this right now—I can barely afford to pay my own bills, let alone a child. I-I don't even know her name!"

There was a moment of silence as the reality of the situation sunk in.

"Starla," Elizabeth muttered. "Her name is Starla."

Donna observed the small, sleeping girl once more. She seemed unaware of the gravity of the circumstances happening around her—the only one in the room who looked content, at peace.

The frazzled woman knew it was useless to protest. Besides, Donna mused, any animosity she had was with *Sondra,* not her daughter. With a deep breath, she returned her attention to the two women standing in the middle of the room and nodded slowly. "Alright," she said. "But you'll let me know the minute she wakes up?"

The doctor nodded her confirmation. "We'll call you if

anything changes with her situation."

Donna thanked her as the social worker handed her a bag of the little girl's possessions. She looked wistfully at the small child and took a deep breath.

# CHAPTER 5

Pelican's research laboratories were located in an interi-
or section of its huge headquarters that had no windows;
even if it wasn't nighttime, it still would have been just
as dark as Angela Hyde emerged from the elevator and
waltzed through a shadowy waiting room. A collection of
motion sensors triggered a series of lights that turned on as
she walked down a narrow hall until she came to a stop at
a locked set of double doors. The woman typed an access
code onto a keypad with glowing buttons. The door clicked
open. A dim bluish light emanated from between the gap,
and Angela disappeared inside.

The lab was cluttered and humming with the sounds
of room-sized supercomputers, bubbling beakers, and the
faintest buzz of a blacklight bulb. When Angela's eyes
finally adjusted to the light, she scanned the room. A slight
motion at a lab table on the far side of the room caught her

attention and she slowly moved toward it.

A young man—in his early thirties—hunched over a row of glass vials into which he carefully inserted a couple drops of liquid from a pipette, one-by-one down the lineup. He crouched patiently with the cylinders at eye level. His bespectacled gaze flitted from one to the next, but he appeared perplexed.

"What's wrong, doctor?" Angela asked, startling the man so that he nearly lost his balance.

"Oh! Angela," he stuttered and rose to his full height. "I didn't hear you come in."

The woman hurried past the pleasantries and inspected the vials for herself. "Please tell me you've got something to show for all this, Roger?"

Dr. Roger Lansing had been working on the project for years, building on a half-decade of prior research before he landed the coveted Pelican job. He avoided eye contact with Angela as he explained: "Well, er, I've made many break-throughs over the past several months, though the most significant were in the last few weeks and—"

"Roger!" Angela glared. "I know when you're lying to me." She waved a sharp finger as if drawing an invisible circle around his face: "*This* is what it looks like. Now tell me if we've got a reason to keep our jobs."

Dr. Lansing was silent for a moment then slowly brought his eyes to meet Angela's. He slid his large glasses tighter to his face then shook his head solemnly.

"Do you *know* what's at stake?" The woman said,

raising her voice slightly. "How much I've poured into this company—into *us*—the sacrifices I've made?"

Roger thought he saw a tear forming at the edge of the woman's eye, but it was too dim to tell. "Sorry, Angie, but replicating a formula for which I don't know the original source isn't the easiest—"

"*Angela*," she interjected through gritted teeth. "Sorry. I told you: it's *Angela* now. Or Miss Hyde, if you prefer."

"Angela's fine," said the nervous doctor. "We're so close!"

"We have one week."

The doctor gasped. "The effects vary too much based on the subject—and it doesn't help that the man upstairs won't answer our questions. We're just not *that* close."

"You *have* to be that close," said Angela, moving closer to the man. "Figure out what you need to make it work and get some test subjects in here. I need the final, *positive* report to my desk before the board meeting."

The young doctor tried to protest: "But the ethics of testing on humans before—"

Angela put up a hand to interrupt. "Public relations can worry about the ethics; I need *you* to work a miracle. Anything to prove that this hasn't all been a waste. This is my last chance—*our* last chance."

Both were silent for a moment, then Angela moved toward the door. She opened it slowly, paused, then finally turned back and said in a loud voice over the thrumming machines: "One week, doctor." Angela left the lab.

The weary scientist took a deep breath.

*She's asking for the impossible.*

In another part of the city, in another darkened building, Officer Marcus Myles peered through the one-way mirror that separated him from his recently-apprehended suspect. The man on the other side of the window was hand-cuffed to a small table that was secured to the floor in the center of the room. His greasy black hair covered his eyes as he hung his weary head. The only other contents of the interrogation room were two chairs—the one under the suspect and another on the opposite side of the table.

"Has he said anything?" Marcus turned to the neatly-trimmed officer at his side.

The second officer ran a hand through his slick, black hair: "Not a peep since you brought him in last night."

Marcus breathed deeply. "You wanna be the tough guy today, Castillo?" Officer Myles turned back to the hunched man in front of them.

"Think you'd better do the honors," replied Officer Rico Castillo. "Something tells me he'll respond better to my sweet-talking if it's in our native tongue."

"Whatever you say, amigo," Marcus smiled, adjusted his loose-fitting button-down leisure shirt, and moved toward the small door around the corner to enter the room. Rico held out an arm to stop him.

"Just make sure you keep your cool," Rico reminded him with a brow raised in concern. "You know things have been getting pretty dicey with these kinds of cases sprouting up all over the county. Situation's got us under the microscope." For the past few months, the whole division had been on high alert as new drug smuggling rings seemed to crop up every other day. In certain parts of the city, one could feel the pressure rising—about to boil over.

Marcus took a deep breath and nodded his understanding, then continued around the corner. He pressed a button and, after hearing a quick buzzing sound, swung open the door and sauntered in.

A single light placed directly over the table was all that illuminated the sparse room. Marcus emerged from the shadows and pulled the empty chair toward him. It grated along the hard floor as he flipped it around and sat with his arms crossed comfortably over the back of the chair—like all of the tough TV cops did.

The suspect with greasy hair didn't look up or acknowledge Officer Myles' entrance. Marcus flashed his badge as he introduced himself, but the man paid no attention.

"I'm Officer Marcus Myles. What's your name?" Marcus asked calmly.

The man across the table didn't reply but took a short breath.

"Hello—anybody home?" The young officer craned his head to try and make eye contact, but the suspect kept his eyes lowered. "Anybody en la casa?"

Again, the man took quick breaths but made no answer.

"You know, this will go a lot better if you respond." Marcus looked across the table at the man's cuffed hands. His right forearm featured a simple, black tattoo—a line-drawing of a familiar emblem: a scorpion. The officer recalled the same icon found on the confiscated paraphernalia the prior day: "What does the scorpion mean?"

Suddenly, the suspect's eyes flitted up toward Marcus then back to the ground—wide open and unblinking. *The signature tell of a person who's hiding something,* Marcus thought. *But he's just told me plenty.*

The officer leaned in. "The scorpion," he repeated. "It obviously means something to you. What is it?"

The man across the table trembled and again refused eye contact or speech.

Marcus slammed his hand on the cool metallic table and raised his voice, startling the man so that he winced: "What does it mean?"

"No English!" The suspect pleaded as Marcus leaned and grabbed the thin chain links that fastened the man to the table. "No English," he repeated a few more times, tears beginning to well at the edges of his eyes.

With a sharp exhale, Officer Myles released his grip on the man's cuffs and stood, stepping away from the table. "No English, eh? You're in luck."

Marcus moved into the shadows once more and rapped on the door to the interrogation room. A moment later, it buzzed and the young officer swung open the door to return to his partner.

"How was that?" Marcus asked with a smile.

Rico shook his head. "They should give you an Oscar,"

he grinned. "And good call on the whole *scorpion* thing. I think I can work him."

Officer Castillo made his way into the confined room and situated himself across from the subject. Everything about his demeanor and posture implied a greater sense of calm to the suspect than his predecessor—*all part of the act.*

Marcus watched from the other side of the glass, his face only inches from it. He turned a dial to increase the volume of the real-time audio being fed through a crackling, outdated speaker.

"Hola," Rico began his introduction in Spanish. "Me llamo Enrico Castillo. Lo siento por mi compañero."

*Sorry about my partner,* Marcus made a mental translation. He had no formal language lessons to speak of, but growing up in Miami meant that he'd picked up enough Spanish to understand most words—if not converse at a basic level.

"Nosotros estamos con la Policía de Metro-Dade y necesitamos que nos digas algunas cosas. ¿Puedes hacer eso?"

*We're with Metro-Dade and we need you to tell us a few things. Can you do that?* The officer spoke tenderly and awaited a nod or word of confirmation.

The suspect finally inched his chin up and nodded.

"Bueno," Officer Castillo smiled. "Entonces, ¿como te llamas?"

His lips were parched and cracked. "Hector," the man whimpered his name.

Castillo nodded and continued in Spanish: "Nice to meet you, Hector. Now, I just need you to tell me about the scorpion—and who you work for—then we can move on. It's already half-past ten and we'd all like to be done with this."

"Diez!" *Ten!* The suspect's eyes shot wide, as if he had a recollection. His eyes darted around the room suddenly, looking for a clock on the walls.

Castillo bent forward and raised an eyebrow.

Hector lowered his gaze and shook his head. "Voy tarde," he muttered to himself, almost a whisper.

The officer raised an eyebrow. "You're late? What do you mean?" Rico turned toward the glass, imagining Marcus matching his look of confusion, then turned back.

"Voy tarde," Hector repeated in Spanish, putting his head between his tightly-cuffed hands. "Oh, no, voy a llegar tarde."

"Late for what?" The officer across the table asked as calmly as he could.

"Él me va a matar," the man finally returned a fearful, wide-eyed gaze to the officer. "Si no estoy allí a las once, me destrozará." *If I'm not there at eleven, he'll kill me.*

*Fifteen minutes from now.* "Who? *Who* will kill you?"

"No sé," Hector mumbled. "Nunca lo vi." *I never saw him.*

Officer Castillo breathed deeply through his nose: "¿Dónde?" *Where?*

Hector shut his mouth and shook his head.

"It's okay," Castillo spoke in Spanish and offered a comforting gesture. "Tell me *where* you're meeting him and we'll make sure he doesn't touch you."

As tears streamed down his cheeks, Hector nodded, took a deep breath, then spoke. "Isla Dodge—el lado este." *Dodge*

*Island—east end.*

Quickly, Rico thanked the man and Marcus buzzed him back through the door.

"They get that van working?" Castillo asked as the door closed behind him.

Marcus nodded. "Mostly," he said, already headed toward the exit.

Castillo grabbed him by the shoulder and he turned. "Mostly?"

"It runs," Marcus assured him. "And they fixed the broken window. Come on!"

"If we're going undercover, shouldn't we make sure—?"

Marcus shook his head as they rounded a corner. "No time," he said, busting through a door into a large ware-house-like room. "You're driving," Marcus instructed, grabbing a set of keys from a pegboard on the wall. As they headed toward the van, Marcus passed the evidence lockers and snagged a black marker and a kilo of the scorpion-branded contraband they'd originally found in the vehicle. "Gotta make this look convincing," he noted with a smile.

The two men quickly piled into the confiscated conversion van. Time was ticking.

# CHAPTER 6

The beat-up van rumbled over the elevated roadway that served as the only bridge to the small, man-made mass known as Dodge Island. *Smart move*, Marcus thought as Rico steered the vehicle away from the mainland. *Easy to keep watch on the comings and goings when all traffic is squeezed through this one pass.* The officers slowed as they watched the downtown skyline shrink in the rearview mirror.

"Get down," Officer Castillo instructed as they neared the island and a conspicuous black car came into view. "Hector was the only one driving when you caught him, right?" Marcus nodded, unbuckled, and shuffled low between the front seats.

From behind the driver's seat, Officer Myles gestured toward the car. "Slow, but don't stop," he said. "It's one of them."

"One of *us* for the moment," Castillo smirked. He maintained his speed and only reduced it slightly as they passed by the dark vehicle, which resembled a squad car except for the fact that it had no markings and its windows were more heavily tinted. A man in a black shirt and a thick mustache glared through his one lowered window.

With a gulp, Castillo waved and smiled.

"Ditch the grin!" Marcus whispered shrilly as the van drifted past. "These are smugglers, not the circus."

"What's the difference?" Castillo said with a playful tap to his partner's shoulder, but Marcus held his breath and pressed himself further into the shadow of the front seats. The man in the black car rolled up his window slowly and the van continued on to the island.

Both officers breathed sighs of relief as they rolled onto the island's main through-road that neatly bisected its north and south halves. The island itself primarily consisted of docks for cruise ships and freighters, while a swath of shipping containers dotted the easternmost edge. At present, there was little activity—*the perfect backdrop for a shady rendezvous*, Marcus thought as he popped his head up high enough to look over the dashboard.

Sinking back out of view once more, Marcus unsheathed the black marker he'd snagged from the station. "Let me see your arm," he said to his partner.

Castillo smelled the pungent odor of the semi-permanent marker and crinkled his nose: "My arm?"

"Hector had a black scorpion tattoo on his right arm," Marcus said as he tried to steady his hand while the van bumped along the road.

"So you're drawing one in Sharpie?" Castillo shook his head in disbelief, "In a moving vehicle, no less!"

"Hold still!" Marcus compared his hurried progress to the design on the wrapped kilo. "If they get close, we're busted."

Castillo's eyebrows jumped. "Busted? This is crazy, Marcus!"

"Relax," replied the other officer. "I took an art class in high school."

"An art class? As in *one, single* art class?" Rico puffed as he felt the cold marker tip snake along his forearm.

With part of his tongue pressed between his lips in a state of focus, Marcus placed the finishing touches on the ink drawing on Castillo's skin. "All done! Like I said, just don't get too close and you'll be fine." There was a hint of doubt in Marcus' voice as he capped the marker and breathed in deep.

At that moment, they reached the shipping yard on the island's east side. Large, durable containers were stacked on top of each other, forming a maze of corrugated trailers that towered into the sky. Castillo brought the van through one of these narrow fissures and allowed the vehicle to idle while the two men scanned the area before them. The isle was surrounded by Biscayne Bay, the body of water which flowed into the Atlantic beyond. From the van's position, a few smaller islands could be seen in the distance—even darker splotches on an almost pitch-black horizon.

Marcus checked the time: "Ten fifty-nine." *Phew.*

Castillo moved his right arm to wipe a bead of sweat from his forehead, but Marcus grabbed his wrist. "Careful!" He said, reminding him of the imitation tattoo. "You'll smudge this masterpiece."

"Sorry—just a habit," the other officer replied, using the back of his left arm to mop the sweat instead. Officer Castillo was shaking: "Tell me something to get my mind off all the ways this could go south."

From his squatting position on the floor of the van, Marcus breathed deeply and searched for something to say. "I, uh, had a date last night," the young officer offered.

Castillo's pulse slowed a little. "A date, eh? With Donna?"

"Yeah," Marcus answered quietly. "I *had* a date, but she stood me up. *And* she didn't return my call this morning."

"Donna?" Officer Castillo raised an eyebrow. "I'm sorry, man. My sister's known her for *years* and she said she thought Donna was right for you and, frankly, I did, too but—"

Suddenly, Rico went silent as a burst of light appeared ahead. Two lights, actually—the twin, circular headlights of a diminutive sportscar near the water's edge. The clock on the dash ticked the time: 11:00.

Instinctively, Marcus ducked lower. "They see you," he whispered. "Stay calm."

"I *am* calm," replied Castillo, tapping his fingers on the back of the steering wheel. "What do I do?"

"Flash your lights back," suggested the other officer.

Officer Castillo complied, clicking the van's brights on for a second.

The sportscar revved its engine, then slowly rolled across the expanse of concrete toward their place in the shadows. As it neared, Castillo recognized the classic look of the vehicle. "He's driving a Porsche Nine-Eleven," he muttered to Marcus with a tone of admiration.

"Should I have expected anything less from a drug dealer?" Marcus joked quietly. "Let me guess: it's cherry red?"

"Yep." Castillo's answer was short, as the car now drew closer. He motioned with his lowered right hand for Marcus to move further behind the seat.

Finally, with its lights out, the polished red Porsche wheeled next to the decrepit van and rolled down its window. With a gulp, Castillo did the same—only halfway, though, to obscure the view inside as much as possible.

From the void of the car's small front compartment, a face appeared. It was no human's face, however; it was a mask, covered in scales to resemble a deep-scarlet dragon. When its eyes locked on Castillo, the masked head cocked slightly. A gravelly voice spoke: "You're different than they described."

Castillo tried not to show his fear as he scrambled for an answer. Then he remembered their suspect, Hector, and his long, greasy shag. "I-I had a haircut," was all that came out. *Haircut? Castillo, you idiot!*

The man in the dragon mask seemed to be studying the neatly-trimmed officer to make a judgment of his statement's veracity. Officer Castillo heard the *click* of a handgun and immediately tensed. Sure, he had his own pistol in the glove compartment, Castillo reasoned, but he couldn't reach it without blowing his cover.

"They said you'd bear the mark on your right arm," the man spoke hoarsely.

Castillo nodded and glanced down at his arm—with a quick flit of eye contact to Marcus—then raised it so the man could see the crudely-drawn scorpion. *This had better work.*

What felt like several seconds passed before the mysterious man said anything. Finally, he seemed satisfied. "Let me see it," the masked man ordered.

Castillo was about to stutter out another reply when the man added:

"The delivery. Let me see it."

The officer nodded slowly. *Marcus!* If he opened the back doors, the man was sure to see him—and the lack of precious contraband. Then the ruse would be over. He had no choice—the masked man clicked open his door and approached the van with the gun held at his side, leaving the tiny red car running. He wore a tailored, burgundy suit and stark-white gloves. "You *do* have the delivery, don't you?" The dragon-masked man raised the gun and held it close to his own chest so Castillo could see it clearly—a threatening move to apply more pressure to the nervous van driver.

Castillo nodded again, somewhat aggressively, and took a deep breath. "Of course," he sputtered. "It's in the back." Then he nodded to the driver-side door as if to ask permission: "I can show you."

The man with the dragon mask waved the gun toward the back and nodded. Castillo looked down at his glove compartment for a moment, then out of the corner of his eye glanced toward Marcus as if to warn him. Finally, he pulled the keys out of the ignition. He clicked open the driver-side door and stepped out. As he did, he stammered: "After you."

To Rico's surprise, the man took him up on the offer and slowly sauntered around the van. With him trailing behind the masked man from a safe distance, he flipped through scenarios in his head—of what would happen when the man discovered Marcus in the back. Castillo kept his right arm—and the false tattoo—as close to his side as possible. He could feel his armpits moistening, and a drip of perspiration trailed down the back of his arm. *Stay calm. Stay calm!*

As they reached the back of the van, the masked man tried the handle. It was locked. "Open it," he demanded with little change in inflection.

Officer Castillo nodded and fumbled around in his pocket for the keys while the man in the mask stepped away and surveyed the waterfront. Bits and pieces of a lively Latin dance track echoed over the lapping waves only a few meters away, but otherwise, the island seemed quiet and tranquil—besides the thumping of Castillo's heart as he inserted the key slowly and unlatched the vehicle's door with its heavily-tinted windows. With a deep breath, the young man pulled open the right-side door just a crack.

The officer peered into the small opening and felt around the floor of the van, trying to stall. To his surprise, his fingers came to rest on a small rectangular package. *Phew!* Marcus had slid the kilo of contraband across the floor. Castillo carefully withdrew his left arm from the shadows, held it out for the contact to receive, and shut the door behind him.

The man hesitantly holstered his gun, then grabbed the

package quickly and turned it over in his gloved hands.

"The rest is yours once I get payment," Castillo said with haste, hoping there wasn't a special arrangement he wasn't privy to.

The dragon mask returned a blank stare—unflinching and quite terrifying, Castillo thought—then inspected the kilo once more. The man seemed ready to speak again when he paused and held out one of his hands. Castillo followed his gaze. There on the tip of his gloved pointer finger was an inky, black smudge.

The officer instinctively nestled his right arm closer to his body, obscuring his sweaty forearm.

"Show me the mark." The masked man hissed.

Castillo's breaths were short, but he kept his arm hidden from view. "I, uh, already showed it to you and I—"

The officer stopped mid-sentence as the masked man reached toward the holstered gun with his free hand. He slowly removed and pointed it at Castillo, who took a half-step back.

"Woah woah woah!" The officer threw his arms up above his head, revealing the blurry, muddled scorpion. As the gun moved closer to his heart, Castillo trembled. *Marcus: do something!*

"Who are you?" The dragon-man clicked off the safety.

*If I could distract him, I might be able to get his gun.* Castillo breathed deeply then exhaled. "Just calm down and I'll explain everything—"

"Where is my contact?"

"Like I said," the officer answered. "If you just stay calm and put the gun down, I'll be happy to—"

Before Officer Castillo could finish, they heard a sudden and prolonged *honnnnnnk!* The masked man turned slightly, stunned and startled as the irritating car horn continued to resound from the front of the van. He pointed the gun away from Castillo's chest for a split second, loosening his grip. At that moment, Rico threw his arm toward the weapon and knocked it out of the man's hand. While Castillo dove after the gun, the dragon-man sprinted toward his sportscar.

Before the young officer could get on his tail, the car skidded and screeched away at full speed.

"The keys!" A voice shouted from the driver's seat of the van. It was Marcus. "Toss me the keys and get in!"

Officer Castillo fumbled around for the van keys and hurled them through the open window as he rounded the vehicle. Marcus caught the keys and ignited the engine as his partner leaped into the passenger seat and slammed the door shut.

"Hurry!" Castillo panted. "Don't let him get away!"

The van peeled away, careening through the narrow avenue between the towering stacks of shipping containers. Ahead of them, the red Porsche zipped around a sharp corner. The cops followed quickly, catching the tail end of the car as it made yet another dip into the confusing, dark maze of the stacks.

"We can't let him get off the island," Castillo said.

"We won't," Marcus assured him, flooring the gas pedal as

the sportscar came into view once more.

As they reached the main avenue that led to the bridge, the distance between the two vehicles began to increase. The hulking van was no match for a compact German sportscar designed for racing.

"We're gonna lose him!" Castillo shook his head.

Marcus shot a glance at the gun in his partner's hand. "The tires," he said quickly. "Blow out the tires!"

Castillo's wide eyes spoke ahead of his lips: "They're a moving target!"

"We *can't* lose him!"

With reluctance, Rico nodded and rolled down his window. With half his body hanging out the side of the van, he aimed the pistol low toward the tires of the car ahead of them. The officer pulled the trigger. The bullet whizzed and nicked the paint off the back bumper. *Shoot!* Castillo aimed again.

By now, the Porsche crossed over onto the foot of the bridge. A second car wheeled between the red one and the van—the same, dark sedan that had acted as sentry when the undercover cops first crossed onto the island. The sedan slowed its speed gradually, hurtling precariously close to the van, where it pulled next to the van's driver side and matched its speed. The black car inched closer to the van, compelling Marcus to veer aside—toward the thin support railing at the side of the bridge.

"He's trying to push us off!" Castillo, still hanging out the window, looked down. They were so close to the bridge's edge that he could now see the rippling water directly below him. He felt dizzy and returned to his seat.

"He's *trying*," said Marcus through gritted teeth. "But we're bigger." With a jolt, he yanked the wheel to the left, creating a deep, scraping gash in the side of the car. The black car hurtled forward with increasing speed to get between the van and the Porsche, then slowed, forcing the van to do the same—or risk ramming into it—while the red sportscar sprinted ahead.

"Get around him," suggested Castillo.

While Marcus attempted to move past the dark car, the sedan sped up, once again widening the distance between the officers and their quarry. As Marcus pushed the van as fast as it could go, the two men heard an alarming noise: a sputtering sound originating near the hood. Both of the cops tensed.

Rico turned to Marcus: "I thought you said they got it working again?"

"It *is* working," Marcus countered. Then, with a hollow metallic crash, the van began to slow until it finally came to a stop at the top of the bridge. The two officers watched as the red and black cars dropped under the cover of darkness and vanished into the city.

Marcus sighed deeply and loosened his grip on the steering wheel. Before Castillo could say another word, Officer Myles turned to him and waved his hand: "Don't."

Whatever wisecrack he was about to say, Rico kept it to himself. Then, after a brief moment of quiet, he turned back to Marcus: "Please tell me you at least got a good look at his plate?"

"I got half of it," Marcus nodded. "Should at least help narrow it down."

Castillo agreed and clicked open his door. "Guess we should start walking—find a payphone and call a ride."

"Sounds like a plan." Marcus offered a weary smile and followed the lead of his partner in disembarking from the troubled vehicle. The two men began the slow descent toward the city.

# CHAPTER 7

Donna arrived back at her apartment building, with Sondra's diminutive daughter trailing behind as they approached the old structure. They'd taken a bus from the hospital and it was now only a few hours before sunrise. The little girl had been silent, sleeping for most of the ride, but now spoke up as Donna juggled her keys and a large bag full of Starla's belongings.

"Is this where you live?" With drooping and uncertain eyes, Starla inspected the apartment building and its peeling paint.

Donna shoved open the unlocked door with her shoulder. "Yep," she puffed. "This is it." She placed their things in a corner, flicked on a light, and turned to the little girl who stood on the threshold: "And I guess it's yours for a little while now, too. You coming in?"

Starla looked around the room with an eyebrow raised,

then took a deep breath.

The aunt walked with purpose back toward Starla and began to motion for the girl to enter as she grabbed the door handle. "Hurry—you're letting the mosquitoes in and the cold air out," she said, prompting Starla to take sluggish steps into the hall. "I'm not paying to cool the whole neighborhood." Donna shut the door quickly.

*Okay,* she mused, leaning against the kitchen counter. *What do I do next?* Her eyes flitted to the cabinet, where she quickly withdrew a glass, filled it with lukewarm water from the faucet, and handed it to Starla.

The girl received it without a word and took a seat on Donna's pink couch.

*What else?* Donna tapped a finger on her chin as she thought. *Ah, sleeping arrangements; guess she can have my bed and I'll take the couch.*

The frazzled woman made a beeline for her bedroom, shouting over her shoulder, "I'm going to get the bed ready for you—make yourself at home!"

With another sip of water, Starla inspected the living room. Around her were a boxy television set, a mismatched armchair, and a remote control on a coffee table that was far too big for the space.

"Do you have any movies?" The child asked Donna from the other room. Before the woman could answer, Starla began to rifle through a small box of videotapes. Most were home videos recorded off television programs via a VCR— the tapes sleeved in flashy, colorful cardstock with titles scribbled across them in smudged ink.

"I think there's a few," Donna hollered back. "Do you know how to work a VCR?"

Starla nodded to herself. The majority of the VHS tapes featured photos of svelte young women clothed in shimmering leotards and vibrant leg warmers. Another had a man in short shorts with a perfectly spherical cushion of brown hair bobbing atop his smiling head. Finding the breadth of genres quite limited, Starla chose a tape and inserted it into the player.

The girl clicked on the TV and settled back onto the couch. A moment later, the volume blared at one of its highest levels as the video began to play somewhere near its halfway point. A deafening pop song issued throughout the apartment, overlaid with the energetic but garbled voice of an aerobics instructor filtered through the blown-out speakers: *"Now stretch, stretch, stretch—"*

Donna came rushing from the back room. "Turn that down! You'll wake the neighbors!" She yelled, grabbing the remote from Starla's tiny hands. The word *VOLUME* appeared in huge, pixelated lettering, while the notches of a bar beneath it shrunk one by one. Soon the room was quiet again, save for the sputtering air conditioner under the window.

"I can't hear it now," Starla muttered.

Donna rolled her eyes then clicked the volume button twice, allowing the faintest notes of the upbeat soundtrack to fade back into audibility. The woman tossed the remote aside, placed her hands on her hips, then returned to the bedroom to complete her preparations.

When she finished, Donna sauntered back into the living room: "It's all ready for you now—" Donna stopped mid-sentence when she saw that Starla had dozed off on the couch. By some miracle, the girl seemed at peace. *Too young to understand what's happening, I guess.* The woman took a deep breath and let out a weary sigh, then moved to the couch, lifted the child, and carried her small, sleeping body to the bed.

When she'd tucked the girl under the covers, Donna swept back a lock of Starla's reddish hair. The woman had never had children of her own and felt ill-equipped to mother one now. *How on earth am I gonna take care of you? I'm barely scraping by as it is.* Donna rose, turned out the light, then quietly closed the door as she returned to sleep on the couch.

The next morning as the sun crept through the windows—only a few hours since they'd gone to bed—Donna was sprawled out on the pink couch, her hair a tangled, wavy blonde mane, when she felt a poking on her arm from a tiny finger. As the woman stirred and struggled to lift her drooping eyelids, she turned to face Starla, who stood behind the couch wide awake.

Donna yawned. "Hey, what're you doing up? It's so early."

"Sun's up," Starla pointed to the first rays of light that snuck through the curtainless windows.

"The sun didn't have a crazy night like we did," the woman grunted as she turned over and closed her eyes. "Go back to bed."

"I'm hungry," said Starla.

Her aunt kept her eyes closed as she answered: "There's some eggs in the fridge."

The girl sighed impatiently. "I'm only seven," she said. "Mom hasn't taught me to cook yet."

"Add that to the list of reasons she and I can't get along," Donna mumbled under her breath. Then, with great effort, she rolled over and sat up. "Alright, fine. I'll make you break-fast. I have to leave for work soon, anyway."

While Donna gathered ingredients, opening and closing cabinets and the fridge multiple times, her niece planted herself back on the couch and switched on the television set once more.

"How do I get to the cartoons?" Starla shouted over the racket of Donna shuffling through a number of different-sized frying pans under the counter.

The woman popped her head up. "Those are on cable," she said.

"What's that?"

"Something I can't afford," Donna replied as she placed the pan on the stove and slammed the cabinet shut. She rose, sauntered to the TV set, and turned on the VCR. "How about you finish the tape you started last night? You fell asleep right when it was getting good."

Starla didn't protest as the workout routine appeared

on the screen again, led by its fit, young instructor. Donna handed the girl the remote and returned to the kitchen, switching on the stove.

Butter in the pan began to sizzle, crackling as Donna took an egg from its carton. Just then, the phone rang. She reached for the phone and, with the egg in one hand, put the receiver to her ear. Donna cracked the egg while she held the phone between her head and shoulder.

A hesitant voice garbled from the other end: "Hello?"

"Hello—Donna speaking."

"Donna!" The man's voice said excitedly. "It's me: Marcus. I was just calling since I hadn't heard from you and—"

"I, uh, can't talk right now, Marcus," Donna replied, preoccupied with guiding the edge of the oozing egg whites with a spatula.

"Oh," Marcus' tone changed. "I guess I should've expected that, since you never called back." He paused. The eggs began to hiss louder. "You *did* get my message, right?"

"Mhm," was all Donna said in response, her attention divided. She sprinkled salt and pepper over the eggs, then slowly slipped the spatula beneath the fried underside of the egg. Biting the edge of her lip, Donna readied to flip the egg. Carefully, she began to lift it.

"Donna? You still there?"

"I can't hear the music," Starla shouted from the sofa.

"Use the remote!" Donna hollered back. "Volume button."

"Who are you talking to—" Marcus stopped mid-sentence, then added quietly. "Oh, I see."

Starla held the button on the remote, raising the volume of the tape's peppy soundtrack so that it nearly drowned out all else in the apartment.

Donna flipped the spatula, landing the egg halfway upside-down so that its uncooked yolk splattered across the edge of the pan. "Cut it out!" She nearly screamed at the little girl, barely moving her mouth away from the phone receiver.

Marcus quavered. "I'm sorry, Donna, I didn't mean to upset you. If this isn't a good time—"

"It's *not* a good time, Marcus." Donna hurled her reply more sternly than she intended. She made eye contact with Starla and silently mouthed, "Turn it down!"

"Then, uh, goodbye, I guess?" Marcus waited for an answer.

The volume on the television lowered gradually until it became a plucky murmur.

"Wait, Marcus—" Donna began to speak, but she heard the tell-tale drone of a dial tone; Marcus had hung up. Exasperated, Donna smashed the phone back onto its dock and scraped the half-splattered egg onto a plate. "Breakfast is served, kid."

Starla moved over toward the counter and looked around: "Where's your table?"

"No table," Donna replied, sliding the plate across the counter. "You get to sit at the counter like a big girl."

Without another word, the little girl pulled back one of the barstools and carefully climbed onto it. She inspected the plate of steaming eggs with a quizzical look but did not pick up her fork.

Donna raised an eyebrow and crossed her arms. "You gonna eat, or what?"

"There's pepper in it," the seven-year-old pointed out.

"Yeah, so?"

"I don't like pepper."

"It's *pepper* not poison, kid," Donna answered, her jaw slackening. "This is what's for breakfast so you can eat it or you can starve."

"That's not how mom makes it," the girl insisted, preoccupied with finally pecking at the edge of the warm egg with her fork.

Donna leaned across the counter. "Well," she puffed, "first of all: I am *not* your mother. Second: don't you have to get to school or something?"

Starla found a small corner of the egg devoid of seasoning and nibbled on it. "It's the weekend," she replied without looking up. "There's no school today."

"But I have to work today," Donna said as she began to pace across the small kitchen, running a hand through her mess of blonde locks. "You're old enough to stay at home alone, right?"

The little girl shook her head.

"What! Are you sure?" Donna paused and tapped her fingers on the laminate counter. Suddenly, the phone rang again.

Donna's heart fluttered. "Marcus?"

"Donna!" The voice on the other line was a woman's—Lisa.

"Oh, Lisa," Donna apologized. "Sorry, thought you were Marcus."

"Don't mention it. Hey, Sue and I were going to hit the beach today. Wanna come?"

"I actually have to get to work in a little and—"

"Can't you ask off?" A second voice—Sue—spoke from the other line. "Weatherman says it's supposed to be a perfect day!"

"Oh, girls, I'd love to but my hours are getting reduced as it is," Donna replied quickly. "And, um, I've had a little situation—"

"Donna!" Sue exclaimed so that Donna had to yank the receiver away from her ear. "Are you in trouble?"

"Not trouble exactly," Donna said, making eye contact with Starla. She exhaled sharply. "It's a long story. But, um, could you guys do me a favor?"

Lisa took on a compassionate tone: "Oh, Donna, you know we're totally here for you!"

"Thanks, girls," Donna said with a relieved smile. "You guys are real life-savers."

# CHAPTER 8

"Anything yet?" Marcus hovered impatiently over the desk of the old office clerk. The graying woman had stacks of printed registries and lists of license plate numbers strewn across her small cubicle space.

"As I told you before lunch, Officer Myles," she replied without looking up, "I will call you the *instant* I have something to report. This goes much faster when I can work... uninterrupted."

"Of course," the young officer stammered apologetically. "And I appreciate that immensely, Marge." He gave a nod, beginning to move back toward the main room of the station. "Remember," he shouted over his shoulder as he opened the door. "We're looking for *any* plates with those three characters *or* a red Porsche. He could've swapped the plate to or from another vehicle."

Finally, Marge looked up, raising her eyebrows and cocking

her head to indicate her irritation. "You got it, Officer."

Marcus nodded, turned back, and took a deep breath before plunging into the bustling main office, his ears met with the sounds of phones ringing and the indistinct chatter of colleagues working through details of their various cases. On a far wall, an officer added pushpins to a huge diagram of the metro area, while another typed up a report on a word processor, straining to view its small display screen.

When he had reoriented himself to the room, Marcus located Officer Castillo and made a beeline toward the glass-walled meeting space where his partner stood over an oblong, rounded table. Rico leaned over a large, unfolded Rand McNally roadmap, focused on a depiction of the small island that had been the scene of the prior night's high-speed chase.

Officer Castillo ran his finger along one of the printed routes, retracing the course the red sportscar had taken. He leaned in close then scribbled something on a notepad.

Marcus scratched his chin. "Have we tried seeing if any of the businesses nearby might've caught something on tape?"

His partner held out his notes: "I'm compiling that list and I'll turn it over to Sanchez and Bishop to start making some calls. Unfortunately, he could've gone anywhere," Castillo pointed at the roadmap.

"But *anywhere* is *somewhere*," Marcus grinned, "and *somewhere*'s a place we can find."

A woman appeared in the doorway: Ruby Sanchez, an investigative officer. "Heard you two had quite the night," she chided as Officer Castillo handed her his list.

"Just another day in paradise," Marcus replied. "Good to see you, Sanchez. Thanks for all your help on this."

"You, too, Myles," Sanchez returned, then moved her attention back to Officer Castillo.

"Start with those closest to the island," he instructed. "Make a note of *any* cameras that might have had eyes on the street last night between ten-thirty and a quarter after eleven. Employees, customers, cameras—any of it."

Sanchez nodded. "You got it, boys." The woman disappeared to her desk.

"Now what?" Marcus asked.

"Now," Castillo said with a deep breath. "We keep digging until we find something."

*Ka-ching!*

Donna flung open the register to close out the drawer as her shift at the diner was ending. She stared down at the array of bills and coins, each in its proper compartment. For a moment, she considered whether Mary and the rest of her small staff would notice a few dollars missing from the drawer. The woman glanced over her shoulder to see if anyone was around: a few contented customers who'd already paid their bill but were continuing a lively conversation; a mother and child sharing an ice cream at the far end of the bar; and Mary, framed neatly through the kitchen door's round, porthole window. Donna returned her attention to the money.

*Just a couple bucks?* Donna hovered her fingers over the twenties, then reconsidered and moved to the ones. *Less likely to be noticed—*

Her heart leaped as she heard the kitchen door swing open.

"Donna!" It was Mary. "Glad I caught you before you clocked out."

The younger woman whipped around. "Sure, what is it?"

Mary's eyes flitted from the open register drawer to Donna, who held her hands behind her back. With a sigh, she returned her gaze to the blonde woman's weary face. "Just wanted to ask if you'd heard anything from Sondra yet," she said with genuine concern.

"Nothing new," Donna replied. "Nothing since we left the hospital."

Mary offered a slight smile. "At least you're getting some quality time with that kid of hers," she said. "That was a very generous thing for you to do for your sister."

"I am *not* doing it for *her*," Donna corrected with the wave of a finger. Then, with a slump of her shoulders, she added: "I'm the girl's only living—er, *conscious*—family. Trust me, I'm not cut out for motherhood." Out of the corner of her eye, Donna glimpsed the register drawer. "Mary, you sure you can't give me more hours this week? I was struggling before but now there's an extra *very picky* mouth to feed and—"

Mary shook her head reluctantly. "Sorry, hun. Like I said, business isn't exactly booming right now." Suddenly, the diner owner remembered something. "But," she rifled through her stained apron and withdrew a blush-pink business card, "I know a lady who's made a killing selling makeups and beauty products."

"You mean like at a department store or something?" Donna took the card and inspected it with an eyebrow raised.

"No, no," replied her boss. "It's one of those door-to-door kinda things. Sell enough and they give you a pink car or something like that. Pretty girl like you'd do well, I should think." Mary pointed at a phone number on the card. "Give my friend Tammy a call and she'll hook you up—the moisturizer is to die for." As she was about to walk away, the woman turned back and added in a mock whisper: "I'll even let you use the phone when you're finished with the register."

Donna thanked Mary, who quickly disappeared back into the steamy kitchen. As Donna counted the money in the drawer, she kept glancing at the small, pink business card on the counter. When she finished with her tally, she took one more look at the cash before closing the drawer with a deep breath. She confirmed the amount on a record log, took the business card in hand, then quickly began to dial Tammy's number.

Even while wearing her three-inch heels, Tammy was a diminutive and dainty brunette. But she was a spitfire, speaking quickly and nearly trotting beside Donna to keep up with her longer-legged strides along the suburban sidewalk in the wealthy Citrus Springs neighborhood.

"Remember, Miss Locke," Tammy said, barely taking

breaths as they passed by a couple of charming old houses, "you're not a saleswoman; you're a *beauty consultant*—the elevated language helps highlight the importance of the work we women do out here." Tammy was clothed in a tight, gray skirt—whose edge rested just around her knees—and a matching blazer. She wore a billowing pink blouse with a small, brimmed hat—that featured an obnoxious rosy ribbon—atop her head.

Donna nodded but couldn't get in a response before Tammy continued, handing her a small, pinkish faux-leather box with a handle on the top.

"This is just the Starter Kit—I've got plenty of extras, so since you're trying to get started right away, I'll let you have it free of charge." Tammy gave the pat of a finger on the top of the box and continued: "Once you're done with these samples, you'll want to purchase the Introductory Beauty Showcase Portable Studio so you have everything you need for a good consultation. It's only two hundred dollars."

At this, Donna gasped. "Two *hundred!*"

"Relax, dear," Tammy pleaded. "It's only a little buy-in, and you'll make that back in sales in *no* time with your looks." This seemed to calm Donna for the moment, so Tammy added in earnest, "So glad to have you on my team, Miss Locke."

"You can call me Donna."

Tammy squealed. "Oh, *can* I? So real and down-to-earth. I feel like we're the best of friends already, *Donna.*"

"That means a lot," the blonde woman replied with a

hint of sarcasm. "I know you don't let just *anyone* on your, er, team."

"Heavens no! I consider myself to be quite inclusive, but Nancy Kay forbids us from recruiting any consultant who's 'openly controversial.' One of the company's 'Golden Rules,' you understand?"

"Of course," Donna replied, trying to maintain a similar level of enthusiasm as they came to a stop in front of a two-story home with a well-kept front yard.

From beside her, Tammy placed her hands on Donna's padded shoulders. "Alright, now is the moment: your first consultation!"

"You're sure this is the right house?"

"'Course I'm sure," exclaimed the shorter woman. She gestured to the landscaping. "Those manicured bougainvillea vines and the fresh mulch are the *sure* signs of a woman running this household—one with a wealthy husband, I might add. Now," Tammy leaned in closer and spoke in a loud mock-whisper, "go give her the beauty show that she *deserves!*"

Donna took a deep breath. "How do I look?"

Tammy inspected Donna's simple summer dress and her hastily-fluffed mane. "A perfect representation of the Nancy Kay way," she smiled, then tapped her chin. "If we had more time, I'd give you a full beauty treatment, but this will do for now."

Donna wasn't sure how to respond.

"I'll be right outside," the woman assured her with a nudge.

Slowly, Donna nodded and sauntered up to the front door. She knocked then glanced back over her shoulder. Tammy silently clapped her hands in delight and bobbed her head with glee. Donna inhaled deeply, turning as she heard the door unlatch and open from inside.

"Good afternoon," she began to the woman of the house. "Do you have a few moments to spare for a, er, beauty consultation?"

# CHAPTER 9

Detective Ruby Sanchez flung open the conference room door and flopped a notepad onto the table, right in front of Castillo.

"Got something?" Marcus asked, moving away from a wall of pinned notations.

"Sure do," replied Sanchez, crossing her arms confidently. "Smith and I called every store, shop, and restaurant within four blocks of the Freedom Tower—the intersection where your Porsche driver and his buddy disappeared."

Castillo nodded. "And?"

"There are three establishments that have video footage from last night," Ruby explained. "If the vehicle passed by, there's a chance they caught some of it. The names, addresses, and contacts are listed there."

"Not bad, Sanchez," said Marcus with a grin as he leaned over Rico's shoulder to inspect Ruby's detailed notes.

Castillo tore the page from the pad and folded it neatly into his pocket. "Thanks, Sanchez. We'll call in if we find anything." He nodded to Marcus and the two hurried out the door.

Donna stared out the passenger-side window of the Cadillac as the picture-perfect neighborhood rolled by, her cheek smushed sullenly against the glass while she rested her head on her hand.

"Are you sure you don't want to talk about it, Donna?" Tammy offered from behind the steering wheel.

The blonde woman nodded and turned back to her. "Yes," she said quietly. "Can you let me off here?"

Tammy pulled to the side of the street and clicked the car into park. "Don't you want me to drive you home?"

"I need to use the phone," Donna answered, already opening the door. Just before closing it, she stuck her head back into the car. "You don't have any spare change on you, do you?"

The sprightly woman nodded and rifled through a cupholder, producing a few quarters, which she placed in Donna's palm.

"Thanks," she replied, slamming the door shut. As Tammy slowly drove away, Donna made her way over to the phone booth, where she quickly inserted the change and dialed the number for her apartment.

The phone rang a few times before someone picked up on

the other end. "Hello, Donna Locke's place. Who's calling?" In the background, Donna heard a pair of high-pitched screams.

"Sue?" Donna strained to hear her over the noise.

"Donna! Thank goodness!" Sue replied hastily. "Are you coming back here soon? Lisa and I aren't cut out for this babysitting thing."

"I'm working on it," Donna shifted the phone to her other ear. "Is everything alright?"

Sue sighed deeply. "We'll be fine. Won't we, Lisa?" Donna couldn't hear Lisa's reply, but Sue continued. "You okay, Don? You sound depressed."

"I tried to do that door-to-door beauty sales thing—"

"Oh!" Sue exclaimed with excitement. "You do Nancy Kay now?"

Donna exhaled sharply. "I *did* Nancy Kay *once*. Never again."

"What happened?"

"It did *not* go well. Her name was *Mauve*—that should've been my first clue. Anyway, the spritz got in her eyes, she didn't tell me she was allergic to our product, and to top it all off I got blush on her *brand new* sofa."

"Let me guess," Sue chimed in. "The new sofa was white?"

"Bingo," Donna replied with little inflection. "Any other ideas for how I can make a quick buck? I've gotta keep this kid alive *and* keep the lights on."

Donna could hear Sue's smile on the other end: "Have you considered becoming a, um, lady of the night?"

"Sue! I'm serious!"

"Alright, alright," Sue chuckled. "Let me think. Oh! I just remembered. I have a friend who has a little brother who did that thing with the knives. You know?"

Donna raised an eyebrow. "Ginsu?"

"Sort of like that but it was, um, a different name. What was it?" Donna could hear Sue rifling through her purse and then flipping through small pages. Finally, she found what she was looking for and read from her notes: "His name is Randy and he works for Cuts-a-lot—he stopped by a while back. He said they're always open to new salespeople!"

With a sigh, Donna opened the small handbag slung over her shoulder and withdrew a pen, poised to scribble on her hand. "Alright, Sue: what's his number?"


A gruff man in a ballcap shouted through the slightly cracked-open threshold: "I told your other *Ginsu* friends already: I won't buy it unless it's *American!*"

Donna stammered a reply. "B-but sir, I already told you, these are *like* Ginsu knives but they're not—"

The door slammed in Donna's face.

*Apparently, they are not interested in Cuts-a-lot knives.* Donna slumped and moved to the edge of the front porch. As she descended the few steps to the driveway, the blonde woman heard a crash of thunder. The sky was heavy and dark, ready to pour out a classic afternoon shower.

Clutching her small wheel cart bearing the full starter

line of Cuts-a-lot knives, Donna hurried down the sidewalk. When she got to the end of the block, she looked both ways before crossing the street. As she reached the opposite corner, there was another booming roar from the sky, followed by a sweeping rush of rain moving toward her. It hit her all at once. Donna was soaked.

Donna exhaled sharply and kept moving, her heels ensuring that she moved as slowly and laboriously as possible. She dragged the heavy cart through a muddy puddle, which splashed on the edge of her dress. The wheels caught on a crack in the pavement.

"Drat. Come on!" She muttered under her breath, forcing the small wheels free. Finally, the cart came loose and Donna tumbled backward, losing her balance and narrowly missing another large mud splat.

On the verge of tears, Donna rose and scanned the area, squinting to see through the rain. Just a couple of blocks ahead she could make out the familiar form of a phone booth. *Thank God.*

The woman hurried toward it and stuffed herself into the small, plexiglass compartment, escaping the downpour. Donna managed to fish out a few coins from her handbag and quickly insert them into the payphone. She dialed the number.

After a couple of rings, a woman picked up: "Hello, Saint Mary's. How can I help you?"

"Yes, uh, hi," Donna said, swiping a lock of dripping hair from her forehead. "This is Donna Locke and I'm just calling to check in to see if Sondra—Sondra Gordon, my, uh, sister—has woken up yet?"

"Hold please," the voice said. There was a click. A calming smooth jazz track began to play through the receiver. A few seconds later, a second click signaled the woman's return. "Hello, Miss Locke. You still there?"

"I'm here," Donna answered.

"Unfortunately, Miss Gordon has not yet woken up," the voice said somberly. "The doctors said they're not sure when she'll wake, but they'll call you if there's any news."

Donna took a deep breath and exhaled through her nose. "Thank you." She hung up the phone and lowered her head as the rain trickled down the transparent box around her. *Help!* Donna pleaded—or prayed, perhaps. Another rumble of thunder rattled the booth, startling her.

When she looked up, Donna's eyes landed on a crisp flyer taped to the inside of the glass. Across the poster in large lettering were the words:

*Need cash? Participate in a new research study.*

At the top of the flyer, Donna's eyes alighted on a logo for a company featuring a bird with an oblong beak: *Pelican Innovations.*

The young, damp woman chuckled. "What the heck," she muttered. She slipped a few more of her remaining coins into the phone and then dialed the number listed at the bottom of the flyer.

Donna was surprised that the phone rang only once before someone picked up. "Good afternoon, you've reached Pelican Innovations." The voice was energized and peppy. "This is Debra speaking. How may I assist you today?"

"Hi, uh," Donna sputtered as she gathered her thoughts. "My name is Donna Locke; I saw your ad for the research study and I'm calling to see if you still need participants."

"Of course," the secretary replied. "We've just launched a new study that's still recruiting. What's your availability?"

"I, uh, I guess I can come in today?"

"Let me see," Debra said as she presumably checked a schedule. "That will work. I just need to make sure you haven't eaten or drank anything in the last three hours?"

Donna thought back to her busy afternoon. "Come to think of it, I haven't." *And I'm starving,* she wanted to add.

"Perfect," continued Debra. "I've added you to the schedule, Miss Locke. There will just be a few forms for you to fill out when you get here. Let me give you the address—tell me when you're ready for it."

The rain had nearly stopped by now. Donna fumbled around in her purse and found her pen, then ripped a corner from the Pelican flyer. "Ready," she said.

Debra proceeded to relay the address to the research labs. To Donna's relief, she was only a few minutes away. As she was about to hang up, Donna added, "Oh, one more thing: what does it pay?"

"For the two-hour procedure and a few follow-up appointments," Debra read off her notes, "you'll be compensated a total of eight-hundred dollars."

*Eight-hundred!* Donna nearly dropped the phone. *That would easily cover the month's bills and leave me with some left over.* The woman was floored and completely forgot about the secretary on the other end of the phone line. After a few moments to regain her composure, she hung up the receiver and hurried off down the sidewalk. *This is what I've been waiting for. This will change everything.*

# CHAPTER 10

Officer Myles paused on the sidewalk in front of a hole-in-the-wall convenience store. Just above the bodega's entrance, Marcus spied a small, wall-mounted camera. *Let's hope this is the one.* The young officer took a deep breath and yanked open the shop door, which jingled a tiny bell. "After you," he motioned to Officer Castillo, who tarried behind him, ushering his partner into the humid space.

The tightly-packed corner store smelled of strong cleaning products, nearly-expired fridge meats, and tobacco. A pair of children concocted a sugary, bubbling cocktail at a soda fountain on the far wall, while an elderly man slid a few dollar bills under a plexiglass window at the checkout counter. When the old man had gone, Castillo approached the shop-tender.

"Buenas tardes," the officer said with a nod, flashing his badge. "Habla inglés?" Castillo could tell the owner looked confused as to why he wanted to converse in English, so he pointed toward Marcus.

"Ah, sí, sí," the shop tender smiled, baring a gap-toothed grin.

"Gracias," Castillo replied. "I'm Officer Enrico Castillo and this is my partner—Officer Myles. One of our colleagues called and said you had video footage from last night?"

The man nodded.

Marcus moved closer. "Do you have a place where we can view the tape?"

Again, the shop-tender gave his silent answer with a nod, then motioned for the two cops to come around the counter via a barred door. When he had opened it and the two men were inside the tight quarters, the shopkeeper pointed to a small, boxy television set that sat yellowing atop a brand-new VCR. The screen displayed a real-time, black-and-white feed of the sidewalk and street just outside the bodega.

"Pretty big deal for a little shop like yours to have this kind of equipment," noted Castillo as he inspected it.

"Lots of problems," the man explained as he rifled through a stack of video cassettes. "Vándalos—kids painting graffiti, swiping candy, Coca-Cola. So it was worth every penny." Finally, he found the tape, which bore a label scrawled in black marker. "Here it is. I should warn you, the picture quality isn't the greatest. Lights on the street aren't too reliable, either."

The shopkeeper inserted the tape into the machine and pressed a couple of buttons, causing the grainy, live image to disappear. The sounds of rotors and clicks indicated that the VCR was preparing to play. Then, after a moment, the tape began. As its recording had started earlier in the day, the shop tender picked up a remote control device and began to fast-forward. A woman stepped up to the counter, so the man handed the remote to Castillo.

"Hit the play button when it gets to the time you're looking for," the man instructed. "You can see what time it is in the corner." His oily finger smudged the glass as he indicated the placement of the timestamp, then attended to the customer.

The two officers huddled in front of the small, squarish screen and watched the scan lines flutter while the footage moved at rapid speed. Eventually, the sunny street gave way to shadows. After a few more moments, Castillo pressed play and checked the time. 10:34. He sped the footage up again until he passed 11:00. The streets were mostly empty and devoid of cars. The officer fast-forwarded again, then hit play at a few minutes after the hour.

"Look there!" Marcus pointed to the corner of the frame, where car headlights began to appear. Slowly, the lights grew larger, illuminating a wider portion of the frame. Both officers leaned in instinctively, straining to get a better look.

The car drove into frame. It moved quickly, but there was no mistaking that it was the same model of Porsche sportscar as the one the men were looking for. Before they could get a good look at it, the car was gone.

"Quick, rewind," said Marcus, though Castillo had already clicked the button to do so.

The footage reversed, sending the car back the way it came. Castillo pressed play once more. There were the lights again, then the edge of the car, then:

"Pause it!"

Castillo pushed the button just as Marcus said these words, freezing the frame with the back of the sportscar clearly visible. "Can you make out the rest of the plate?"

Officer Myles leaned in closer and squinted his eyes. The image pulsed a little, but the characters seemed clear enough: ZAQ 17B. "Or is that an '8' at the end?"

"Should be a number," answered Castillo.

"Then '8' it is," replied Marcus with a smile. "What are the odds?" He quickly withdrew a small notepad and a pen then scribbled down the plate number.

The two officers thanked the shopkeeper and asked to use his phone. "Claro," he said, pointing to the small rotary phone at his side. "It's old but it still works."

Marcus dialed the number for the station. "Marge," he said when the woman picked up. "We've got the full plate number. Can you run a search on this for us and figure out who it belongs to? We're on our way back in."

"Sure thing, Officer Myles," replied Marge. "I'll try to get an answer for you by the time you're back."

Marcus fed her the license plate number over the receiver, thanked her again, then hung up the phone. With a final word of gratitude to the shopkeeper, the two men hurried back to their car.

The modern structure that housed Pelican's labs was enormous, towering over Donna as she approached the covered front portico where valet runners waited in the shade. A cool, ocean breeze swept through her hair as she was ushered through a set of wide, glass double doors into the bright and spacious lobby. The scale of it all was overwhelming at first, but Donna quickly oriented herself and made a cautious beeline to a long receptionist's desk, her heels clacking along the freshly-polished tile floor.

"I'm here for a, um," she searched for the right words. "The, um, experiment? I'm one of the guinea pigs and—"

"Sign in here, please," the receptionist cut her off, sliding a slim clipboard across the marble countertop.

"Oh, um, sure," Donna scribbled her information and then handed it back to the woman on the other side of the counter.

"Take the elevator to Level 13," the receptionist instructed with a sharp hand motion, barely glancing at the blonde woman across from her.

After a moment to verify that there was no further information to follow, Donna clutched her purse and took off in the direction the woman had indicated. She arrived at the twin elevators and pressed the button to call one to the lobby floor. It arrived almost silently, with a pleasant chime and the faintest murmur as the doors swished open. A woman with big hair exited clutching the hand of a small boy; both had small, round bandages on the cruxes of their arms, Donna noted as she entered the elevator.

When the huge, shiny doors closed, Donna pressed the button for Level 13. To her surprise, the elevator barely rattled at all; instead, the woman experienced the faintest feeling of floating as the car whirred upwards. It was only a matter of seconds before the elevator emitted its calming ding as the doors slid open.

Donna was greeted by another receptionist as she stepped into the small, sparse waiting room: "Hello. You must be Donna?" This receptionist was much friendlier than the one downstairs and Donna thought there was something familiar about her voice.

"Yes," Donna answered, extending her hand to shake the woman's own. "That's me. Donna Locke—I'm here for the test."

"Of course," the woman replied as they shook hands. "It's a pleasure to meet you in person. I'm Debra—we spoke on the phone." Her smile was almost aggressive, Donna thought. Debra handed over a clipboard and gestured toward a row of empty seats along the wall. "If you'll just fill out these consent and intake forms that will help us get to know you a little more, we'll get you going right away."

Donna took the forms and flipped through the stack; it was thick. "So do we get paid *before* or after the test?" There was a hint of humor in her voice.

Debra replied earnestly: "You'll get your first installment after the procedure, then the rest once you complete the two follow-up appointments."

*Procedure? That sounds intense.* Donna was starting to question whether this was the wisest choice she could make, but her thoughts returned to her young niece and the bills that seemed to be piling higher with each passing day. She took a seat and began to fill out her information on the forms. Near the end of the packet, Donna encountered several pages of legal language in small type. She squinted through reading a few lines before deciding to skip to the end, where she scribbled her signature to affirm she'd read and agreed to the terms.

Debra noticed how quickly Donna had skimmed the legal jargon. "Are you sure you don't want to read all of that?"

Donna sighed, slightly irritated at the question. "Those things are all the same, aren't they?" She smiled. "Besides, the sooner we get through this, the sooner I can get something to drink."

Debra's smile cracked only slightly. "Actually," she began apologetically, "you'll need to wait twelve hours before you can drink anything after today's procedure is complete."

"Twelve hours!" Donna hadn't intended to raise her voice quite that loud. Thankfully, there was no one else in the waiting room to disturb. "Sorry. I won't drink anything. Where do I go from here?"

Debra walked over to a nearby door and typed an access code. The door clicked open and Debra ushered Donna into a small examination room. Donna followed and sat in a padded, leathery chair in the center of the room. The receptionist placed a few pages from the clipboard on the counter in the corner. "Dr. Lansing will be with you shortly," she said with her signature overbearing smile as she shut the door behind her and returned to her desk.

The exam room was cold, and Donna was grateful that she'd mostly dried off from the brief trickle of rain that had abruptly halted her career as a knife saleswoman. Before she could think on the matter much more, there was a click of a latch and the door swung open. This time, a young man—not much older than Donna—entered carrying a small, metallic briefcase.

He seemed nervous as he walked across the room to greet her. "Hello, I'm Dr. Roger Lansing," the man said, setting the case on the counter and adjusting his large, thick glasses. "And you must be Miss..." he looked at the notes left by Debra. "Miss Locke?"

"That's me," Donna replied, crisscrossing her legs.

"Wonderful," he said. "First we'll need a quick blood sample to use as a control." The doctor produced a small device. "Your finger, please?"

Donna complied and held out her hand. Roger placed the device to her finger.

*Click!* Donna winced.

"Got it," Dr. Lansing assured her and returned to his briefcase while Donna shook out her hand to allay the sting. While the doctor fiddled with something inside the case, the woman tried to get a better look.

"Am I allowed to know what this test is all about?"

Roger chuckled nervously. "Unfortunately, we've got

to keep the details to a minimum," he said as he withdrew a large cylindrical syringe from the case. "When we say too much, some patients claim to experience certain sensations that aren't really there—a placebo effect, you understand?"

Donna nodded but tensed when she saw the large needle that the doctor now screwed onto the tip of the syringe. "Are the stories true?" The woman asked, her breath quickening at the sight of the sharp tip moving toward her.

"What stories?"

"That one of your patients grew a third arm," Donna tried to force a grin, but it quickly melted away. She gulped.

"Third arm? Nonsense!" Dr. Lansing looked her in the eyes. "I'm not *that* good of a scientist." Then, realizing the implications of his words, he sputtered: "But the research behind this test is sound, I assure you. There'll be no additional limbs as far as we're concerned."

This seemed to assuage Donna for the moment, so the doctor moved the syringe toward her arm. An unidentifiable liquid sloshed inside the tube. Dr. Lansing rubbed a small antiseptic wipe on her skin then tossed it into the trash. "This may sting for a moment," Roger noted.

Before Donna could respond, she felt the sharp jab as the needle sank into the soft flesh of her arm. She scrunched her face. The doctor moved quickly, injecting the serum until the syringe was empty. Then, all at once, it was done. Dr. Lansing wiped the spot once more then slapped a small adhesive bandage on it.

"There," he said with an air of relief. "That wasn't so bad, was it?"

Donna placed her hand over her arm instinctively. "I've still got only two arms," she jested through gritted teeth.

"Now," began Roger as he turned his back to clean up the counter, "I'm sure Debra mentioned that you'll need to refrain from consuming any liquids for at least twelve hours. You may eat a small amount, but stay away from dairy products and that sort of thing—they can cause strange dreams and such. We'll call to schedule a follow-up meeting for later this week."

The blonde woman acknowledged that she'd be on the lookout for the call and both of them moved toward the door.

"Oh, and one more thing," Roger sputtered as he opened the exam room door, motioning for Donna to exit ahead of him. "This may make you quite drowsy, so be careful operating motor vehicles or heavy machinery."

"I'll do my best to avoid driving my industrial tractor," Donna quipped, then the two parted ways as they returned to the waiting area. The doctor disappeared through another keypad-protected doorway off the waiting room while Donna checked out with Debra.

The kindly receptionist handed Donna an unmarked envelope. "Your compensation's in there," she said with a smile. Donna thanked her then headed back to the elevator.

Inside, she ripped open the envelope to find that her first installment of Pelican's payments was larger than she'd anticipated: $600! With a sigh of relief, Donna clutched the check. She reached the ground floor and disembarked from the elevator. The city bus arrived just out front as the golden hour rays began to seep through the large, glass lobby space. Donna stepped outside and hopped on the bus back to her apartment, staring out the window as the city whizzed by.

# CHAPTER 11

As soon as they reached the station, Officers Myles and Castillo hurried to the desk where Marge waved a slip of paper with a smug grin.

"What did I tell you?" She said in a sing-songy voice.

Marcus leaned over her desk: "You found out who the Porsche was registered to?"

"Well, the plate isn't registered to a Porsche, that's for sure," Marge shook her head. "But the good news is that we've got the name and address—right here in the county, too."

"Someone thought the flashy sportscar would distract us from them swapping the plates," Castillo noted. "They're no match for Marge. You're a lifesaver, you know that?"

"All in a day's work, boys," she replied, handing the address to Marcus. "The name mean anything to you?"

Officer Myles inspected the handwritten note and read the name aloud: "Vander Newport." He shook his head and looked at his partner.

"I haven't heard it before, either," Castillo replied.

"Well he lives just up the street," said Marcus, noting the address. "What do you say we pay a little visit to Mr. Newport?" As they moved to gather their things, both men thanked the ever-resourceful office assistant: "We couldn't have done this without you, Marge!"

"I know," she smirked. "And don't you forget it!"

The officers occasionally departed from their usual use of the squad car when on assignment in certain neighborhoods, opting instead for a more stylish ride that would draw less attention than one branded with the emblem of local law enforcement. Of course, a shiny, government-owned convertible drew its own kind of attention. But, combined with their casual, non-uniform attire of Ray-Bans and breathable linen button-ups in a muted rainbow of pastels, curious eyes would never guess they were police at a first glance—which was exactly what the two men hoped as they buzzed down the breezy artery toward the ritzy Bayshore neighborhood.

Located in a quieter section of the island, these streets were lined with elaborate villas tucked away behind generous setbacks. Almost all of these lots touched the bay or a connected inlet, with their own private docks to show off pristine, white vessels moored on the water.

Mr. Newport's compound featured a tall hedge that

obscured views from passersby on the street and a metal, automated gate that kept unwanted guests out. Marcus pulled up to a small callbox and pressed its singular round button. Rico glanced up toward the lampposts that guarded the road and noticed a pair of cameras.

A moment later, there was a beep and a man's voice crackled over the speaker: "Newport residence—may I ask your name and the nature of your call?"

"Uh, yeah," Marcus held down the button, nearly shouting his answer into the speaker, with a glance to Castillo. "This is Officer Marcus Myles with Officer Castillo, Metro-Dade. We just need to ask Mr. Newport a few questions—nothing to be alarmed about."

The silence lingered just long enough for Marcus to wonder whether his response had made it to the person on the other end of the callbox. Then, the garbled voice answered succinctly: "Of course. One moment, please."

The speaker clicked off. The officers heard a *buzz*, then the gate began to slide open. When the gate had locked into its open position, the car slowly rolled down the long driveway toward a loop near the front door. Marcus and Castillo quickly stepped out of the silver convertible, leaving the top down, and made a quick scan of their surroundings as they approached the steps.

"Nice place," remarked Officer Castillo, gesturing toward a trickling fountain and the coral-carved tiles that bordered it.

Before Marcus could respond, the large front door swung open. The men were greeted by a well-groomed man that appeared to be a butler. "Good afternoon, officers," said the man—his voice recognizable from the brief exchange via the callbox. With a flourish, he opened the door wider and motioned for them to step inside: "Right this way, please."

The two men followed the butler through the expansive foyer and into a sitting room at the back of the house with a stunning view of the inlet. "Please make yourselves comfortable. Mr. Newport will be with you momentarily," the butler said and then vanished to another part of the house.

Rico stepped to the large sliding glass doors and gazed at the sparkling waters. He noted a pool, the brand-new dock, a pristinely-kept speedboat, and the lack of cameras. When the young officer turned back to his partner, he was startled by the sudden, silent appearance of a man in the doorway who he presumed to be their host.

"My apologies, gentlemen," he said with a disingenuous smile as he sauntered toward Marcus. "I was just putting away my pet—he can get a little too excited when we have guests." The man extended his hand. "I'm Mr. Newport. Emilio tells me you're P.D.?"

"Officer Marcus Myles," he answered as he shook his hand. "And my partner—Officer Enrico Castillo."

"Pleased to make your acquaintances." Mr. Newport's gaze lingered longer as he greeted Castillo, but then he took a seat on a low, white sofa. "Now, to what do I owe the pleasure of a visit from the Metro-Dade Police?" The man wondered aloud, then paused. "Please," he motioned for his visitors to join him on the couch.

Marcus and Rico hesitantly obliged, then the latter spoke: "Thank you, Mr. Newport. We're investigating a case and, to be frank, we've stumbled upon something that may connect you to a crime."

"I beg your pardon!" Mr. Newport raised his eyebrows and fluttered his eyes dramatically: "You think someone has set me up?"

"It's possible," continued Castillo.

"You ever owned a red Porsche Nine-Eleven?" Marcus interjected.

Their host seemed somewhat caught off guard, but answered confidently: "I can't say that I have—at least not outside of my dreams, of course." He chuckled to himself.

Marcus continued. "Someone's been driving one around with a plate that's registered under your name." He gave a nod toward the man. "Any idea how that might have happened?"

With his mouth agape, Mr. Newport waited a moment before nodding. "Yes, actually."

Both officers turned to one another and tried not to show their surprise at the man actually offering them the possibility of useful information.

"I was out for a night on the town a couple weeks ago," Mr. Newport continued, his eyes drifting toward his freshly-washed boat outside, "and when I returned to the car the plate was gone—almost didn't notice it in the dark. I filed a report with the authorities right away but they were never able to find it." He turned back to the two men. "I'm surprised your colleagues didn't alert you when the plate turned up on this red Porsche—though, perhaps I shouldn't be surprised."

Marcus tried to ignore the not-so-subtle jab at his fellow Metro-Dade coworkers. "Do you remember what the date was—when the plate went missing?"

Mr. Newport thought for a moment. "Come to think of it, I do," he said. "It was April 3. I remember because it was my dear Rufus' birthday."

"Rufus is your...?"

"My boxer," Mr. Newport interrupted. "Had him since he was born."

The officers nodded as they took in the information. Mr. Newport again filled the silence.

"I do hope you're not implying I had something to do with whatever crime has been committed?"

Castillo shook his head. "Just following up," he smiled.

"And shall I presume you located the stolen plate, then?"

Marcus breathed through his nostrils, "It, er, *eludes* us for the moment, but we'll let you know if it turns up again. Thank you for your time, Mr. Newport." Officer Myles rose as the other two men did the same and all expressed their goodbyes.

The butler, Emilio, appeared once more to usher them to the door. Once outside, Marcus and Rico loaded back into the silver convertible. Mr. Newport stood on the top step, looking down on them as the car's engine roared to life.

"Be careful out there," the man waved and offered the same, disingenuous smile as he had when they arrived.

"You got it," Marcus hollered back then revved the engine.

The little car peeled out of the driveway then slowed as it returned to the gate. A glance in the rearview mirror revealed that Mr. Newport continued waving. Then the car whipped down the street and left the compound in a trail of exhaust.

"Never seen someone look so guilty in my *life*," Marcus said to Rico.

His partner chuckled then placed a hand to his chest dramatically in a half-hearted impression of their former host: "Surely you don't think I, *the* Mr. Vander Newport, could have done anything wrong, officer?"

Marcus grinned and shook his head. After a moment, he spoke up: "Now we've just gotta figure out a way to prove he's connected to this whole thing. I have a feeling we'll be back here soon enough."

Both men turned their gazes ahead as the car careened through a maze of hedge-walled streets, then zipped along a canal lined with low-rise condominiums.

"So," Castillo said after a few moments of quiet. "You gonna give Donna a call back or what?" He nudged Marcus with his elbow.

Marcus took a deep breath, his eyes focused on the road before them. "I told you: I don't think she's interested, man—she told me to back off. I'm really into her, but I think maybe there's someone else in her life."

"Then if she's not ready for you, Myles, I guess it's time you expand your horizons."

Marcus raised an eyebrow. "Expand my horizons?"

"Yeah," Castillo smiled. "Get out, put yourself out there,

hit up a club or two."

"I don't know, Castillo—"

"C'mon, you'll have fun—I promise."

Marcus searched for excuses: "We've got a lot of work to do on the case and—"

"It can wait," his partner nodded. "I've got your back; time to dance, partner."

Finally, Marcus laughed and nodded his reluctant agreement. The sun was beginning to set, so both men flipped down their sun visors as the salty air wafted into the car. Castillo clicked on the radio, adjusted the station until he heard the sound of wailing electric guitars, then cranked up the volume and let out a loud shout as he felt the breeze in his hair.

From inside her apartment, Donna opened her front door, allowing a wave of warm, humid nighttime air to rush inside. She turned to usher Sue and Lisa out the threshold to relieve them of their babysitting duties, but instead found them saying an extra set of goodbyes to little Starla near the couch. "Alright, alright," Donna chided. "Time to go—girl's got school tomorrow... right?" She made eye contact with Starla, who nodded, then picked up a clunky camera she'd been inspecting on the coffee table.

"*You* make good choices," Lisa called over her shoulder as she headed for the door, then leaned toward Donna. "She's a special one, that kid."

Donna inhaled deeply and hugged Lisa. "Thanks," she said. "Thank you both for everything."

Sue came in for her own embrace. "Don't mention it, Don. Turns out babysitting is a lot more fun after you get through the first couple hours of chaos."

"Any tips?" Donna asked with a grin.

"Give her whatever she wants," Lisa said with eyes wide, stepping over the threshold. "Keeps the crying to a minimum."

The blonde woman shook her head and began to close the door. "I'll remember that one," Donna said. "Thanks again, girls. I owe you one—*big* time." With that, she blew a kiss to the duo then shut the door and swung the latch. With a deep sigh, she turned back to Starla, who now placed the big camera to her face. "So, you behave for Sue and Lisa?"

"We had fun together," replied the girl, trying to find a good grip on the camera with her tiny fingers. "I like your friends." She turned toward Donna and held down a button. *Click!* The flash momentarily blinded the woman.

"Hey! Point that thing someplace else!" Donna exclaimed.

The faint murmur of rotors inside the camera churned, producing an instant square photograph that hadn't yet fully developed. Starla yanked it from the camera's mouth-like opening and inspected it. "Isn't there supposed to be a picture?"

Donna puffed and planted herself on the couch next to the girl. "It's a Polaroid," she said. "Let me see that." The girl obliged and handed the device to her aunt. Immediately,

Donna turned the camera around so that it faced the seated pair. She pressed the button, casting another blinding flash, this time on both of their faces.

"Gah!" Starla squealed and giggled.

Donna set the camera down. "See? Not so great to be *blinded*, huh?" She pulled out the newly-created photograph and began to shake it. "It's supposed to help it develop faster," she explained. "At least, that's what everyone says."

Starla watched intently and did the same for hers. Gradually, the grayish squares morphed into clearer images. The two held up their photographs for the other to see; one showed a frazzled Donna while the other depicted the pair together on the couch.

Donna smiled to see the little girl so amused, then inhaled deeply. "So, ready for bed?"

"Mom always reads me a book before bed," said the girl matter-of-factly, placing the photo on the table.

Donna quickly scanned her apartment looking for anything resembling a children's book but saw nothing. "I'm not exactly a literature buff, kid—"

"Just a minute," Starla interrupted and ran to her backpack. She rifled around for a moment before returning with a thin, square book in hand. "We can read this one. It's one of my favorites." She held it out for Donna.

"*Where the Wild Things Are*," Donna read from the cover. She raised an eyebrow and glanced at Starla. The girl looked up at her with big, sparkling eyes and freckled cheeks. Finally, Donna caved. "Alright," she said. "One story then it's off to bed."

Starla clapped with delight then hurried to the back bedroom. Donna followed, book in hand, and the two nestled under the covers, their backs supported by a mound of limp pillows. Donna took a deep sigh and then began the story.

They were only a few pages in when Donna glanced down at Starla. Her eyes were closed and the tiny girl rested peacefully against Donna's side. The woman smiled softly, swept a lock of ruddy hair from the girl's face, then carefully and slowly slid off the bed. With one final look at the sleeping girl, Donna turned out the light and closed the door. *Maybe things aren't so bad,* she thought. *Maybe things might work out after all.*

# CHAPTER 12

Debonair was one of the newer dance clubs on South Beach, housed behind a low-rise Art Deco facade adorned with symmetrical sequences of nautical portholes, decorative stucco ridges, and stripes of pink neon lights. The glow cast harsh shadows over Marcus and Rico as they ambled up the sidewalk in the salty night air, their steps nearly in sync with the synthesized drum loop that emanated from within.

"You sure about this place?" Marcus lingered on the sidewalk, surveying the youthful smiles and massive hairstyles of those coming and going while he adjusted a pastel pink blazer.

"C'mon, Myles," said Castillo, playfully tugging the other off-duty officer by the edge of his collar. "Let's have a little fun. Plenty of fish in this sea." Here the man gestured at a flock of primped women in sequined party dresses and scrunchied ponytails who entered the nightclub ahead of them.

Marcus rolled his eyes and sighed, then followed his partner's lead into the thumping, dark space. Inside, the club's reflective walls resembled fun-house mirrors, accented by neon squiggles of green, blue, and hot orange. A mirrorball cast flickers of sparkling color on the mass of sweating bodies that congregated in the center of the room. The officer glanced toward an upstairs balcony area, which was mostly populated by young couples slow-dancing, then took a deep breath.

Castillo noticed Marcus scanning the room. "You looking for someone in particular?"

Marcus didn't make eye contact as he allowed his gaze to jump from woman to woman. The back of a blonde woman's hair caught his attention enough for him to stop, zero in, and continue to ignore Castillo's question. When the woman turned, Marcus sank, lowering his shoulders and his hopes.

"I said: you looking for someone?" Castillo repeated.

The man shook his head then glanced toward a hallway near the building's entrance. "Just need to make a call," said Marcus, already moving away.

As Marcus vanished into the throng, Rico threw his hands up in frustration and made his way toward the bar.

When Marcus had located the club's payphone, tucked down a hall that was still far too loud to carry on much of a conversation, he withdrew a few loose coins from his pocket and slipped them into the machine. He started to dial, then realized he hadn't yet memorized the number to Donna's current apartment. Marcus stuffed his hand into his back pocket, removed his wallet, then carefully slid a small business card out of it. On the front, the card advertised a local establishment—Jaci's Pizza. Marcus flipped the card over, revealing a word scrawled hastily in blue ink: *Goldielocks*. Beneath it was a handwritten phone number preceded by Miami's signature 305 area code.

Marcus tapped in the number from the card and pressed the receiver to his ear. With the music thumping almost tangibly around him, he could barely make out the sound of a ring. Then another ring. Then another.

By the final ring, Marcus exhaled deeply and clicked the receiver back into its place. He lingered for a moment, took another breath, then issued back down the hallway.

The revelers dotting the central dancefloor seemed to take a collective breath as the disc jockey transitioned to a new track—another pulsing, throbbing pop beat. Marcus spun around, searching for his partner. He strained his eyes to locate Castillo in the dimly-illuminated space.

As he squinted to look up to the balcony, Marcus took a step back and nearly lost his balance. His elbow collided with another and he felt a cold splash over his entire arm.

"Oh!" A woman's voice exclaimed as she whipped around.

Marcus turned, too, as he inspected the sleeve of his blazer, now soaked in once-fizzing cola. He was too caught off guard to be angry. When he'd finished his rotation, he raised his eyes, meeting those of the lady who now stood before him. For a moment, Marcus could hardly think or breathe; she was beautiful—a mass of tiny, black locks framing her dark eyes as she held out a white cloth napkin as a peace offering.

"I am *so* sorry!" She winced when she realized the extent of the spill.

"It's my fault—I guess that's why they say to keep your eyes on the road," Marcus grinned, nearly shouting over the pulsing music, then raised his soaking arm to accept the napkin. "It couldn't have been *water*, could it?"

The woman smiled and shook her head. "Rum and coke."

"A classic," Marcus replied, dabbing at his sleeve.

Slowly, the woman took a step backward. "Well, I'd better go. I've caused enough trouble here."

"Hey, wait," the young officer said, moving toward her. "Where you going?"

"Gotta get another drink to dump on someone," she quipped. "I hope you find 'em." With that, she turned, but Marcus interjected before she could get far.

"Wait—find *who*?"

"Whoever you're looking for," the woman said dismissively, ready to turn away again.

Marcus furrowed his brow, confused.

The woman stopped, then moved a step closer and took a deep breath. "I know you're with someone," she said finally.

"Excuse me?" *How does she—?*

"Come on," the woman continued. "You're preoccupied, not watching where you're going, *and* you're not even a *little* bit tipsy? You were looking for someone—whoever you came here with."

The DJ's track throbbed and swelled.

"Oh!" Marcus exclaimed finally. "You mean *Castillo?* He's my partner—"

The woman raised an eyebrow.

"At work, I mean," he stumbled. "No, we're just—he's one of my closest friends—my wingman, you know?"

The lady laughed and shook her head. "What's your name?"

He took a deep breath and flashed his winning smile. "I'm Marcus," he said, relieved.

"What are you doing tomorrow night, Marcus?"

He started to think and speak at the same time, but nothing intelligible came out. "Uh—"

"Buy me a drink tomorrow night—eight o'clock?"

He hesitated, thought of Donna. *She said she can't do this—us.* Marcus breathed in and finally nodded. "Just name the place."

"The Jade Lion," she answered. "You been there?"

"I know where it is," Marcus affirmed.

As soon as he said this, the woman started to slink away, but Marcus interjected once more.

"Wait," he hollered. "I didn't get your name!"

With a coy smile, the woman took one step toward Marcus. "It's Angela," she said. "See you tomorrow." Angela flashed another smile and added, "There's more napkins at the bar," then swiftly disappeared into the crowd of dancers behind her, leaving Marcus mesmerized.

*Angela,* he mused, allowing the rest of the room to evaporate for the moment while his thoughts zeroed in on the enigmatic beauty of the woman who had just vanished into the crowd.

*See you tomorrow, Angela.*

The first golden rays of the Florida sun crept through the windows of Donna's apartment the next morning, casting linear beams across her curled-up body and the pink sofa on which she slept. She tossed and turned before blinking groggily as a shadow cast itself over her: the shape of a small girl.

"Starla, what're you doing?" Donna groaned. "Up early *again?*"

"I'm getting ready," the girl replied, slipping on the same pair of socks that she'd worn since the day she came from the hospital.

"Ready? What time is it?"

"It's almost time for school," answered Starla, nodding toward a digital clock.

Donna's heart jumped and she sprung upright. "Oh, gosh! I'm sorry—I overslept!" She quickly tossed aside a blanket and began to pace around the living room. "So how does this work? Do we walk there, ride the school bus together, hail a cab—"

"It's fine," Starla assured her. "Your friends helped show me how to get to the bus stop—I can do it all by myself."

"You can?" Donna stood with a look of disbelief, raising a skeptical eyebrow. Then, as the girl grabbed her backpack and headed for the door, her caretaker added, "Okay, well, just remember, um, don't be out too late, make sure you keep your shoes tied, and uh—" She searched for whatever other wisdom she could remember receiving at Starla's age. "Don't talk to strangers."

The girl flashed a toothy grin and opened the door. "I won't, Aunt Donna."

*Aunt Donna.* That was the first time she'd heard it out loud, yet it somehow seemed...

"Right," Donna replied, following Starla out to the landing. "I forgot; you're seven and you can do everything but cook," she mumbled under her breath and watched the girl descend the steps down to the ground level. The woman hung her body over the railing to holler to Starla one last time. "And stay away from boys!" She shouted with a smile. Donna couldn't be sure from a distance, but it looked as if Starla's cheeks grew rosy. Finally, the girl turned and contin- ued her journey down the sidewalk before disappearing around a corner.

Donna returned to the apartment and latched the door behind her. She felt a dryness in her throat and realized she hadn't had anything to drink since early the prior day. Her stomach gurgled. As the twelve-hour timeframe prescribed by Dr. Lansing had expired, Donna moved to the kitchen and grabbed a glass from the cabinet. She quickly filled it with water from the faucet then began to chug, barely taking a moment to breathe before filling the glass a second time.

When she'd drank her fill, Donna set her glass on the counter and moved toward the refrigerator. Before she could open it, though, she felt a churning in her gut. She nearly retched and lost her balance, catching herself with a grip on the edge of the counter. As she leaned there for a moment, contorting her face from the pain, she took a deep breath. Slowly, she hobbled down the hallway and collapsed in front of the ivory toilet with the bathroom door wide open. She had barely lifted the seat when she felt an extremely unpleasant expulsion of digestive juices forcing their way up her throat. Then, unable to hold these back any longer, Donna opened her mouth and released the soupy cargo into the toilet bowl.

Donna felt immediate relief and loosened her white-knuckled grip on the sides of the toilet. She closed her eyes and took deep breaths. Suddenly, she began to experience a light tingling in the tips of her fingers. When Donna opened her eyes to inspect them, she let out a sharp scream and quickly threw her hands up in the air. She leaned away instinctively, distancing herself from the porcelain throne as if it held some terrible curse, for the toilet was no longer its normal, off-white color; it now appeared to be coated in shimmering, sparkling gold.

# CHAPTER 13

*What the—?*

Donna held her mouth agape as she took another long look at the now-golden toilet and craned her neck to view it from every angle, hoping to prove to herself that this was some sort of strange apparition.

*It has to be a dream... right?*

Finally, she stood up and held her hands in front of her, palms up. There didn't seem to be anything different in their appearance, and the tingling had faded considerably. *Did I do that?* For what seemed like several minutes to her, Donna's gaze flitted back and forth between her outstretched hands and the shimmering metallic toilet.

*How on earth—?* Then it hit her: *The lab. The experiment!* It was the only explanation. *But why did it happen now and not sooner?* Pushing this thought aside, Donna focused on the more pressing one: *Can it happen again?*

Keeping her hands with fingers wide in front of her, Donna quickly began to scan the small bathroom. Her eyes alighted on a pink, plastic toothbrush in a cup, its bristles frayed and worn. Slowly, cautiously, the woman stepped toward it. Then, with a deep breath, she extended her hand to reach for it.

The instant Donna's fingers touched the thin shank, the toothbrush began to transform before her eyes. She quickly lifted the light, plastic handle from the cup. It rapidly become heavier and—more significantly—changed its coloring and physical makeup. She held it in front of her face to get a closer look. The object she held in her hands was no longer a mundane, ordinary toothbrush; now it was made of solid gold.

Donna gasped. *This can't be real!*

And yet there was the evidence of its reality: a toilet and a toothbrush both miraculously turned to gold in front of her own eyes. As she held the gilded toothbrush, Donna looked up into the mirror. Her thick, blonde hair was its usual, tangled mess—that was nothing new—but inside there welled a novel, foreign feeling she struggled to describe.

*Luck? Fate? No.* She took a deep breath and looked her reflection in the eyes. *Hope: the possibility of a better future. Finally, I can live the life I've wanted for so long.*

As she came to this realization, Donna quickly began to scan the room. She placed a finger on the bathroom's stainless steel doorknob. Instantly, it turned to gold. Donna let out a gasp of delight then made her way down the hall and back to the living room. Along the way, she touched a pair of wooden picture frames that quickly faded from a dark stain to a brilliant, yellowish metal.

*Unbelievable!*

For several minutes, Donna hurried around the large front room, fingering all manner of ordinary objects. In every instance, the items upon which she placed her hands morphed into gilded versions of their former shapes. Hoping to test the limits of this newfound ability, Donna glanced at her elbow. She then bent down toward the coffee table and placed the elbow—instead of her hand—to its surface. There was no shimmer or gilding this time, however. Next, the woman carefully placed her bare foot on the table. In the same way, there was no change in the furnishing's makeup.

*So this strange power is only in my hands—my fingers? The golden touch.*

Donna's stomach rumbled. She remembered she hadn't eaten anything since early the prior day, and all of the running around had made her tired. The woman moved to the kitchen counter, where she kept a basket of a few wrinkling apples on display. Out of habit, Donna reached for one of the shiny, red fruits and brought it to her mouth. She closed her eyes to enjoy a large, juicy bite, but then felt a sharp pain in her jaw as she bit down.

*Ow!*

Donna inspected the apple and realized that it, too, had turned to gold.

*That could be a problem...*

Thinking quickly, the woman moved around to the other

side of the counter and pulled open a silverware drawer. Donna ignored the new gold knob that appeared, then fished for a fork. By the time she held it up to inspect it, it was now no longer silver. Donna gripped the golden fork firmly and jabbed it into another apple in the basket. To her relief, the apple remained its natural color. With a deep breath, Donna took a massive bite. The apple was perfectly sweet and crisp, and Donna savored every mouthful.

She finished the last morsels of fruit, then the phone rang, startling her. Donna reached for the receiver then caught herself at the last minute. *That would not be good,* she thought as the ringing continued and she wondered how she might pick up the phone without touching it with her hands. Donna scampered around the kitchen and the living room, wringing her hands while the phone's chimes resounded throughout the apartment. She remembered the speakerphone button and was about to try and press it with her elbow when the sound ceased, followed by a *click!* and then a long beep.

The answering machine relayed a voice Donna didn't recognize: "Hello, this message is for Donna Locke. We have a slot that opened up on tonight's lineup at 8:15. Let us know if you can make it. If you have any questions, call me back at The Jade Lion booking office." Then the voice rattled off a phone number that Donna didn't have a way to transcribe.

*Surprised they want me back,* she thought. *But now I can finally pursue my dream without worrying about the measly pay. I can finally be Goldielocks without worrying about making a living—*

Her thoughts were interrupted by the phone ringing a second time. Donna didn't want to miss the booking agent again—this gig was important, after all—so she eyed the phone intently then reached out her elbows. It took a few tries, in which she managed to dislodge the phone from its mount. The phone clattered onto the counter, receiver-side up. Donna was so flabbergasted that she almost forgot there was someone on the other end. She reached out her elbow once more and finally landed on the speakerphone button.

"Hello?" A familiar woman's voice came faintly through the speaker.

Donna moved closer and answered back: "Hello, this is Donna—"

"Oh, Miss Locke! This is Debra, from Pelican Innovations."

"Debra," Donna repeated, recalling the energetic receptionist. "Uh, how are you?"

A little confused by the question, Debra replied: "I'm fine, thank you. I was just calling to see if you had time for your first follow-up meeting this afternoon. Dr. Lansing thought it would be a good idea—"

*What if they take this away? I can't let them know!* Donna's thoughts interrupted. *I can't lose this—*

"Miss Locke?"

"Yeah, I'm here."

"How does two o'clock sound?"

Donna thought it over for a moment, then nodded, "Two o'clock sounds perfect."

"Great!" Debra replied enthusiastically. "We'll see

you then!"

Donna heard the *click* as Debra hung up on the other end of the line. With a deep breath, Donna exhaled and took another look at her hands. Her fingers felt a slight and momentary tingle, then it was gone.

*This changes everything. I can't lose this.*

Officer Myles paced in front of the large map of the city's streets. The faint sounds of chatter and telephones ringing grew louder all of a sudden as the door swung open. Officer Castillo appeared in the threshold.

"Sanchez found something I think you should see," he said, nodding his head to signal for Marcus to follow him.

The two men wove through the maze of desks until they came to one with a boxy computer where Detective Sanchez strained to read from the screen.

"What'd you find, Sanchez?" Marcus asked.

Ruby pointed to the on-screen report. "This is a list of all license plates reported missing in the last year," she said.

"And?"

"You said Mr. Newport reported his plate just a couple weeks ago," she continued. "We keep these files up-to-date— you can thank Marge for that. Sure enough, he *did* file for a missing plate."

Marcus raised an eyebrow. "You're serious?"

"Dead serious," Ruby answered.

Officer Myles paced for a moment before returning to lean

close to the screen once more. "What's the recorded date and time of the incident?"

Ruby clicked the bulky mouse and called up more details about the report. "2:15 p.m. on April 3. That mean something to you?"

Marcus snapped his finger and pointed at Castillo. "You remember what Mr. Newport said about the stolen plate?"

"Yeah," Castillo nodded. "He was out for a night on the town."

"Exactly!" Marcus smiled. "A *night* on the town—he said it was dark when he came back to the car and noticed the plate missing."

"You don't think it could've been an error in the report?" Officer Castillo didn't want to jump to conclusions too soon.

Detective Sanchez reached into a file folder, withdrew a piece of paper, and shook her head. "Marge is too good about double-checking the data," she said, pointing to the sheet. "The hard copy has the same time, too. If it says the incident happened at 2:15 p.m., then that's when it happened."

"Newport didn't think we'd call his bluff," Marcus muttered as he began to pace again.

"So what's he hiding?" Castillo interjected. "And what's his connection to all this—the van, the drugs, the freaky dragon mask?"

"I don't know," replied Officer Myles as he tapped his chin. Then he turned back to Castillo. "But," he added, "I bet if we keep an eye on him, he's bound to let something slip."

"What do you have in mind?"

"A stakeout," answered Marcus. "Watch that compound of his—note any comings and goings that seem suspicious. If he's in with the cartel, we'll find out soon enough."

"You're gonna wanna get out there as soon as possible," chimed Ruby. "Now that he knows you're on to his scent, the window's closing—hopefully you didn't already miss your chance."

Castillo turned to his partner. "Well, shall we?"

Marcus nodded. "We'll take shifts," he explained. "Two of us at once would draw too much attention. I'll take this afternoon; you okay taking tonight?" The officer gave a conspicuous wink to his partner.

Detective Sanchez perked up: "Oh, I see—looks like *someone's* got a date." She gave a playful swoon and batted her eyelashes. "Who's the lucky girl?"

Marcus rolled his eyes. "Don't worry about it, Sanchez," he grinned.

She pressed: "What's this, the third date? Second?"

"First," Marcus finally obliged. "She's someone I ran into the other night—we kinda hit it off, I guess."

"I see," Sanchez nodded, then shifted her gaze to the other officer. "Whatever happened to that friend of your sister's, Castillo? I thought you set them up." She pointed a finger at Marcus, but Castillo didn't answer right away.

Finally, he sputtered, "Didn't really work out, I guess." Rico added a light punch to his partner's shoulder. "That right?"

Marcus, who had suddenly become somber, offered a faint smile then nodded quickly. "Yeah. Right." Then, once again bringing their imminent mission to attention, he said: "Ready to get to work?"

Castillo nodded.

"Well, have fun out there, boys," said Detective Sanchez. The two men thanked her for her help and hurried off to prepare for the stakeout.

# CHAPTER 14

Donna had some time until the laboratory appointment at Pelican, so she decided to make a little detour on her way there. Before leaving, however, she first took another look around the apartment. In her bedroom, Donna found a smattering of Starla's belongings strewn across the floor, including a few of the girl's toys.

Her eyes caught a small, plastic action figure coated in a cheap and fading metallic paint. Donna picked it up with two fingers and felt the lightweight toy android become heavier as its makeup shifted to one of solid gold. She recognized the character from a popular space film that had come out a few years prior. *This will go for a good price, I should think.*

The woman gathered a couple more ordinary items from around the house, transforming them with a single touch into invaluable treasures. She threw them into a voluminous and sturdy handbag whose threaded texture had also been transfigured into woven, semi-malleable gold. Then, with much care and difficulty, Donna managed to exit her apartment, accidentally turning the old brass doorknob to gold on her way out.

It was a warm and sunny day, but Donna chose to walk to her destination rather than risk nudging up against someone on the bus and causing a panic. She paid little mind to the fact that she was still in the clothes she'd woken up in. She wasn't sure she had much of a choice in the matter, anyhow. That was a logistical problem for another time, though. Now she came to a stop on the sidewalk and looked up to read the sign on a small, nondescript building painted in a red-orange hue:

*Manolio's Pawn Shop and Jewelry*

She clutched her shimmering handbag of golden items close to her chest to avoid drawing too much attention as she waited conspicuously for another customer to enter or exit the building. Several minutes passed. Finally, she saw someone leaving. Donna nearly sprinted toward the open door. It was closing fast—too fast for her to fit herself through the gap. Donna reached out with her foot and wedged it between the gap.

*Ow!* She winced at the minor pain, then used her leg to open the door the rest of the way so she could shimmy herself through the space and into the shop hands-free. A tiny bell jingled as the door slammed shut behind her.

The building smelled like the bedroom of a teenager who's tried and failed to hide the smell of cigarettes from their parents by spraying an ungodly amount of air fresheners; the smoky scent prevailed. Donna glanced around at the stacks of old and used electronics that formed rudimentary aisles down the length of the compact space. A bin of twenty-five-cent records caught her eye near the entrance, but she quickly passed it by and located the check-out counter.

Donna tapped her foot anxiously while the customer in front of her completed a transaction, then she stepped up to the counter and dumped her wares in front of the young clerk. "How much can you give me for all this?" She quickly took a half-step back and threw her hands to her sides.

The young man's jaw nearly dislodged itself and his pupils enlarged as he inspected the glittering mass of items before him. "Are you for real?"

Donna wasn't sure whether to interpret the man's words as serious or sarcastic. "Um, yes," she said diplomatically. "It's all real—real gold."

He suddenly seemed interested in only one item in the pile, which he picked up carefully with a gloved hand—the golden robot action figure. "This has got to be one in a million or something," the clerk said with awe. "Do you *know* what you have here?"

"Um, of-of course," Donna stuttered. She didn't know. "It must be a prototype or something."

"I have *never* seen a solid gold Threepio before," the clerk said, seemingly to himself, a huge, dumbfounded smile wiping across his face.

"So, it's valuable?"

"Shyeah!" The clerk answered. "With the new movie coming out, it'll be in even higher demand. You a fan?"

Donna realized she couldn't remember the name of the movie from which the droid came. She improvised, "Sure, I've been watching Star Trek for years."

The young man raised an eyebrow then shook his head in disappointment.

"So?" Donna tapped her foot.

The clerk took a small magnifying glass to verify the details upon the golden surfaces of the action figure, then looked Donna in the eye. "Five hundred dollars."

Donna staggered backward but caught herself. "Five *hundred?*"

"Yeah; that's what I said."

The woman could hardly believe it. A few days ago, she was struggling to make her rent payments; now, unpaid bills seemed to be becoming a thing of the past. By some miraculous turn of events, her life was suddenly changing. *The possibilities are limitless. This is totally unreal.*

Donna quickly agreed to the amount without much more thought, and waited as the young man took the figurine and disappeared somewhere in the back of the store. A moment later, he returned with a huge wad of bills—five hundred dollars in cash.

For a moment, Donna wondered how she'd receive the payment without turning the cash—or the clerk—to gold.

Finally, she took her golden bag and held it open in front of her. "Just drop it in there," she instructed. The man obliged, raising another curious eyebrow. "Thanks, and have a nice day."

Donna started away from the counter when the clerk called after her: "What about the rest of this stuff?" He gestured to the smattering of golden objects from her bag.

"All yours," Donna forced a quick smile, then continued walking.

Satisfied with the day's yield, Donna hurried out the door, pushing it open quickly with her right hand. As she stepped onto the sidewalk and heard the jingling of the door as it slammed shut, she froze. It was the same, hollow metallic sound as when she'd entered. Donna slowly turned around and examined the door, her eyes wide. She held up her bare hand and examined it, then looked back at the door. The frame of the door was the same, peeling, painted red-orange as before.

*Not gold!* Donna's breathing became tense. She glanced back at her hand. It wasn't tingling this time. Quickly, she hustled back to the door and swung it open with her right hand again. She inspected the backside of it but found that it, too, was still its proper color and makeup. Donna shuffled her handbag so that she could try using her left hand, but it was the same. *Nothing. I don't understand—*

"Are you okay, lady?" The clerk shouted from inside while Donna held the shop's door agape.

Donna's eyes were fixed on her hands as she replied

absently, "I'm not sure—thanks." *This is terrible. I need this power to come back. This was supposed to change everything!* The woman let the door swing shut once more and started back down the sidewalk, recalling the appointment. As she made her way on the route to the lab, she resolved that she could not tell the doctor about any of the day's uncanny events. *It's too risky. They can't know, or they'd try to take it away for good— and now I've got to find a way to bring it back.*

The laboratory seemed colder to Donna that day as she sat down in a chair in the waiting area across from Debra's desk. She began to shiver and immediately wished she'd brought a sweater. After a few minutes, the lab door opened and Dr. Lansing greeted her with his typically-dodgy smile and scattered manner of speech.

"Right this way—you know the drill," he said as he led Donna into the same small examination room from the prior day. He fiddled with unpackaging a fresh sampling kit while he began with what had become mindless, routine questions: "So, have you noticed any changes since yesterday?"

Donna situated herself in the sterile, stiff chair and tried to conceal her gilded handbag under the seat as much as possible while she played dumb: "Changes? What sort of changes?"

Dr. Lansing glanced over his shoulder. "You know, any symptoms, side effects, hallucinations—anything like that."

"Hallucinations?" Donna hadn't considered the possibility that her escapades could have been figments of her imagination. *It all seemed so real.* The woman craned her neck to look back at the bag underneath the chair to verify its golden makeup, but the doctor interrupted before she could steal a look, appearing at her side with a small syringe.

Roger wiped the small patch of skin and plunged the needle into Donna's arm. She winced as the doctor continued his questions: "Have you had any?"

"Any what?" Donna took labored breaths and felt dizzy all of a sudden.

"Hallucinations," he said.

She took another deep breath. "I don't know..." Donna leaned her head over the chair and finally saw the edge of her purse. Sure enough, it was composed of glittering gold.

"You don't know?"

"I don't think so," she clarified. "I mean, *no*. I haven't had any." The last thing she needed was for the doctor to think she was crazy. *Then they definitely wouldn't let me get away with having this ability. Now I just have to figure out how to get it back...*

Dr. Lansing inspected his newly acquired blood sample, holding it up so that the fluorescent panels on the ceiling provided a vibrant backlight. He squinted, shifting the large glasses tighter on his face.

"What are you hoping to see?" Donna inquired.

"Sometimes," Roger explained, still holding the vial close to his face, "one is able to see changes in the blood right away with the naked eye. In other instances, it takes time and a closer examination to see how something's been altered. My hope is that my hard work has resulted in meaningful, visible change." He turned back to Donna with a sad, forced grin. "But maybe I'm just a little too optimistic."

Donna sensed there was more behind the man's words, but she wasn't sure she wanted to pry. She opted instead for a cheerful yet cryptic encouragement. "I think someday you'll be able to look back and see that all your hard work was, er—" Donna searched for the right word, "*worth* far more than you think, Dr. Lansing."

"Please, call me Roger," he said with a more genuine smile. "And you really think so?"

"I *know* so."

Roger sighed. "Well, now, if only you could sway our investors or Ang—uh, Miss Hyde. They're not convinced that my efforts over the past several years are going to pay off."

"What do you mean?" The woman was now very interested in what the doctor had to say. "Do you mean they're going to shut this down?" *And take away the possibility of this miraculous gift returning?*

"I'm afraid so—*if* I can't prove these tests are producing results." Dr. Lansing drifted into a thought, then returned his attention to the blood sample in his hand. "I'm sorry, I shouldn't have said all of that. All of those details are supposed to remain confidential from our subjects so it doesn't affect your perceptions of the formula's effects—" He rambled on as he packed up the test kit. Finally, he turned back to Donna. "All set."

"That's it?" Donna breathed a sigh of relief. She'd made

it through the appointment without letting slip what had happened.

"That's it," Roger affirmed. "We'll have Debra schedule a follow-up for around this time next week." As they exited and Donna gathered her things, he added, "And thank you, Donna."

"For what?"

"For believing in me—in the science."

She nodded and they returned to the waiting area. Debra smiled as they came near. "Gorgeous handbag, Donna," she commented. "The gold threading on that material is *so* chic."

"Uh, thanks," Donna sputtered and pushed it closer to her side, hoping the doctor wouldn't notice.

"Well," Roger said. "I'll leave you to it. Have an excellent afternoon and a good night." Dr. Lansing smiled, waved, then returned through the mysterious doors at the other side of the large space.

*Perhaps the key to bringing this back is in there*, Donna mused, trying to catch a glimpse inside as the doors shut quickly. *I will find a way. I need this.* Then she remembered something. She turned to Debra. "Can I borrow your phone—and a phone book?"

Debra shuffled under her desk as she answered eagerly. "Of course!" A moment later she plopped the large, thick book on the counter. Donna thanked her and flipped through the book to find the phone number for The Jade Lion.

# CHAPTER 15

Marcus checked the clock on the van's dashboard. It had already been a couple of hours that he'd sat parked along the road leading to Vander Newport's compound-like residence—from there he could easily see whether any visitors came or went. He and his vehicle wore the trappings of an electric utility company to avoid suspicion, but he knew it was only a matter of time before someone noticed. To his relief, a voice crackled over the radio.

"Almost there, Myles. Hit the beginning of rush-hour traffic." It was Castillo, on his way to take the night shift.

Marcus smiled and clicked the radio to reply: "Perfect timing for my commute home—thanks for that."

"Relax," answered Castillo. "You've got plenty of time to groom yourself before the big night." He chuckled to himself. "You see anything?"

"No one in or out," Marcus replied. "Hope you get a little

more action."

"That's why I became a cop, after all."

The intercom clicked off again and Marcus took a deep breath. A few moments later, he caught sight of a van in his rearview mirror—a van with an identical electric company logo. Its driver flashed its brights twice—Castillo's signal— and Marcus turned on the engine. As Rico looped back, the two disguised officers passed one another with a quick nod, then Marcus drove away.

Rico parked his electric utility service van on the opposite side of the street from Marcus' prior stakeout position, a little closer to Newport's property. As he leaned over the dashboard, he could see the cameras with their aim fixed on the area around the front gate; Castillo's vehicle was just out of their reach. The officer took shaky, deep breaths then leaned back in his seat.

It had been a long day, so it took every ounce of Rico's willpower to keep from dozing off. As the first hour passed, he felt his eyelids drooping. Through the drowsy slits, he finally saw a movement near Newport's gate. His eyes widened and he sprung forward to get a better look through the tinted window.

The gate opened. This time, someone was approaching from inside. As a black car inched down the driveway, Rico ducked lower to avoid being seen. Over the top of the dash, he observed as the small car turned into the street and drove slowly past him with the windows down. The driver looked familiar to Castillo: *the butler from earlier—going home for the night?* When he was sure the car was out of sight, the young officer slowly returned to his upright position to continue his watchful mission.

Another hour or so later—Castillo was losing track of the time—the gate began to open once more. It had grown dark, but the officer could still make out the metallic blue coloring of the classic car that edged onto the street. As the car passed by, Castillo saw the silhouette of the wealthy Vander Newport in the driver's seat of what appeared to be some breed of Ferrari. *Nice,* Castillo nodded his head in admiration as he held his breath instinctively.

In the rearview mirror, Officer Castillo caught the quick flash of red from the brake lights as the Ferrari peeled around a hedged corner and disappeared. He turned his eyes back to the residence. *So now I just wait some more?*

Castillo tapped his fingers on the steering wheel of the utility van and inspected the mounted cameras above the gate. At that moment, he recalled his observation the prior day: there were no cameras on the backside of the house—along the waterway. Quickly, the officer glanced down the street to the house directly next door to Newport's; its lights were off and he hadn't seen any vehicles enter or exit the premises during his entire shift. *Snowbirds,* he mused. *Gone for the summer a little early?* He was fairly certain of it—and it helped that they didn't have a fence to prevent entry to their backyard.

The officer took a deep breath and exhaled slowly. Breaking and entering with so little concrete information was highly frowned upon by Metro-Dade policy, but Castillo felt certain of Vander Newport's connection to the smuggling operation; all he needed was to find some evidence. Officer Castillo unlocked the driver's side door with a *click* and started to open it.

Suddenly, a bright light blinded his vision, bouncing off the rearview mirror above him. Castillo panicked, covered his eyes, and slammed the door shut. He hurriedly crouched low, out of view. The car drove past—uncomfortably slow— then vanished down another street.

*On second thought...* Officer Castillo began to reconsider the risks—like being spotted by a passing civilian.

*No. I have to do this. There's got to be something inside that can prove he's part of this.* With a final survey of his surroundings, Officer Castillo clicked open the door, quietly shut it behind him, and slinked across the silent road in a shadow between two streetlights.


Donna leaned over the bathroom sink in front of her, pausing to stare at herself in the mirror as she powdered her face. Her slightly-swollen eyes drifted down to her toothbrush sitting underneath, its neck now crafted of what looked like solid gold. She shook her head. The morning's events seemed like a dream; and yet here was the evidence that it had all truly happened—that it was real.

Little Starla appeared in the open doorway. "When did we get a new toilet?"

"Um," Donna searched for a response as she quickly continued the application of blush to her cheeks. "This morning. Do you like it?"

"It looks expensive," replied the girl.

"Yeah, well it was," answered Donna. "Figured we spend so many hours of our lives on it, might as well look nice, right?"

Starla nodded, then cocked her head. "You look sad, Aunt Donna."

Donna closed her eyes, took a deep breath, then set down the makeup brush. She turned to the girl and crouched to her level. "I am sad, kid."

"How come?"

She inhaled deeply, searching for the words. "Well, your Aunt Donna thought she had a way to take care of you, to provide all the things your mother would have—I mean, *has.* But, no matter how hard you work, sometimes things are just too good to be true."

The seven-year-old seemed to be taking all of her words to heart. "But you *are* taking care of me."

Donna exhaled slowly and forced a slight smile. "I'm trying my best, kiddo," she answered. "But I can't give you everything you need—you deserve better. Someday, when you're older, you'll understand what I mean." The woman tousled the girl's hair then rose to finish getting ready.

As Starla hurried back to the living room, Donna shouted after her: "Keep an ear out for the door—babysitters should be here any minute now."

"I'm not a baby," the girl hollered back.

"You know what I—" Donna's hand slipped and she accidentally swiped lipstick over her chin. She puffed, then heard a knock at the apartment door. "Can you get that?"

Starla answered the door, revealing the gregarious duo of Sue and Lisa.

"Hey, girl!" Lisa exclaimed as she entered the apartment. "Ready for a fun little girl's night?" The women took turns giving Starla hugs as they dropped their purses on the counter.

Sue held a pizza box in hand with a couple of decks of playing cards on top. "You like pepperoni, right?"

Starla nodded enthusiastically as the aroma filled the room.

"Good," continued Sue. "Afterwards we can teach you Go Fish or Texas Hold-'em or—"

Donna appeared in the hall, snapping a shiny earring into place. "Oh, thank you guys again," she gushed and embraced her friends. "It's been a crazy day and I *really* need this gig tonight."

"Don't mention it, Don. We're always here for you, remember?" Lisa raised her brow for emphasis.

The blonde woman nodded then brushed out a wrinkle in her glittering, sequin-covered dress. "How do I look?" Donna spun around slowly, the metallic circles creating a shimmering, golden disco-ball effect on the walls.

"Like a million bucks," Sue quipped. "Go get 'em, Goldie."

"I told you before, Sue; it's *Goldielocks*." Donna threw a thin trenchcoat over the ensemble to make herself appear less flashy during transit.

"I dunno, Don," chimed Lisa. "Sue may be on to something. People remember things better when there's fewer syllables."

"Thank you for the grammar lesson," Donna smiled, slinging a small handbag over her shoulder. "Gotta go—I can't be late again." The woman blew kisses to her pair of friends, then opened the door. As she closed it behind her, Donna stuck her head through the gap and added to Starla: "Be good, okay?"

The little girl smiled. "Will do, Aunt Donna."

Donna took a deep breath and nodded. She shut the apartment door then hurried off into the night.

# CHAPTER 16

A giant hedge ran from the front of Newport's property to the inlet and docks in the back, creating an impassable barrier between his yard and the next-door neighbor's. Officer Castillo considered his options; there was no way to climb over the hedge without creating a great amount of noise—or getting scratched up by the thorny branches. He stood at the back edge of the neighbor's lot and looked down into the dark, rippling water just a few feet below the level of the backyard. Castillo felt a lump in his throat as he realized getting into the water was his only viable option.

He took another glance around to make sure he wasn't visible to any of the neighbors, then Castillo removed his shoes and began to unzip the coveralls that bore the utility company insignia. He would risk tracking in too much water if he kept the uniform on. *And besides,* he reminded himself, *I've got a change of clothes in the van.* Castillo reached into a pocket and withdrew a tiny flashlight. When he was stripped down to only his boxer shorts, he tucked his discarded trappings under the base of the hedge and once again moved closer to the water.

Carefully, the young officer placed the small flashlight between his teeth, crouched, then began to lower himself into the inlet. His toes met the water first—surprisingly cold for springtime in Miami—then Castillo allowed the rest of his body to descend into the gloomy ripples. He sunk slowly until the water met his chest, paused, then quickly dunked the rest of the way. Castillo breathed his momentary relief as he kept himself afloat, neck-deep in the water, then waded toward Newport's backyard dock.

A metal ladder led up to the dock, situated opposite Newport's freshly-cleaned boat. Castillo avoided the ladder's slippery, algae-covered lower steps, instead pulling himself up to rest his bare feet on a higher rung. Before clearing the safety of the shadows, he took another look to verify the absence of any cameras. *All clear*, he confirmed, then sloshed across the dock's planks toward the house.

The home was completely dark. Castillo took the flashlight in hand and clicked it on, peering through the sliding glass doors. He saw silhouettes of the modern furniture on which they'd sat the prior day then allowed his eyes to scan what little else he could see. The officer jumped when he thought he saw movement through a doorway off the side of the living room. He swung the beam of his light in that direction. Nothing. *Just the shadows of swaying palm trees playing tricks.*

Rico took another deep breath to calm himself then moved on to the next order of business: getting inside.

First, he jiggled the sliding door handle. *Locked.* Next, he moved past a glassy swimming pool toward a more opaque glass door near the side of the house. Castillo turned the handle slowly. To his surprise, it clicked open. *I'm amazed this guy doesn't have an alarm system set up*, he thought. *Could definitely afford one.*

He shined the light inside. It was a small bathroom. Remembering that he was sopping wet, Castillo stood on the threshold and reached an arm toward a stack of towels above the toilet. He quickly dried himself off as much as he could, then carefully folded the towel and put it back in place. The officer, clad only in his damp boxers, entered the house and closed the door behind him.

The air conditioning was set to full blast, and Castillo's teeth chattered as he passed through the bathroom's interior door to enter the hall. He rounded a corner and discovered a set of tile-covered stairs that led up to the second story. Castillo winced as a few droplets of water fell from him to the ground, but he kept his focus on the top of the staircase. He carefully shifted his weight and raised one foot to ascend the stairs. Suddenly, he felt the opposite wet foot slide out from under him. He reached for the railing and grabbed onto it as tightly as he could with a muffled exclamation. After a moment to catch his breath, Rico again stood up and proceeded to climb the staircase with greater caution.

At last, the officer reached the top of the stairs. The second-floor landing was covered in a light-colored carpet. Castillo glanced in either direction to inspect the surroundings. There were four doors: one appeared to be a linen closet and a second led to another bathroom. Officer Castillo concluded that the other two were bedrooms and made his way toward the nearest one.

Castillo peered into the room. Glass blocks on a far wall let in a hazy combination of moonlight and streetlight, and his flashlight came to rest on a queen-sized bed with a duo of lucite end tables at either side. Twin ceramic lamps adorned them, but the officer dared not turn either on. He shifted to another side of the room, illuminating a long, smooth dresser beneath an enormous, rectangular mirror. Castillo grinned when he saw his faintly-lit, half-naked reflection. *I can't believe I'm crawling around some rich guy's mansion like this.* He shook his head, ran a hand through his damp, dark hair, then carefully began to open each of the drawers to feel beneath the stacks of clothes for a secret hiding place.

In a middle drawer, the officer's hands felt something beneath a stack of t-shirts. By touch alone, it seemed to be a large paper folder of some sort. Castillo removed it without disturbing the shirts, then placed it atop the dresser. Sure enough, it was a manila envelope; its seal had been sliced open. The officer reached inside and emptied the contents on the surface, careful to keep them in order: files, notes, receipts, and other assorted slips of paper. Castillo could not immediately tell whether these had any bearing on the case at hand, but he slowly flipped through them to see if anything stood out.

Most were typed forms and spreadsheets that looked like account records, though there were no discernible indicators of what they referred to. As he neared the end of the stack, a small piece of ripped paper fell out. Castillo lifted it and held it up to the flashlight's beam. In quickly-scrawled handwriting, it read:

*Sure about S.G.? Awaiting update.*

The message didn't immediately mean anything to Castillo, but he studied it closer. The bottom corner of the scrap featured half of an emblem of some type of bird—the other portion had been torn off. It was hard to make out for sure, but Castillo thought it looked familiar. Wanting to investigate it further, he folded the fragment and tucked it under the waistband of his shorts.

Castillo carefully returned the envelope and its contents to the drawer and closed it quietly. With his flashlight in hand, he walked back to the hall then descended the steps—this time gripping the railing the entire way down. As he wondered where to look next, he recalled the events that first led them to Vander Newport's home: the sportscar and the license plate. Castillo oriented himself to the house and moved in the presumed direction of the garage.

When he opened the small door from the hall to the

garage, Castillo was surprised that it didn't smell musty like most such storage spaces in South Florida. *Figures,* he thought. *Probably air-conditioned.* The officer shined the light across the expansive space; there was enough of it to fit three cars—and accompanying retractable doors that opened to a driveway on the side of the house. But at the moment there was only a single car inside, covered in a neutral shroud. *The Porsche and his missing plate, perhaps? Only one way to find out.*

The damp officer weaved his way around a stack of boxes. He moved to lift the front edge of the sheet but was startled by a loud creaking sound. A light came on above him. One of the garage doors was opening slowly.

*Someone's home!*

Castillo panicked and sprinted across the garage toward the door, slipping as his wet feet pressed against the concrete. The officer tumbled across the floor, bruising his knee, then forced himself the remaining distance to the door. He threw it open, jumped inside, and closed the door behind him silently, catching a view of the front headlight of the approaching car before it shut. Panting, the officer glanced at the forming welt on his bare skin, then hurried toward the nearest doorway.

He found himself in the kitchen. Before him was a large island with a rounded edge. Castillo heard the sound of the car's engine cut out and he stumbled behind the counter. He ducked. The door from the garage opened and closed. Footsteps clacked across the tile floor and Castillo took shallow, quick breaths. He hadn't been able to make out the color of the car, but he presumed it was Newport.

Castillo closed his eyes and expelled a quiet sigh as he heard the footsteps fade into another part of the house. When he opened his eyes, he jumped and hit his head on the edge of the counter; there in front of him stood a massive dog! The officer rubbed the spot on his head as the dog stared him down from behind a plastic gate. Though it seemed to be contained in the pantry alcove, Castillo immediately grew more fearful. He remembered Mr. Newport's delay in greeting them the other day—he was putting away his pet, he told them. *He can get a little excited,* he'd said.

"So *you're* the security system," Rico whispered under his breath through the throbbing of his head. Castillo poked his forehead above the island to see if he could discern the identity of the visitor but saw no one.

A moment later, the footsteps returned, moving toward the kitchen. A light flicked on and Castillo froze, pressed as close to the island cabinets as possible. The large canine whimpered and the officer slowly brought a finger over his mouth in an attempt to communicate with it.

"What is it, Rufus?" A voice said from behind the counter.

It wasn't Newport's voice, Castillo noted. The dog snarled.

The man's voice continued with a preoccupied air, "Go back to sleep." The dog seemed to comply and lowered its head, but kept its gaze fixed on the intruder before him. "I'm only here for a moment."

Finally, Castillo could discern the familiar voice; it belonged to the butler. *Emilio was his name, wasn't it?*

The officer couldn't see what Emilio was doing, but heard a few clicking noises echo across the kitchen tiles from the butler's location. Then the room became silent. Officer Castillo nearly held his breath, only expelling and inhaling the minimum amount of air needed to stay alive—and that as quietly as possible.

"Hello?" Emilio asked suddenly.

*He's seen me! How?* Castillo tensed even more. *Do I run? Answer back?*

"Excellent, and yourself?" The butler said.

The young, shivering officer closed his eyes for a moment of relief, then listened closely as he realized the butler was on the phone.

"No, that exchange never occurred; there was a, um, complication," Emilio continued. "Nevertheless, I'm prepared to meet at your designated location. 8:17—precise, as usual. I'm en route with the package."

Castillo heard Emilio hang up the phone. The kitchen went dark. Then the butler's footsteps clacked across the tile once more and faded back down the hall to the garage. The door opened and shut. The officer turned back to the guard dog, whose canine gaze remained transfixed on him, its dark eyeballs glistening in the limited moonlight. As Castillo started to move, the dog let out a low growl.

"Shh!" Castillo implored.

The dog barked, much louder this time.

"Quiet, Rufus!" This did little to assuage the large pet. "He'll hear you! Cut it out!"

Realizing his demands were unlikely to be met, the under-dressed cop rose and sprinted across the kitchen. He hurried through the living room and back down the hall. Castillo's foot slipped on the tile as he rounded a corner and he went sailing across the floor.

*Smack!* For a few seconds, he lay flat on his back, hoping the commotion had not attracted any extra attention while he applied pressure to his knee. Rufus continued his barking. In the darkness, it was hard to make out, but Castillo could see the beginnings of a small, bloody wound where a patch of skin had scraped away—on the opposite knee from the bruise from earlier. He winced, confirmed there was no blood on the tile, then rose and continued through the small back bathroom until he was again outside the back of the house.

Castillo heard the garage door closing, then the purr of an automobile engine moving slowly down the long driveway. Realizing that time was of the essence if he was going to follow the butler to this secret rendezvous, he sprinted to the dock with a minor limp and descended the ladder into the inlet's cool, dark water. In no time, the officer was back on the neighbor's property; to his relief, he found his belongings right where he had left them. He fumbled his way into the electrician's jumpsuit and hurried back to the van.

As he slammed the van door shut, Rico watched as the tail lights of Emilio's car disappeared around a hedged street. He ignited the engine and floored the gas pedal, wheeling after the butler. He checked the clock; it was 7:55.

# CHAPTER 17

It was a few minutes before eight o'clock when Donna arrived at the alley entrance to The Jade Lion. After a firm knock on the door, the woman was greeted by the large bouncer, whom she recognized from her previous visit to the club.

"Hey there, uh, *pal*," Donna addressed the man. "Can I call you pal?"

"Get inside," the bouncer replied, sidestepping her question.

"Did you notice I'm early this time?" The woman attempted to break the man's hardened expression to no avail.

"You know the drill," the big man said as he closed the door and led Donna down the dark hallway. "Be ready to go on stage two minutes before your slot."

The man swung open the green room door and Donna thanked him. She removed her neutral-colored trenchcoat and hung it over the back of a chair, then spent the next few minutes touching up her makeup and hair. With a final inspection in the mirror, Donna headed backstage. *There's no way I'm going to let that man short my pay again.*

Another singer began her final song as Donna made her way to stand behind the curtains, just offstage. She lingered in the shadows and watched to see what she might glean from observing the other performer's stage presence. From between the curtains, Donna could see slivers of the crowd— mostly wealthier male patrons with dates much younger than them. By this time many had moved on to their second or third drink. At the far side of the room, the woman's eyes caught a familiar face.

*Marcus!*

Donna was caught off guard. She had intended to reach out after he'd called, but the past few days had been hectic. *Besides, he wouldn't understand my situation—Starla, the experiment. Maybe when things settle down...* Still, the young officer sat alone, handsome as ever. *Dressed to impress—impress who?* There was a glass of water beside him, but he hadn't yet ordered any drinks, Donna noted.

Donna remembered that she had a few minutes until she needed to go on stage. She eyed a half-finished cocktail on a side table and took a large swig; the ice had melted so that the drink was incredibly watered-down, but Donna didn't seem to mind. *Here goes nothing.* She made a beeline for a side door that led to the main room.

Marcus perked up when his eyes met Donna's from across

the wide, dim space. She smiled and waved, but suddenly felt a terrible, queasy feeling. Donna's gut began to rumble; she was going to be sick. Thinking quickly, the blonde woman ducked behind a half-wall and discovered a copper ice bucket. She dumped the ice into a nearby planter and placed her face directly above the now-empty bucket, holding back her hair as she retched and let loose.

*Please tell me Marcus didn't see that.* As she finished, Donna wiped her mouth with a thin napkin and peered over the wall. *Oh, gosh!* Marcus was moving toward her. Donna looked at the napkin in her hand and gasped; it—and the copper ice bucket—had turned to gold!

*It's back? How?* Donna scrambled in a mixture of delight and sudden anxiety. *This is* not *a good time for this to happen—*

"Donna!"

*Oh, no!*

Marcus appeared around the corner as Donna tucked the bucket and napkin behind the planter and flung her hands behind her back. "Marcus! What are you doing here?"

"Uh," he mumbled over the music, moving nearer to the woman. "I-I could ask you the same question."

Donna made a shifty glance, looking for a way to run. "Well, uh, I asked first."

Marcus sighed and took a step closer. "I just—it's been a couple days since..." He trailed off, then started again: "Did you mean what you said on the phone?"

The woman started toward him. "Marcus, I—" She stretched out her hands in an apologetic posture, then held herself back. "It's just that there's a lot going on right now—and I'm not sure you would understand."

"Of course I'd understand," he replied, taking another step forward. "I'd *try* anyway."

The two were mere inches from one another. Donna wanted so badly to reach out and touch him. *Kind, sweet Marcus. He deserves better than this.*

The man's hand moved from his side toward Donna's. "Is everything alright?"

Donna's fingers tingled and twitched instinctively—involuntarily. "Sure," she replied softly.

They were close enough that Donna could feel his cool, minty breath on her cheek. His big, dark eyes had her mesmerized—their dreamy look was one of the things that drew her to him in the first place. Marcus inched his hand closer to hers as the band's performance built to a crescendo.

"Marcus?" A woman's sharp voice pierced the moment—Marcus and Donna took an instinctive step back from each other.

Donna pulled her hand away. The young officer turned to find Angela, the beautiful woman from the dance club, moving toward them. The band played the song's final notes as the room erupted in applause.

"There you are, Marcus," Angela said, arriving at his side wearing a smile and a radiant, purple dress with imposing shoulder pads. "Sorry I'm late—traffic." She raised an eyebrow as she saw Donna, adorned in her sequined dress and feathered blonde hair. "And who's this?"

Marcus took a deep breath, then exhaled. "This is, uh," he smiled. "This is my... friend Donna."

"Donna Locke," the blonde woman nodded.

Angela extended her hand toward the other woman. "Pleased to meet you, Donna Locke," she said with a feigned smile. "I'm Angela Hyde."

*Hyde—I've heard that name recently...* Donna did not reciprocate the gesture of greeting but nodded. "Nice to meet you, too." Then, holding her hands behind her back, she added, "Well, I've gotta get backstage."

As she hurried away, Donna turned back and shouted, "It was good to see you, Marcus."

"Good to see you, too," he replied with a bashful smile, adding "friend" more softly.

When Donna had vanished back through the open side door, Angela turned to Marcus with a skeptical look. "Friend?"

Marcus exhaled through his nose. "We went out for a while, but that was a long time ago," he assured her. Then, with one hand, Marcus motioned toward his table where his glass of water sat collecting condensation. "Shall we?"

Angela raised her eyebrows—still unsure of the veracity of Marcus' story—but nodded and followed Marcus back to the table.

As he piloted the huge, lumbering utility van and attempted to change out of his damp jumpsuit, Castillo maintained a reasonable distance between him and the car driven by Mr. Newport's butler Emilio; the cop needed to avoid suspicion and keep a visual on the little black car at the same time.

But Emilio wasn't making it easy. He swerved in and out of traffic, ducking behind large trucks whenever he could. At one point, Castillo followed the butler around the same block multiple times. The officer was sure he hadn't been seen. *He's just following protocol, taking precautions,* Castillo assured himself.

Finally, the small car came to a stop in a parallel parking space on a tree-lined street in front of a small, pinkish apartment building. It was a few more minutes before the headlights turned out and the man exited the vehicle. While he waited, Castillo slipped on a pair of dry slacks. In the shadows, the officer saw that Emilio carried something that looked like a small briefcase. The butler checked his watch before walking briskly down the dark sidewalk; it was a few minutes past eight.

Now fully dressed, Castillo waited until Emilio neared the end of the block before hurrying quietly behind him. The butler crossed an intersection but continued down the same block once he crossed, so Rico maintained sight as he scurried along in the dark. Officer Castillo paused near the butler's car and peered through the window into the backseat. There was something tucked halfway underneath the back of the driver's seat, as if it had begun to slip out during the ride. Castillo produced his small flashlight, double-checked that there were no passersby in sight, and pointed it through the window as he clicked it on.

The light reflected off something small and metallic on the floor of the car. Castillo craned his neck and adjusted the flashlight until he could make it out clearly: an open box full of shiny bullets—*likely for a handgun, judging by the size*, the officer noted as a shiver went down his spine. He instinctively felt for his own gun, strapped at his side underneath a light jacket. *Hopefully it won't come to that.*

With little time to lose, Castillo nearly sprinted down the road to catch up with the mysterious man. Emilio looked both ways before crossing a street at the end of the next block. Rico was gaining on him, but time was running out.

Donna arrived at the edge of the stage just as the prior performer was leaving. The usual emcee—the club owner who smiled with only half of his face—announced that they would take a short break before the next act began, then strode toward Donna.

"Where you been?" He said without even a hint of his signature half-grin as he produced a pocket watch.

"I know you don't like it when people are late, so I was actually here *early*," Donna answered hastily. "Your buddy at the door can vouch for me. Just ran into an old friend, is all."

"Yeah, sure," the man said. "You know he doesn't like when people call him buddy—"

"I know—sorry."

The man offered her a half-faced smile as he eyed her

from head to toe. "The dress is an improvement," he said of the gold-sequined frock. "It suits your brand. Good job, Goldielocks."

His inspection made her feel strange and exposed, but she tried to ignore it. "Th-thank you," she sputtered.

"Ready to go?" He leaned his head toward the stage.

She nodded, then followed as the man moved through the curtains.

"Oh—one thing," Donna said. The man turned to face her. "I thought I might try switching up the name a little."

"Now?" Neither side of the man's face even hinted at a smile.

"Just shortening it," she pleaded. "If that's not too much to ask?"

The man rolled his eyes and puffed.

Donna accepted this as an answer. She took a deep breath then offered a smile. "Call me Goldie."


The expansive, lounge-like room was abuzz with lively conversation and the clinking of glasses when the club's owner took the stage once more. "Ladies and gentlemen, may I present to you for the very first time," the man paused for effect. "The stunning, the magnificent... Goldie!"

Marcus clapped and smiled as the spotlight narrowed on Donna and her shimmering gold-sequined gown at the center of the stage. Her blonde hair seemed to float and glow as she stepped up to the microphone while the band started to play. Then, with a deep breath, she began to sing.

"Your *friend* has a unique voice," Angela said after a few bars, pulling Marcus and his thoughts back to their table.

"Mhm," the young man forced a smile, then took a drink from a bottle of beer. "She's very talented. She told me she's wanted to be a singer since she was a girl."

Angela leaned in and took a sip of her drink. "What about *you?*"

"Have I wanted to be a singer since I was a little girl?" He grinned.

Angela was about to speak when she chuckled, causing a burst of gin and tonic to spray through her lips. Marcus handed her a napkin and she thanked him. "No," she tried again. "I mean, when you were a kid, what did you want to be when you grew up?"

Marcus leaned back in his chair as Donna's sultry voice enveloped the room. "What did I want to be?" He repeated the question under his breath. "An astronaut?"

Angela raised an eyebrow. "You don't sound too sure."

"Been a while since I've thought about that," he smirked. "You?"

"You promise not to laugh?"

Marcus chuckled. "I'll try not to," he assured her, taking another drink.

"When I was a girl," Angela said, taking a deep breath, "I wanted to be a CEO."

The edges of Marcus' lips began to curl as he tried not to expel the beer from his mouth. Quickly, he swallowed then let out a breathy snicker.

"Hey—you said you wouldn't laugh! Women can be CEOs, too, ya know?"

"No, no, it's not that, I promise," Marcus apologized. "Just the way you said it—"

"Sure," she smiled, and shook her head. Angela glanced over his shoulder toward the stage, then took another sip. "Hold that thought," she said, grabbing her purse and rising from her seat. "Just gonna go freshen up before this gin and tonic permanently adheres to my skin."

Marcus obliged and watched as she sauntered toward the restrooms near the entrance to the club. His attention returned to the stage, from whence Donna's captivating voice reverberated across the room. For a moment, he thought they'd locked eyes, but the glimmering stage lights made it difficult to tell for sure.

Just then, Marcus felt a frantic tap on his shoulder. "Marcus!" He whipped around, expecting to find Angela or a waiter. To his surprise, it was his partner—Officer Castillo—hunched low near Angela's empty chair.

"Rico?" Marcus said in a loud whisper, looking around to make sure the other tables were out of earshot. "What're you doing here? You're supposed to be watching Newport's mansion."

Castillo nodded, out of breath. "I know, and I did watch it—"

"Wait a minute," interjected Marcus, noticing droplets of water along the man's forehead. "Why are you *wet*?"

"Longer story than I have the time for right now,"

Castillo loud-whispered back. "I overheard a call and then followed Emilio and he led me here—" He paused, allowing his eyes to focus on the stage beyond them. "Is that Donna?" He turned back to Marcus. "I thought you said you were branching out?"

"I *am* branching out, she's just in the ladies' room at the moment." The off-duty officer took a deep breath. "So tell me what you're doing here *now*, Rico!"

"No time," he muttered as he glanced at a clock on the wall. He started to move back into the shadows, then crouched at the table again. "Listen, if something happens to me, just remember: the butler did it!"

"The butler?"

"You know, Newport's butler, his valet—*Emilio*."

"He's *here*?" Marcus scanned the dark room but couldn't get a good view from his seat.

"Yes, somewhere," Castillo nodded rapidly. "He has some sort of *package*. And I think he's armed."

"Who's he meeting?"

"Don't know," replied Castillo. "But I'm about to find out." He started to hurry away again, but Marcus grabbed his wrist.

"Wait for me," he said with a smile.

"What about your date?"

"We'll be back before she even notices I'm gone," Marcus said with a nod as he began to rise. "You and I—we're partners, remember?"

Rico nodded and smiled. Marcus took one more swig of

his beer then the two vanished to the edge of the room to search the club.

# CHAPTER 18

Marcus and Rico approached a bar on the far side of the room. From here they had a better vantage point of the entire dimly-lit space.

"So where did the butler go?" Marcus asked his partner quickly, keeping his eyes averted to avoid suspicion.

"Think he got a table on the other side," Castillo nodded. "One of us should sweep that area while the other keeps a visual on the exit. Can't let him see us—he'll remember us from the house."

"I'll sweep," said Marcus.

"Be careful, partner."

Marcus nodded, felt the handgun concealed under his blazer, and pushed off from the bar. He moved casually but quickly, blending into a gaggle of guests that stood mingling in front of a rounded countertop. The officer glanced over his shoulder to make sure Angela had not yet returned, then shifted to Castillo who meandered toward the club's entrance. Marcus paused in a shadowed corner. Finally, his eyes landed on a man in a white fedora and matching linen suit. The hat provided just enough obscurity that Marcus had to do a double-take; but, sure enough, it was Emilio.

*Gotcha.*

The butler's back was turned to Marcus, but his silhouette was unmistakable. The officer locked eyes with Castillo across the room and nodded. He took a deep breath. Next came the hard part: waiting for the suspect to make the exchange.

They didn't have to wait long, though. Right as Donna finished her first song, the room erupted in applause and, in the commotion, Emilio placed the fedora on the table, rose with the briefcase in hand, and started toward a door at the side of the room—one that presumably led backstage. Marcus took another quick look at his table. *No Angela yet—good.* He rapidly signaled to Castillo to maintain his post, then hurried along the edge of the room after the butler as he disappeared through the door.

Donna's voice faded as the door closed behind Marcus. The hallway was dark, save for a few flickering fluorescent lights placed at wide intervals down its length. The officer looked one way, then the other. There was no sign of the butler; Emilio had vanished.

Biting his lip in frustration, Marcus chose a direction and headed toward another door. A red glow filled this room and the music grew only slightly louder. A set of thick curtains adorned the areas to Marcus' left and right, and a stack of large wooden crates formed a divider along the wall straight in front of him. *He could be hiding behind any of those,* the officer noted. He threw back the nearest bundle of curtains: nothing but a set of ropes and wires. Next, his attention turned to the crates.

As Marcus neared the wooden boxes, he heard voices— two men, from the sound of it, speaking in hushed tones. Slowly, the officer removed the gun from its hiding place and raised it as he rounded the corner.

"Metro-Dade—hands up!" Marcus demanded of the two men as they came into view.

Both complied with fearful expressions. One of the men was large and burly—like a bouncer or bodyguard—while the other was short and wore a half-faced grin; Marcus recognized him as the emcee for the club. Neither of the men was Emilio.

"Listen, officer," stammered the shorter man. "We don't want any trouble. Nothing we're doing here is illegal—you can put that down." He faintly bent a finger from one of his raised hands to point toward the gun.

Marcus took a step forward. "Where's the butler?"

The face of the bigger man contorted: "Butler?"

"He ran through here," Marcus started to reply, realizing mid-sentence that the men's confusion was genuine. *They don't know. Drat—*

Marcus spun around at the sound of a small commotion behind him as he heard an object hit the ground. There was a hollowness to the sound. *Like an empty briefcase,* the officer thought just as he saw the familiar, black case tumble open from the foot of the second set of curtains. His eyes quickly darted from it to a figure vanishing through the half-open drapery.

The determined officer hurried after the figure. Marcus threw back the curtains and pressed forward. Suddenly, he froze, blinded by a blazing spotlight. He put up his hand to shield his eyes from the harsh light, giving him the clarity to see two things: that he was now onstage—in front of the entire club *and* Donna—and that the butler was making his escape into the curtains on the opposite side. The band continued to play.

"Marcus?" Donna whispered out of earshot of the microphone. "What are you doing?"

He didn't answer. The man had a sudden lump in his throat as the crowd began to murmur. Perhaps it was a flashback to a traumatic grade-school memory of stage fright. Or, more likely, the fact that he was off-duty and yet now stood in front of a crowd of nearly a hundred people wielding a loaded handgun in full view.

Donna leaned toward him with a look of concern. "You okay, Marcus?"

Marcus slowly nodded his head and forced a smile, which quickly faded to shock and adrenaline when he saw the tip of the butler's handgun peeking out from the far-side curtains.

"Donna, down!" He shouted.

A few moments earlier, Castillo posted up near the club's entrance, outlined by warm lights as he made methodical visual sweeps of the huge area. He watched as Marcus disappeared through the side door, tailing Emilio closely while the crowd applauded at the conclusion of Donna's first song. There was a flurry of motion—*the perfect time to see if that fedora holds a clue or fingerprint that might be helpful.* Castillo started toward it from the opposite side of the room.

He moved as casually as possible, tossing a glance in every direction as he approached the table where Emilio had set the white hat down. He was nearly upon it when he froze: a woman crossed his path. She appeared to be making a beeline for the table, but Castillo couldn't be sure. In the dim light, all the officer could discern of her appearance was her mass of dark hair and a sleek, purple dress.

Castillo moved closer but angled himself away to keep from looking too suspicious. The woman was now only inches from the table. She took a glance over her shoulder; Castillo diverted his attention elsewhere, pretending to watch the performance on stage. The woman reached for the white fedora and carefully slid it from the table with both hands. She continued walking past the table as if nothing had happened.

The officer muttered something crass under his breath, then started to follow the woman in purple while she made a turn through the center of the dining area. *If I could just create a distraction, maybe I can grab it—*

A gunshot went off and Donna felt the bullet whiz past as she threw herself into a low crouch, careful not to let her tingling hands touch the floor.

The clubgoers gushed a collective shriek and rose from or ducked beneath their seats, while the band members froze, clutching their instruments. Marcus knelt into a position behind one of the curtains and stole a glance at the shooter: he confirmed that it was Emilio—judging by his build and the light linen suit he'd been wearing—though now he wore a mask to conceal his face. *The mask of a red dragon!*

Another shot rang out, ripping a hole in the curtain just above Marcus' head. Donna scampered off-stage and hunched at the officer's side while he took aim.

"Date went that bad, huh?" Donna nearly shouted over the roar of the frantic throng.

Marcus took a shot, narrowly missing the butler by only a few inches. "I dunno," he said as he readied for another. "I might give it a second shot."

He fired again, then ducked back. *Speaking of Angela,* Marcus quickly squinted to pierce his gaze through the lights and into the scurrying masses. *Where'd she go?* The officer didn't have much time to think on the answer, as another gunshot tore through the curtain again—this time narrowly missing the top of his head. *Too close.*

By this time, Marcus had only a couple of bullets left in the round. He knew he had to make his next shot count.

The officer took a deep breath, pressed up against the thick, velveteen curtain, then swung his whole body around as he pulled the trigger. The shot met its mark, creating a tiny, dark hole in the chest of Emilio's loose, white blazer. The butler staggered backward into the shadows and Marcus sprinted toward him across the stage.

When the officer pushed through the curtains, he saw a smudged scarlet trail on the floor, leading down a narrow hall. Marcus raised his gun and quietly crept into the flickering light. He peered around the corner and saw Emilio sprawled on the floor. Marcus hurried toward the butler, kicked his gun out of reach, then pointed his own firearm at the man as he removed the dragon mask. Underneath, Emilio was barely breathing.

"Who were you meeting?" Marcus demanded.

Emilio took a labored breath, wincing in pain. He didn't answer.

Marcus insisted again, "Tell me who you were meeting here. What was the package?"

The butler was fading fast. His eyes began to roll back into his head as they fluttered shut. Marcus felt for a pulse. Nothing. He was gone.

As the officer took a deep breath, he heard footsteps from behind. He turned to see Rico and Donna moving quickly toward him and Emilio's body.

Donna gasped and gestured toward the bloody, lifeless butler. "Is he...?"

Marcus nodded. "Yeah," he muttered with somber reverence. "He's gone." The officer felt the pockets of the body and turned to his partner as he rose. "No sign of any package, either."

With a deep sigh, Castillo shook his head. "Nope," he said. "And no fedora."

"What do you mean?" Marcus tilted his chin.

"I don't know what happened," continued Castillo. "One minute I had it in view; next, some lady swooped in and grabbed it; there was the gunshot, the commotion, then it was gone."

"What lady?"

"I don't know," replied Castillo earnestly. "Never seen her before."

The other officer's gaze drifted. "The package," he said softly, shaking his head. "The fedora was hiding it." After a moment, Marcus turned to Donna. "Sorry you had to see this."

"No, I'm okay," she replied, clearly frazzled. "I-I should go." Donna started in for a hug, then quickly stepped back. She offered a timid wave then hurried back down the hall.

"What's with her?" Castillo asked when she'd gone.

"Longer story than I have the time for," Marcus grinned, then sighed. "Let's call in the crew and get things cleaned up." Castillo agreed and disappeared to find a phone while Marcus took another long look at the lifeless butler. *Now what?*

# CHAPTER 19

By the time she returned to her apartment, Donna noticed that her newly-regained power had faded away once more. She lingered for a moment outside the door, her head hung in a deep sigh of silence, before finally entering to relieve her babysitters. It was late and Starla had already been put to bed, so the women exchanged whispered pleasantries as Sue and Lisa gathered their things and headed home.

When the sun spilled through the living room the next morning, Donna woke up slowly. She rose and contorted her body in an attempt to relieve a knotted feeling in her spine. *I'm getting too old to sleep on the couch after a late-night gunfight.* The woman tousled her tangled blonde hair and glanced at the kitchen clock with half-open eyes.

"Starla!" She exclaimed, shouting toward the bedroom when she realized the time. "You're late for school—!" Donna paused as her droopy eyes met a sticky note on the counter.

*Left for school. I made breakfast.*

Donna took a deep breath, smiled, then shook her head. Before her was a plate of toast, cut into two buttered, ragged halves. She took a bite. It was a little cold, but Donna was grateful. *Proud, even.*

While she munched on the crispy but lukewarm bread, Donna moved back to the couch and sank into it. She picked up the remote to turn on the television, but set it down slowly when she noticed something else on the table: a small Polaroid picture.

The woman held it between her buttery fingers—the image of Donna and Starla, captured in a moment of laughter and innocence. She could almost hear the girl's little giggle. The photograph brought back recent memories—the earliest days of their time together. It was all so unexpected; Donna hadn't felt ready or prepared to take on the sudden challenge of parenting another human being, and yet it happened all the same. She knew their time together was limited—that things could change again in an instant—but she wanted to treasure every single moment.

The phone rang. Donna tossed the photo back on the table and hurried over to pick up the receiver.

"This is Donna," she said.

"Donna Locke?"

"Yes, who is this?"

"I'm calling from Saint Mary's," the woman's voice replied.

"It's about your, uh, sister?"

"Sondra—yeah," Donna's pulse quickened. "What about her?"

The receptionist seemed to pause before finally answering. "We think she might be waking up."

*Waking up?*

"You should get over here as soon as you can," the woman finished.

For a few seconds, Donna held the receiver but said nothing. *But what about Starla—?* Finally, she nodded and said, "Sure. I'll be right over."


Officers Myles and Castillo stood over a table covered in notes and files. On one wall of the conference room, they had pinned photographs of Vander Newport and his butler Emilio—obtained from the archives of the Department of Motor Vehicles. Nearby, Rico had used pieces of scotch tape to adhere a copy of the fragment of paper he'd procured from Newport's dresser. Now, the officer moved toward the ripped note and studied the partial symbol that was torn in its corner.

"I know I've seen that bird before," Castillo muttered to himself.

"Let me get a good look," asked Marcus as he stood over his shoulder and withdrew a magnifying glass. With one eye squinted he inspected the half logo. "You're right—it's *very* familiar." Officer Myles smiled and hurried to a phone book, where he began to flip through—starting near the middle of the alphabet.

Castillo shook his head and crossed his arms. "Why do I get the feeling you've figured it out and aren't telling me yet *just* for the sake of suspense?"

"Because," Marcus replied, his finger running down a page before he flipped again. "I just want to be sure..." He flipped once more then pointed at the page with a smile. "A-ha!"

With a reluctant sigh, Castillo moved toward him and inspected the phone book's open page. Marcus' finger rested on a listing with an image—a logo featuring the full bird from the scrap.

"Pelican Innovations," Rico read aloud. "Not bad, partner."

"It's only plastered on *every* advertisement and television set in the city these days," Marcus chuckled.

Castillo turned their attention back to the matter at hand. "So, what's the connection? How is Newport—or his butler, for that matter—tied to Pelican?"

"No idea," the other officer replied, moving toward the door. "But I bet Ruby can crack it." Marcus stuck his head through the door and hollered to her: "Sanchez, you got a minute?"

A moment later, Detective Sanchez arrived.

"Thanks, Sanchez," Castillo began. "Can you pull some information on Pelican Innovations for us? We're talking tax docs, employee directories, anything with names of those who've associated with Pelican—specifically the names Vander Newport or Emilio Esquivez."

Ruby grinned. "I'll see what I can do." She returned to her

desk to gather the requested intelligence.

After some time had passed, Detective Sanchez returned with a stack of folders, binders, and loose documents and threw them on the table with a thump. "That's everything I could find in public records for Pelican," she said. "I'll keep digging for more, but there's bound to be something in there."

"Ruby, you're truly a gem—the crown jewel of Metro-Dade," Marcus said with an exaggerated smile.

"Thanks, Myles—glad I could help," Sanchez replied, rolling her eyes as she vanished once more.

The two officers began to dig through the stack, forming piles to organize by the information's apparent relevance to the case at hand. The entire tower of pages stood nearly a foot tall when Ruby had dropped it off, so the process was tedious and lengthy.

"Bingo!" Castillo exclaimed as he held up a spiral-bound booklet for Marcus to read its fading printed cover:

*Pelican Innovations Employee and Board Directory, 1979.*

"Good job." Marcus pointed to the pelican logo in the corner. "See? It's everywhere."

Rico shook his head. "How about *you* do the honors, then, partner?"

Marcus yanked the directory from Castillo's hands, unfolded it on the table, and began to flip through it. A table of contents detailed the many different departments and initiatives housed under the Pelican Innovations umbrella;

the officer wasn't sure where to look, so he combed through, running his finger down each page and list.

Following a page on the mission and values of Pelican, Marcus flipped to another that outlined the members of the organization's board of trustees. Quickly, he worked his way down the names until his eyes lit up at one: "Vander R. Newport," he read aloud. "So he's been on Pelican's board for years—go figure."

"No kidding?"

"Yeah," Marcus continued, reading from a brief note beside Newport's name. "Looks like he's been with them since they started in the sixties."

"So Newport's connection to Pelican goes pretty deep," Castillo added, tapping his finger on the table before moving back toward the taped-up items on the wall. "But the note I found must have come from someone *else* within Pelican; it was a note *to* Newport—people don't usually hold on to handwritten notes they write themselves. It says, '*Sure about S.G.?*' It's a question—someone asking Newport if he's sure about whatever S.G. is."

"I'll keep looking, then," Marcus nodded. "Maybe there's something more in here that can help us out."

He returned to scanning and flipping through the pages of the directory. Under a *Department of Experimental Research and Development* listing, Marcus paused on a name near the top. His jaw slackened as he read it again. "Rico—what did you say Emilio's contact at The Jade Lion looked like again? I mean, the one who picked up the fedora—the package."

"Um," Castillo began, half-attentive as he sifted through a stack of tax documents. "She was a woman, average build, dark eyes, dark hair with tight curls—she was gorgeous, actually, and—"

"What was she *wearing?*" Marcus' breaths were short. He couldn't bring his eyes from the page.

"A dress," replied Castillo. "Purple dress and a purse over her shoulder. Why?"

Marcus was speechless. In silence, he slid the directory closer to Castillo, keeping his finger on the name.

"Angela Hyde," Rico read aloud. His eyes grew wide when it hit him: "Wait, you mean *Angela* Angela—your date?"

The other officer exhaled sharply and kept his head down. "I'm almost positive," he muttered.

"So she works for Pelican," Castillo offered. "But you think she's involved with the whole Emilio thing?"

"Your description matches her perfectly," Marcus replied, taking quick breaths.

"Hey, there were other people in purple dresses at the club—"

"No," he shook his head. "It's her. She was so precise when she asked me out—already had the place *and* the time." Marcus began to pace, then paused. "She used me."

Castillo offered a soft smile. "Doesn't mean what you had wasn't real, partner."

"But from everything I can tell right now, she's a criminal," Marcus retorted. "Or an accomplice to one, at least. Hard to redeem that."

His partner gestured back to the booklet on the table. "We still don't know for sure if there's a connection between her and Newport," Castillo pointed out. "Employees at her level may not even *interact* with board members in a company like Pelican. We also don't know what the mysterious *package* contained. And for all we know the butler was acting alone."

Marcus shook his head slowly, deep in thought. "You said you found the note in Newport's dresser, though."

"Yeah," Castillo affirmed. "And?"

"Maybe it's totally unrelated, but I can't shake the feeling that there's something important about it," Marcus said softly, moving toward the note on the wall. "That he would hold on to that and keep it somewhere so personal, so intimate. Now we just have to figure out what S.G. stands for."

Castillo raised an eyebrow. "Maybe it's not a *what*," he suggested. "Maybe it's a *who*."

# CHAPTER 20

The hospital waiting room was unusually crowded when Donna arrived, but she managed to make her way to the front desk and check in with one of the receptionists. The woman instructed her to wait for a moment while she verified Donna's identity. As she stood tapping her foot, Donna glanced around the lobby and inventoried a mother and her swaddled newborn child, a pair of gruff-looking men with tattoos, a coughing toddler, and an elderly couple reading one of the many outdated magazines strewn across an end table.

"Right this way," the receptionist instructed as she reappeared swinging open one of the double doors.

Donna followed her down the bright hallway, which was lined with stripes of light pink and teal that matched the generic seat cushions back in the waiting room. The pair dodged a tangle of carts and nurses as they shuffled by, then they arrived at the familiar room. The receptionist smiled then hurried back to her post while Donna pressed through the half-ajar door.

She was greeted by the slow, steady beep of a heart rate monitor. A doctor hunched over Sondra's near-lifeless body and turned when Donna entered.

"You're the sister?" The doctor asked.

Donna nodded. "They said she was waking up?"

The doctor gestured toward the monitor. "Her levels spiked momentarily, which can be a sign that she's regaining consciousness."

"But?" Donna sensed there was more.

"*But* they've gone back down again. If you like, I can give you two a moment—if you need anything or if her rate rises again, just press that button."

Donna said a quick "thank you" as the doctor smiled and returned to the hall. Hesitantly, the blonde woman settled into the seat next to Sondra's bed and tried to tune out the tone from the monitor.

Her sister was pale—her skin like unpolished ivory. Donna leaned over to brush a strand of Sondra's light-brown hair behind her ear.

"Never thought *I'd* be the one taking care of *you*," Donna said with a chuckle. "You were always the perfect one."

Donna paused, as if waiting for her comatose sister to respond.

"I know you didn't, um, understand all of my choices in life," she continued hesitantly, "but I needed to forge my own path. Living in your shadow was—" Donna searched for the words, bending back in her chair. "It was the *worst*. I felt like I was never good enough—for you *or* for mom and dad. Even at the end, you had something special with them that I just never could."

Donna shook her head and rose. "What am I even saying? You can't hear me, can you?"

Sondra's eyelids didn't so much as flutter.

*I figured.*

The conscious sister began to pace around the room.

"I guess I should've had this conversation sooner," Donna spoke toward the floor as she stepped from one ugly tile to the next. "You were there for mom and dad when they needed you; I wasn't. Seems like a common theme, lately. I couldn't even be there for Marcus. Sweet, handsome Marcus. He must think I hate him or something. I really blew it, but I couldn't tell him the truth—not now. Now he's got some newer, sleeker model. Truth is, I still care for him." She shook her head then sank back into the chair.

"Then there's Starla."

The heart rate monitor registered an extra blip, then it was gone. Donna leaned forward. She could've sworn she saw her sister's lips form a slight smile, but it must've been in her imagination. With a sigh, the blonde sister slackened her posture once more.

"She's a special girl," Donna muttered. She craned her neck toward Sondra and grinned: "I kinda like her, believe it or not." The woman imagined her sister making a snide remark, then continued. "You know, when I got this call, I actually got nervous. I was afraid you'd wake and then they'd take her away from me—just like that. I know she's yours, and I know that'll happen sooner or later, but I mean it, Sondra: that girl's the best thing that's happened to me in a long time."

For another long moment, Donna's gaze lingered on her sister's peaceful, slumbering expression. "Someday I'll get to tell you all of this for real," she whispered. Then, with a gentle squeeze of the hand, Donna rose and walked quietly back into the hospital hallway where she turned to shut the door behind her.

As she spun back around, Donna nearly bumped into a pair of men walking by.

"Sorry!" She spouted as the duo moved slowly past the room, casting a curious look at the plaque indicating Sondra's room number. Frazzled, Donna scampered back toward the waiting room.

Before she could make it to the end of the hall, however, Donna paused and looked back over her shoulder. She recognized the men. Both had large tattoos peeking from beneath their dark shirts. *The men from the waiting room,* she noted. They now lingered in front of Sondra's room, consulting a piece of paper before slowly pushing on the door.

*Sondra!*

Donna sensed she was in danger. "Security!" She shouted as she ran back toward her sister's room. "Someone call security!"

As soon as she began shouting, the two men whipped toward her then took off running down the hallway in the opposite direction. Donna hurried as fast as she could with a cadre of hospital staffers following closely behind, but when she reached a bend in the maze of halls, the woman stopped to catch her breath. The men were gone. They had vanished.

*What do they want with Sondra?* Donna wondered between breaths. *She's not safe here. Maybe I'm not safe here, either.*

The lab was quiet, save for the buzz and whir of a massive floor centrifuge. Dr. Roger Lansing adjusted a pair of safety goggles on his face—with his glasses underneath—before craning his neck toward the controls. He watched the small display screen flash a countdown in a yellowish glow while the machine brought its cargo to a halt, ending its spin cycle. Roger unlatched the seal, then delicately removed the several small vials inside—blood samples now separated and stratified into more refined and distinct elements.

As the young doctor arranged the ampules at another workstation, he heard the signature swoosh and click of the door to the lab. He didn't bother looking over his shoulder as he was too focused on aligning the vials with another row of varying liquids on the tabletop.

"Well, doctor," said a woman's voice—it was Angela's. "I really hope you're going to tell me we have a miracle on our hands."

Dr. Lansing squinted to read a label on one of the vials

before unscrewing its cap and inserting a narrow pipette. "And I really hope you're going to tell me I have more than a few days to finish this project."

Angela stood behind him with her arms crossed. "Not a chance," she said. Then the woman sauntered closer. "If this doesn't work—" She paused.

"Give me some space, please," Roger said, nudging his elbow toward her as his hands were full. Angela took a half-step back while the doctor began to place a single drop from the pipette into each of a series of translucent liquids lined up in vials along the counter.

Dr. Lansing watched closely, his gaze shifting from one to the next, over the course of several seconds. When nearly a minute had passed with no visible changes, Roger sighed, returned the original vial to its place, then repeated the process with the next sample.

"Roger," Angela began again, now pacing behind the hunched man. "I brought you with me to Pelican because I believed we could achieve something great together. If you mess this up, it's both of our jobs—no, our entire *careers*—on the line."

"*You* only got the job at Pelican because of what *I* achieved," Roger corrected, his gaze unwaveringly fixed on preparing the next set of tests.

"We were a team," snapped Angela. "We *are* a team."

"Come on, Angie," Dr. Lansing said, shaking his head as he watched for a reaction. "Maybe you're right—maybe it wasn't my research that got us in the door. Science isn't sexy enough to get noticed on its own merit these days."

Angela breathed deeply, her cheeks turning flush. She was about to spout some seething reply when she sensed an abrupt change in the doctor's demeanor. Roger stood and hunched more closely over one of the samples.

"What is it?" Angela asked quickly.

"I-I—" Dr. Lansing stuttered, trying to form words.

"Roger?"

He stepped away from the beakers to finally face Angela. He wore a dumbfounded expression and pointed at one of the vials. The liquid—and the glass that contained it—had turned to solid gold!

Angela held her jaw agape as she approached, reaching for a pair of safety goggles, which she held over her face. "Roger, what am I looking at?"

He let out an involuntary snicker of delight. "I think I found your miracle."

The pair stared in silence for a few moments as Dr. Lansing tapped on the substance with a metal instrument to ensure its solidity.

"Is that really—?" Angela couldn't bring herself to finish the thought. She was baffled.

"Yes," the doctor said with confidence. "It's gold."

"And how did this, um, happen?"

"Well, let's see," Roger began, verifying the original contents of the vials. "When this particular blood sample extraction was combined with a certain ratio of dihydrogen monoxide, the two differing compounds interact and seem to form a—"

"Roger, slow down," Angela interrupted, impatient. "What did you say the blood interacted with?"

"Dihydrogen monoxide," replied the doctor matter-of-factly.

"Dihydrogen monoxide?" Angela raised an eyebrow. "You mean *water?*"

"Precisely," he smiled. "The patient was given one dose of Formula 29 over the weekend, upon the first appointment, then tested the day after." Roger inspected the vial with the subject's remaining blood in it. "Absolutely fascinating."

"So what you're saying," Angela began to pace frantically, "is that when this subject was given the formula *and* water, his blood turned to gold?"

"Eh," Dr. Lansing was about to give a more scientific explanation, then nodded his head. "Something like that. My hypothesis is that water is some sort of agent to activate the latent properties of the formula. Perhaps allowing one to turn things to gold simply by touching them."

"You're serious?" Angela cocked her head.

The doctor nodded slowly, but surely.

"Do you know what this could mean—to be able to manufacture as much gold as we want?" She shook her head in awe. "You may have just saved our jobs—and our reputations." Angela paused and inspected the golden vial once more. She shook her head in disbelief, then turned to the doctor. "Whose blood is that?"

Dr. Lansing gulped then stuttered, "I-I'm not sure our

confidentiality agreements allow for that—"

"Who's the subject, Roger?" Angela demanded, towering over the doctor.

He took a deep breath, closed his eyes, then opened them once more.

"Her name," Roger said with slight hesitance, "is Donna Locke."

"Donna Locke," Angela repeated with a puff of disbelief. "The girl from the club—Marcus knows her."

"M-Marcus?" Roger inquired.

Angela ignored him, clenched her teeth, and turned to the doctor. "We can't risk that power being discovered by her or anyone else. Get her in here—and *fast!*"

# CHAPTER 21

It was late afternoon when Donna finally returned to her apartment, tense and out of breath. Had someone followed her there from the hospital? Was she safe? Why were those men looking for Sondra's room? Such questions lingered as the woman threw the deadbolt into place and began to pace around the living room.

*Thunk-thunk-thunk!* It was a sharp knock on the door. Donna's heart rate leaped. She took a deep breath and cautiously approached the door. On the way, she picked up a small ceramic vase and dumped out the dried, wilted flowers that rested in it. The woman held the vase above her shoulder like a baseball bat.

"Who is it?" Donna shouted to whoever stood on the other side of the door.

Immediately, a reply hollered back: "Don! It's us!"

Donna's posture immediately relaxed. Her arms slackened

and she unbolted the door. In the threshold stood Sue and Lisa, wearing nervous expressions.

"Careful, Donna, you could hurt someone with that!" Lisa's puffy red hair bounced as she spoke and pointed to the makeshift ceramic weapon still in Donna's hands.

"That was the idea. Sorry about that." Donna set the vase down then ushered the women inside while she stuck her head through the door to look both ways. Then, satisfied that the women had not been followed, Donna slammed it shut and once again turned the latch to secure the deadbolt.

"Don, what's going on?" Sue inquired. "We came as soon as we could when we got your call from the hospital."

"Yeah," Lisa added. "What happened? Why are you so shifty all of a sudden?"

There was a moment of silence as Donna caught her breath then motioned toward the blush-pink couch. Her friends sat down with some reticence while Donna began to pace again.

"Sorry, I didn't want to say too much over the phone," she explained. "It's just—a lot's happened over the past few days and now I think someone's out to get my sister—"

"Out to *get* her?" Lisa interrupted. "Sondra? I thought she was in a coma!"

Sue chimed in: "Donna, you're not making sense."

"Just let me explain," said Donna, making exaggerated gestures with her hands. The two women obliged and settled back into their seats on the sofa. "The things I'm about to tell you are going to sound crazy, but I need you to believe me. Can you promise me you'll do that?"

Sue and Lisa nodded slowly, still unsure what sort of information Donna was about to reveal to them.

"Remember how Sue suggested I look into participating in one of those studies at Pelican?" They nodded to affirm that they did. "Well, a few days ago I was at my wit's end and decided to go for it."

"Pay well?" Sue asked.

"It paid *incredibly* well," Donna nodded. "But that's not what I'm getting at. They had me come in to get the first treatment and take a blood sample, told me not to eat or drink—you know, the usual stuff you'd expect. The next day, I woke up and felt nauseous and—you're not going to believe this—I could turn things to gold with my hands!"

Both women on the couch raised their eyebrows with concern.

"You mean you got super good at doing things with your hands?" Lisa wondered, wiggling her fingers.

"No," answered Donna. "I mean the *actual* golden touch—anything I put my fingers to would turn to pure, glittering gold."

Sue stood up and started toward her: "Donna, you sure you're okay?"

"I'm fine. I can prove it to you—" The blonde woman took off down the hall and returned a few moments later with a toothbrush—the one that had been turned to gold. "See?"

"I see what looks like a very expensive and highly impractical toothbrush," Sue quipped, taking her seat once more.

"Exactly," Donna continued. "It was just your average

plastic toothbrush the other day—frayed bristles and all—until I touched it."

By this time, her friends were still somewhat skeptical, though the toothbrush provided interesting evidence to the contrary.

"So, how about you turn something else to gold—that vase?" Lisa suggested, pointing at the piece across the room.

Donna was getting frustrated. She exhaled quickly. "That's not how it—I mean, it comes and goes—the power, I mean."

"I see." The red-haired woman nodded her head slowly.

"Sounds pretty incredible, Don," Sue added. "Guess we'll just have to take your word for it. But, uh, what's got you so frantic all of a sudden? Did something happen at the hospital—with your sister?"

The blonde woman took a deep breath and nodded quickly, her body beginning to tense again as she recalled the day's recent events. "I think she's in danger—Sondra, I mean. I went to visit her because they thought she was waking up. And just as I was leaving, there were these two men with tattoos—they were hovering outside her door. When I shouted for security, they took off—sprinted down the hall and disappeared. That's when I called you guys."

"Donna! Is your sister safe now?" Sue stood and started toward Donna again.

"I don't know." Donna looked away and shook her head, beginning to pace once more. "Security was going to keep a closer eye on her, post up near her room, but I just don't know what to do—I'm afraid. I kept thinking I saw someone following me, but maybe I'm overreacting."

"You are *not* overreacting, girl," Lisa joined in comforting her friend. "What about the kid?"

"Starla? She'll be home from school—" Donna craned her neck to glimpse the clock, "—any minute now."

"Donna, if someone's stalking you, we should report it." Now also beginning to pace, Sue turned back to the others. "And if you're not ready to do that, can we at least call my brother—or Marcus?"

Donna thought for a moment, biting her nails, then nodded. "Sure. It's probably for the best." She moved toward the phone in the kitchen and dialed the number written on the old receipt on the counter.

As the phone rang, Sue paced around the room while Lisa slid onto one of the seats along the counter. Finally, Donna perked up as she heard the click on the other end of the line.

"Marcus?" Donna's voice was hesitant, trembling slightly.

"Donna," he replied. "I'm surprised to hear from you after last night—and I'm sorry again that you had to see all of that."

"Yeah, it's alright—I'm alright," she said, a slight quivering in her voice.

"You sure? You don't sound alright. And you've been acting strange for a few days now."

Donna took a deep breath. "Well, I guess I'm not alright."

"Wanna talk about it?" His voice was calming and genuine—another trait that drew Donna to Marcus.

Donna's friends raised their eyebrows and urged her to

continue.

"Marcus, I—something *happened*," she started, then changed direction. "I mean, I think my sister's in trouble."

"Sister?" Marcus replied, his voice garbled slightly through the receiver. "You mean the one you haven't spoken to in years—what's wrong with her?"

"It's a long story, but I think someone's trying to spy on her—or *hurt* her." Donna briefly relayed the encounter with the tattooed men in the hospital. "Is there anything you can do—you know, get someone to patrol her room or keep an eye outside my apartment?"

Marcus exhaled as he took it all in. "Sure, Donna, I can try. Remind me of her name again?"

"Her name's Sondra," Donna replied. "Sondra Gordon— different last name."

"Sondra *Gordon*?" Marcus repeated as if the name meant something to him. "You mean, her initials: they're S. and G.?"

"Yeah, she was married and, um—" Donna trailed off then, prompted by another set of eyebrow expressions and motions from her friends, turned the subject to another that was on her mind: "Marcus, I'm sorry about last night, too."

"Donna, what—"

"I said you wouldn't understand everything going on," she continued, her breaths shallow and her cheeks rosy. "But it wasn't fair to keep you in the dark like that. The truth is, I have this kid—"

"A kid?" Marcus gasped on the other end of the line.

"She's my sister's," Donna scrambled defensively. "And

I'm taking care of her until all of this is over. Listen, Marcus, I was confused and overwhelmed and made a *lot* of mistakes, but last night made me realize my true feelings for—"

There was a rustling on the other end, then voices. "I'm sorry, Donna, I have to go—"

"Oh." Donna came to an abrupt stop. "Alright, well then, um—"

"I'll make sure to pass on your concerns about your sister," he said quickly. "We'll look into this."

"Thank you, Marcus—"

He hung up the phone and the buzzy dialtone began. Donna inhaled deeply and returned the receiver to its dock.

"Well? Sounded like that went well!" Lisa smiled.

Donna shook her head. "I shouldn't have said anything about last night," she muttered, coughing to clear her throat. "But he said they'll 'look into' things with my sister, whatever that means."

"If he says they'll look into it, then they'll look into it," Sue assured her.

Donna nodded and coughed again. "Sorry, my throat's a little dry," she said, opening a cabinet. "Haven't had anything to drink all day—can I get you guys something?"

Sue leaned against the counter. "What's on the menu?"

As Donna set three clear glasses on the counter, she glanced in the fridge. "Water, water, and more water."

"Waters all around," Lisa grinned.

"This one's on the house," Donna said, channeling her waitressing talents to quickly fill the cups from a plastic pitcher. When they had each grabbed a glass, the three women held them up.

"To the best of friends," Lisa toasted. They smiled and clinked glasses, then each took generous gulps.

As Donna set her half-empty glass down on the counter, she heard a noise at the door. She started, realizing someone was jiggling the lock. "Who's there?" She shouted. But there was no reply.

A moment later, the door swung open. Silhouetted by the angelic late afternoon light, Starla walked in with a smile and slung her backpack toward the wall.

Donna was relieved to see that it was Starla, but then she felt a sudden lump forming in her throat. A queasy feeling came over her, starting with a roiling in her stomach which moved to a tingle at her fingertips.

*No!*

Starla made her way around the room, embracing Sue then Lisa before rounding the counter to move toward Donna. For Donna, the moment seemed to happen in slow motion. It should have been a moment of pure delight—it *would* have been under different circumstances. But now, as her surrogate daughter drew nearer with that demure, oblivious smile, Donna tensed and took a step back.

"Let me show you what I made for you," the girl said. "In my backpack—come see, Aunt Donna!"

"No, Starla—!"

The child reached for Donna's hand to guide her. The woman couldn't pull her arm back in time. In one horrific instant, Donna felt the touch of Starla's tiny fingers on her own. Closing her eyes, Donna instinctively turned her face away.

The moment passed, a lengthy silence. The air in the room was like a thick, tense fog.

Then, at the muffled gasps of her two best friends, Donna slowly and carefully opened her eyelids. She couldn't breathe. In front of her stood the frozen likeness of Starla, golden and solid. Lifeless.

*Lifeless. Just like the toothbrush and the toilet and the toy robot—*

"Oh my goodness," Sue muttered, clenching Lisa's hand in her own.

Donna's mouth hung agape. She couldn't bring herself to speak. Slowly she sunk, crouching to the level of the statuesque golden girl in the middle of her kitchen. There was every detail, as if etched in precious, cursed metal: the once-ruddy strands of wispy hair; her bright and jovial eyes; and the smile of youthful innocence now snatched away forever.

"Starla." The word was barely a breath. Donna nearly placed her hands to the girl's face but allowed her fingers to hover just a few inches from her instead.

Donna's friends slowly rose from their seats at the counter and orbited the shimmering schoolgirl with their mouths agape.

"Uh, Donna," Lisa said. "What just happened?"

"It's just like she told us," Sue whispered. "Her touch turned the girl to gold."

Lisa kept her eyes on the inanimate child. "Yeah, but I didn't think she was being serious. I thought it was a weird joke or something—"

"Does this *look* like a joke?" Donna cried suddenly, gesturing to her niece while tears began to form in the corners of her eyes. "This is *not* a joke! The kid is—*Starla* is solid gold and there's no way for me to turn her back and it's all my fault."

Lisa pointed at the girl. "You mean she's..."

"Gone," Donna nodded, pursing her lips. She wiped her tears with her arm to avoid touching her face with her own hands.

The phone rang. Donna jumped, startled. She looked at her hands, then at the phone, but did not pick it up.

"You want me to get that?" Sue asked.

Another ring.

"Uh, can you just put it on speakerphone?" Donna nodded with her chin.

*Brrring!*

Sue wasn't familiar with the feature so she scrambled to look over the device. Donna tried to point from afar, frazzled as the ringing continued. "The one in the bottom corner. Just—"

*Brrring! Brrring!*

*Click.* "Got it!" Sue and Lisa backed away.

"Hello?" A woman's voice broadcasted through the phone's clunky base.

Donna moved closer, wiping a bit of snot with her forearm.

"Uh, yes, hello, this is Donna—who is this?"

"This is Debra calling from Pelican Innovations. How are you today, Donna?"

The blonde woman held her mouth agape, but couldn't think of a response. "Uh—"

"The reason I'm calling," Debra proceeded without waiting for an answer, "is to set up your next follow-up appointment for this afternoon."

*This afternoon?* Donna's eyes betrayed her shock. "But I thought that wasn't supposed to be until next week?"

Debra didn't respond immediately. Then, after what sounded like a mumbling conversation with someone nearby, she continued. "Dr. Lansing is requesting that we move it to today. He, er, has a full schedule next week so he wants to get it in this afternoon, if you can make it before we close."

"Just a minute." Frantic, Donna shoved her elbow into the device to temporarily mute the phone. Then she turned to Sue and Lisa and whispered loudly: "They know!"

"Know?" Sue's eyebrows contorted.

"I just had an appointment *yesterday*! They know about the power—the gold—they *have* to!"

"Don't you think they *should* know?" Lisa suggested. "Or do you think the gold was just a side effect of whatever they were *actually* working on?"

"And," added Sue. "More importantly—maybe they can help you! Fix this—turn Starla back!"

For a moment the kitchen was silent.

Finally, Donna shook her head. "There's something that

doesn't feel right about all of this. First, someone's after my sister; now Pelican's after me. If they find out what I've done—to Starla—they'll—"

"They'll *what?*" Lisa leaned in.

"Remember the body they never found? That's going to be *me* if I go in for this appointment." The blonde woman paced near the counter. "No. I've gotta go—I have to run."

"Where, Don?"

Her fingers were tingling. Donna glanced down at her sweaty palms, then elbowed the button to unmute the call. "Debra?"

"Yes?"

"I'll, uh, be right over in thirty minutes," she said unconvincingly, then clicked the button to hang up with her elbow before the secretary could finish her reply. "That'll buy us a little time." Donna hurried toward the door.

Sue followed a few steps behind. "Wait, Don, where will you go?"

"I don't know yet," she said softly, turning back. "I need to figure out how to reverse this—to get away until this fades again. Somewhere they won't find me."

Neither of the other women knew how to respond.

"I need a huge favor," Donna pleaded. "Can you watch over Starla—keep her safe?" The woman looked longingly at the child, immortalized in that moment of pure joy that was cut short.

"What if they come looking for you?"

"You'll think of something," nodded Donna, trying to

force a smile. "Just don't let her out of your sight, okay?"

"I don't think that should be a problem—" Lisa muttered, glancing toward the immobilized, gilded girl.

Donna inhaled deeply. "If I could hug you both, I would."

Her friends smiled. "Be careful."

"I will," Donna replied then grabbed the already-golden handle, swung the door open, and vanished into the gusty, humid afternoon just as the sun began its descent.

# CHAPTER 22

Most of the lights in the large office building were already turned off as the Pelican Innovations staff left for the day. Dr. Lansing hovered over the reception desk, wringing his hands as Debra pressed her ear to the phone.

"Anything?" The doctor asked.

Debra shook her head. "I can't get through," she answered, then hung up.

"She could still show right?" He wondered in a hesitant, jittery tone.

The receptionist sighed and looked at the clock, then gestured to a row of offices where the lights were turned out. "It's been an hour, doctor."

Roger began to pace, then the elevator at the end of the hall swished open and chimed, casting a harsh reflection across the polished tile floor. Out walked Angela in a shoulder-padded pantsuit and imposing heels; she moved with a determined gait toward the doctor.

"Where is she, Roger?" Angela demanded as she arrived near the desk and crossed her arms.

He stuttered an answer: "I-I don't know. She hasn't shown up yet—"

"I can see that."

"Miss Locke said she'd be here an hour ago," Roger explained. "I'm sure she just hit a little traffic and—"

"Traffic?" Angela cackled. "No. Miss Locke played us—she's discovered what she can do now and has no intentions of coming back." The woman leaned closer and spoke in a harsh whisper. "You should've kept a closer eye on your subjects, Roger. This wouldn't have happened if you were doing your job properly."

"You asked for the impossible; I delivered." The man replied as confidently as he could.

"If this gets out," the woman continued, "we'll both be out of a job *and* any hope of a career. The board meeting is tomorrow. We need that woman to show what this formula can do. I won't let *years* of climbing the ladder be ruined by yet another in a long string of incompetent and careless men. That may be fine with you, but it isn't fine with me!"

Roger was silent for a moment, an expression of hurt coming over him. "*Careless?*" He muttered, repeating Angela's scathing remark. "So after all this time, that's what you think of me?"

The woman's brows were narrowed but she said nothing.

"You're right," he continued. "Maybe I *was* foolish—for

thinking I could rekindle what we had if I just did enough favors for you."

Angela shook her head. "We never *had* anything, *doctor*."

The man took an instinctive step back and tried to think of what to say.

"Um," chimed Debra—who had listened quietly to their exchange since Angela arrived. "Can I go home now?"

"In a moment, *Debra*," said Angela through gritted teeth. "Get me Miss Locke's address then pass me the phone. It's time we put things into more capable hands."

Dr. Lansing took quick breaths as he watched the receptionist obediently sift through a file, hand it to Angela, then move the phone closer to her.

"What are you doing?" Roger asked.

"Following protocol," the woman answered. Roger's eyes shot wide.

Quickly, Angela dialed a number from memory. The line only rang once before a click signaled that someone had picked up on the other end.

"I need an extraction," Angela muttered cryptically then rattled off the address of Donna's apartment. A moment later, she hung up the receiver and started back toward the elevator.

"W-wait," Roger scrambled after her, then stopped halfway and shouted. "Where are you going?"

The woman reached the elevator, turned with an irritated glare, and replied down the echoing hall: "I'm going out for a drink. Oh, and you're fired, Roger." Angela pressed the elevator call button and the doors swung open. She stepped in, glanced back once more, and added, "Debra, you can go home now." The doors closed and Angela Hyde was gone, leaving Roger and Debra in the dark reception area.

The dance club was just as lively as it was a few nights before as Marcus and Castillo arrived at the glowing entrance. On the sidewalk, the officers were bathed in the blinding, pink neon rays of Debonair's sign as Officer Myles scanned the area.

"I don't see her," Castillo sighed.

Marcus shook his head and tapped his foot. "Maybe she's already inside."

"You think she's hitting up the same club twice in one week?"

"I got the impression she was a regular," explained Marcus, taking a glance through the open window of a passing car. "I never got her number, so this is the best I can do, alright?"

A group of men with slicked-back hair and linen blazers passed by, heckling loudly as they disappeared into the establishment's thumping gateway.

After a few more moments, Castillo spoke again: "Shouldn't we be checking up on Donna's sister?"

"Hospital security said they'll reach out if there's anything fishy," answered Marcus. "We need to find Angela—she's connected to all of this somehow. She *has* to be. She knows something; we've just gotta get it out of her."

"*If* she even shows," noted Castillo, somewhat irritated.

"Don't worry; you'll get your chance to dance, partner."

Officers Myles and Castillo started for the entrance but paused when they heard a shout.

"Marcus?"

They turned. It was Angela, hurrying toward them in a vibrant red dress, clomping gracefully atop a set of high heels.

"Hey, Angela," answered Marcus as she reached them. "I was, uh, hoping we'd run into you again."

Angela caught her breath, then smiled as she turned to Castillo. "*We?* This must be your partner." She extended her hand.

"Castillo," the officer nodded nervously as they shook.

"So we're on a last name basis, huh?" Angela smirked.

"It's Rico, actually—but everyone calls me Castillo—or Officer Castillo."

"I see," the woman nodded with a raised eyebrow. "*Officer Castillo*—you weren't involved in that shootout at The Jade Lion last night, now, were you?"

He moved to reply, but Marcus interjected: "Angela—about that: I wanted to apologize—"

"How about you take me for a walk?" She interrupted. "It's a beautiful night—moon's out, there's a cool breeze... if Officer Castillo's alright with us slipping away for a bit, that is?"

Rico nodded hesitantly as Marcus smiled at him as if to say, "it's okay."

"Sure," Marcus said as they started down the sidewalk. "Let's walk."

Castillo watched from a distance, tapping his fingers nervously, before finally deciding to wait in the squad car while the couple walked a few blocks then crossed the street to get closer to the water. The crashing of the waves just beyond the natural dunes created a peaceful respite from the bustling South Beach nightlife only a few yards away.

"Listen, Angela," Marcus started. "Like I said, I'm sorry about the other night—"

Angela held up a hand to stop him. "Please, Marcus," she said, placing her hand in his. "Call me Angie."

Marcus took a nervous gulp and smiled. "Totally, uh, Angie," he replied. "What I was saying is that I'm sorry I had to run off like that the other night at the club—I didn't even get to see you off."

Angela nodded. "I understand," she affirmed. "You had a job to do. But what happened exactly? One minute I left to use the ladies' room, the next I heard gunshots!"

The couple meandered down the wide sidewalk under a row of bristling palm trees, dipping in and out of the dappled moonlit shadows beneath them.

"Well, I, uh, can't say too much," Marcus replied. "You know—top-secret intelligence and all that."

"Come on, Marcus," Angela nestled her chin against his shoulder. "Just one little morsel? It was all over the news today, so it hasn't exactly been kept under wraps."

The officer let out a labored sigh. "If I tell you my secrets," he said, "you have to tell *me* a secret about yourself."

"Deal!"

"Alright, then," Officer Myles nodded. "There's this smuggling ring that Castillo and I have been investigating for months. A few days back, we finally got a lead. Coincidentally, one of the suspects in that case was meeting his informant at The Jade Lion—"

"The same night you just *happened* to be there on a date with me," Angela interjected with a smile. "What a strange coincidence."

"Exactly." Marcus tried not to show his true thoughts on the matter—*that Angela was the one who decided on the time and place.*

"Did you get him?"

"Who?"

Angela chuckled. "This *informant.*"

"Oh, uh, no." The officer lowered his head. "The informant got away—or maybe never showed—and the suspect died from a gun wound before we could get anything out of him."

"Sorry to hear that," the woman answered softly.

Marcus took a deep breath, then stopped walking. He turned to face Angela. "Your turn. Tell me about your work—what you do."

She nodded. "Sure," Angela answered. "I, uh, work for a little local company called Pelican Innovations—"

"*Little?*" Marcus scoffed playfully. "Hardly!"

A car drove by blaring a raucous maraca-laden rhythm and a tone-deaf singer. After a moment, it slowly faded as the vehicle disappeared.

Angela grinned. "I guess you're right," she continued. "I've been with Pelican since they actually *were* a small lab. Worked my way up. You know, there aren't many women who've made it as high up in the food chain as I have."

Marcus affirmed her: "Somehow, I'm not surprised you've done it, though."

"Thanks," she smiled, squeezing his hand.

"Oh, hey," Marcus feigned a moment of sudden inspiration. "You ever heard of a guy named Vander Newport? I think he's on the board or something..." He watched the woman's reaction for any sign of recognition or wavering.

To the man's surprise, Angela nodded. "Why, yes—Mr. Newport and I go *way* back," the woman explained as they resumed walking. "He's an old family friend—and you're right; he's been on the board for Pelican since the beginning." Angela turned to Marcus with her eyebrows raised. "Can you keep a secret?"

Marcus nodded nervously. "Of course."

"Well," she continued, "I think he may have, you know, *pulled some strings* to get me my first job at Pelican."

"Is that so?" Marcus assumed a facetious air. "You mean that Miss Angela Hyde, self-made CEO of Pelican Innovations, actually owes her success to a *man*?"

She chuckled. "Stop it! I've worked hard for this. And I'm not CEO—*yet!*" Angela took a deep breath. "Sorry, I've told you *way* too much."

"Let me guess," Marcus replied. "If you say anymore, you'll have to kill me?" He flashed a roguish smile.

"Something like that," Angela rolled her eyes and smiled. After a few more moments of quiet walking, the woman asked: "Hey, what's going on between you and that *friend* of yours—Donna, was it?"

Marcus slowed his steps. His shallow breaths intermingled with the salty air. "What about her?"

"You seemed to suggest that you two had a history," Angela noted. "And I couldn't help but notice that she seemed a little skittish when we met. Is she okay?" The woman tapped the side of her head with her pointer finger. "I mean, *up here,* and everything."

"She's got, um—" Marcus paused. "She's got a lot going on. Her sister's not doing great, and she's taking care of her sister's kid, too, apparently—"

"A kid?" Angela perked up, then moved in closer. "And you still have feelings for Donna?"

The question caught him off guard. Marcus exhaled sharply. "Uh—w-we were barely even *together,*" he stammered. "Now, I'm here—with you."

Angela looked into his big, brown eyes, as if trying to determine whether he was telling the truth. Then, apparently satisfied, she nodded and breathed deeply. "That's all I wanted to know."

The two continued on a bit longer before they reached a turn in the path.

"I could use a drink," Marcus suggested.

Angela nodded and the two turned to walk back toward the club, arm in arm.

# CHAPTER 23

Donna sprinted down the street, jumping from shadow to shadow under the young oaks that lined the neighborhood. She hadn't planned for a trip like this when she had readied herself for the day; the loose flip-flops that Donna slipped on her feet when she left the apartment were beginning to rub the sides of her feet raw. Still, the woman pressed on with unbridled determination. When she reached the end of the sidewalk, she looked both ways before hurrying across a crosswalk to the other side of the street. Her cheeks were dripping and wet, yet she couldn't bring herself to risk touching her own face to dry her tears.

Donna hurried past a low-rise hotel with a smooth, rounded corner, not stopping to glance up toward its wide, illuminated second-floor windows nor to peer through a trio of octagonal portholes. Finally, she was now only a block from the ocean—not far from the diner—when she stopped to take a breath.

The salty air was refreshing, but Donna felt the continued tingling in her fingertips that reminded her all was not well. With a fresh teardrop forming at the edge of her eye, the blonde woman rushed between a pair of passing pedestrians, ascended a low sand dune, and arrived at the darkened beach.

She took a deep, salty breath. It was nearly pitch-black as a cloud billowed slowly over the moon. Donna reached the water's edge, carefully slipped her feet from the well-worn sandals, and sunk her toes into the cool, wet sand. The waves lapped over her feet. Donna strained to stare out across the undulating dark violet ocean before her. Then, involuntarily, she began to sob.

Donna took a few steps back and sat down, planting herself in the sand. With her hands held out at her sides, she cried out, "Why is this happening to me? This isn't what I wanted!"

Then, in a softer, quieter voice, she added—prayed: "I don't know what to do. Please, if you're out there—help me."

The current rippled and lapped just out of reach of her toes. Donna whimpered as she listened attentively to the sound of the sea—a sound she'd long associated with pleas- ant memories of family trips to the beach, of comfort, of peace, of good things.

Through the lulling cadence of the waters, Donna heard a shout:

"Miss Locke?"

She turned toward the voice.

"Miss Locke, is that you?" It was a man walking toward her.

"Y-yes," she answered hesitantly, rising to her feet to inspect the shadowed stranger.

The windswept clouds above shifted again, allowing the silver light of the moon to illuminate and reflect off his large glasses.

Donna finally recognized him. "Doctor?" She stepped back with a start.

"Yes, it's me," he flashed a dorky, earnest grin. "But what are the odds—I mean, what are the *chances* of you—"

"Of us *both* sulking by the sea?" Donna finished his thought and took another step back. "How did you find me here?"

Dr. Lansing moved closer. "I'm sorry, I didn't mean to frighten you. I promise I wasn't even looking for you, but it is quite serendipitous, don't you think?"

"How so?" Donna raised an eyebrow.

The doctor's eyes glanced to her fingers, stretched awkwardly at her sides. "Is it true?" He gestured toward her hands.

Donna tried to stall while she thought of a way to make her escape: "Is *what* true?"

"Did the experiment *do* something to you? Give you some sort of *ability*?"

The ocean tumbled at her side as Donna considered her reply. She took a deep breath, then turned and began walking quickly in the opposite direction up the beach.

"Wait, Miss Locke—!"

"I'm not telling you *anything*!"

"I just want to *talk*—"

"Oh, really?" Donna replied over her shoulder above the harsh breeze. "And then you'll make me disappear like your other experiments while you make off with loads of cash and slap a patent on my dead body?" She trudged on with determination.

"Miss Locke—" Roger stuttered, then started again, trying to keep up. "Donna, isn't it?" She didn't reply. "I assure you, this isn't about the money or even the research anymore—I could care less about all that now." He continued shouting over the wind toward Donna's back. "There's more to life than all the opulence and glitter anyhow."

At this, Donna stopped walking and turned quickly. "What's so wrong with wanting a little glitter, huh?" A hint of sarcasm in her tone was lost on the doctor.

"We spend our lives working for what we believe will bring us the happiest, most fulfilled life," he sputtered, "and we miss that it's happening right in front of our very eyes."

Donna inhaled deeply, then shook her head and continued trudging through the thickly-caked sand. Roger hurried after her once more. Without stopping again, the woman asked him, "Why are you following me, doctor?"

"I want to see if it's true," he said plainly. "I need to know that all I've sacrificed was *worth* something."

He watched as Donna slowed her pace, slumped her shoulders, and pivoted to face him. Her cheeks glistened with tears and seaspray. "Do you have a dollar, doctor?"

Curious, the man began to feel for his pockets. "A dollar—?"

"Or a coin or a trinket—something small?"

After a moment of searching, Dr. Lansing produced a ballpoint pen. He held it out toward Donna. She hesitantly extended her hand, palm up. The doctor placed the pen over her hand and let it fall into her grasp. The ordinary object suddenly became brighter and heavier, shimmering in the moonlight—gilded from end to end. Donna took the gilded pen between her fingers and held it up for the doctor to inspect.

The doctor's jaw hung agape as he orbited his head around the object in Donna's outstretched hand. "I don't believe it," he muttered. Then, holding out his hands, added, "May I?"

Donna dropped the gold pen into his palms. He flinched, unprepared for the weight of it. "Solid gold! Remarkable." Roger inspected the item with utter awe, the rest of the world fading away around him.

"*That's* what all of it was worth," Donna said. "Happy?" She was about to continue up the beach when he replied.

"Wait. Something *happened*, didn't it?" He spoke softly. "It turned something—or someone—to gold?"

"Yes," Donna snapped. "So I don't need your lectures about it, doctor; I'm fully aware that gold is not all it's cracked up to be!"

The doctor became somber. "You lost someone." He finally understood. "Someone you love very much."

In another passing moon-shadow, Donna gave a labored, tearful nod. "Her name was Starla," was all she could manage to say. Then, after a few deep breaths: "I don't know how it happened. One minute things were normal, the next there's a tingling in my fingers and things start to turn to gold at the touch!"

"Dihydrogen monoxide," the doctor whispered to himself.

"Excuse me?"

"Dihydro—I mean, *water*—" Roger said. "That's how it happened. It's the compound that activates the effects of the formula." Realizing Donna was still trying to understand, he added, "Water is what activates your, um, *powers*."

Donna reflected on the past few days. The glass of water the day after the experiment—that's when she first felt it. And there was the drink at the club before she went on stage... *He's right—water is the secret ingredient. But that's no help to Starla.*

"I lost someone in all this, too, you know," Roger said. "This was all *her* idea—she asked me to bypass all the usual reviews because she thought this could save our careers—*her* career. All those years, I thought that Angela Hyde *actually* cared for me. That we *had* something—we were partners. Turns out she was just using me like all the rest." Here, the man lowered his head and mindlessly turned the golden pen in his fingers.

"Wait," Donna said as she leaned in. "Did you say *Angela Hyde?*"

The doctor perked up. "So you've had the unfortunate pleasure to meet her, too?"

"Meet her! She's the woman who stole Marcus from me." Donna shook her head. "What am I saying? I pushed him away myself. No. I had the chance, but I blew it. And now everything's gone to hell. I'll never hold Starla again or be able to have a normal life—to be close to someone—with this... this *curse!*" She waved her hands in front of herself and began to mourn once more, again unable to wipe her tears.

This seemed to spark an idea in Roger's mind. "You may yet," he said, tapping a thoughtful finger over his lips.

Through her tears, Donna managed to mutter: "What?"

"I've just remembered something," the doctor continued. "There may be a way to help you—and your poor girl."

Donna shook her head and clenched her fist: "If you're about to suggest I stop drinking water for the rest of my life, then you can go—"

"I'm serious, Miss Locke." He held up his hands in peace.

"Sorry," she backed down. "Go on."

The doctor lowered his hands. "For every compound we develop in the lab, we also prepare another intended to coun-teract it—in the event that something goes wrong during testing. It's a sort of failsafe, if you will."

"There's an *antidote?*" Donna asked. "For this curse?"

"Sure, you could call it that," Roger affirmed. "Anyway, it's all very complicated and the formulas are proprietary and not easy to remember or recreate by any means, but I seem to recall that there were *two* doses for your particular iteration kept on hand."

"Two? That's perfect!" Donna beamed. "One to fix me and one to turn Starla back! Lead the way."

The doctor seemed hesitant.

"What is it, doctor?"

"You see, Angela and I didn't part on the best of terms," he began. "She fired me, actually, so it isn't quite as easy as us just *waltzing* into Pelican's vault."

Donna raised her eyebrows. "But... there *is* a way, right?"

Roger smiled nervously. "Of course," he said, shoving the golden pen into his pocket. "I'll tell you on the way." He turned and beckoned Donna to follow him.

As the two started back up the dune, Dr. Lansing paused. "Wait—where did you say your girl is now?"

"My apartment with my friends—why?"

In the moonlight, it was difficult for Donna to see, but Roger's face became flush and pale. He pressed his glasses up the arch of his nose.

"Doctor, what is it?"

"Angela sent a team of armed men there just a bit ago," he muttered.

"Armed?" Donna's eyes grew wide. "What for?"

"To *extract* you."

"Extract me? But I—"

"The girl, Donna!" Roger raised his voice. "She needs something to show for our work and if she can't have you she'll take the girl instead!"

Donna nearly lost her footing on the thick sand.

"Starla! My friends are with her. We have to get back there," Donna snapped. "You have a car?"

"We can't afford to waste any time," the doctor shook his head. "Find a payphone—call your friends and tell them to bring the girl to Pelican headquarters. We haven't much time to lose before they're on to us. I only fear that we aren't too late."

# CHAPTER 24

The women in Donna's small apartment were uncharacteristically quiet. While Sue paced the living room, Lisa twirled her red hair with a finger and orbited the golden version of Starla that stood motionless in the kitchen.

"I still can't believe this thing is real," Lisa muttered, using her fingernail to scrape at the gilded surface of what was once the girl's shirtsleeve. "But it's real alright."

Sue shook her head. "Would you get away from her? Donna told us to keep her safe."

"What? I'm just taking a closer look!"

The dark-haired woman stormed over to Lisa. "Not even! You're scratching up this poor, perfect kid!" Sue placed a pensive hand to her chin and inspected the gilded girl. "Though, you know, I think I have an idea."

Without another word, Sue hurried down the hall toward the back bedroom. Lisa heard rustling and the sound of squeaky closet doors opening and closing. A few moments later, the other woman arrived holding a bunch of large hats and a feather boa.

"Don't ask me why Donna has these in her closet," Sue instructed sternly. "But," she said as she placed a wide-brimmed, floppy hat on Starla's head, "I think it looks marvelous on her, don't ya think?"

Lisa raised an eyebrow. "I thought you said we should be more careful?"

"Relax," continued Sue as she threw the fluffy boa over the girl's shoulders. "Just having a little fun to pass the time."

With a shake of her head, Lisa snatched a ball cap from Sue's armful stash and swapped it onto Starla's head in place of the other hat. It fit perfectly over the girl's short, wavy hair—once a beautiful reddish color. "I think that's a little more *her*."

Before Sue could respond, the phone rang behind her, causing her to leap and let loose the remaining items from her arms, which scattered across the floor. As she scrambled to pick them up, Lisa hurried across the kitchen to grab the phone.

"Wait!" Sue shouted as the two women nearly tripped over one another. "Don't answer—it could be the lab calling again!"

Lisa caught her balance on the counter and stabilized herself. "But it could be Donna or Marcus with an update!" She didn't wait for her friend to answer. Lisa picked up the receiver and carefully placed it to her ear.

"Hello?"

The line was crackling a little, but the reply came quickly: "Hey, it's Donna!"

Lisa misheard. "Donna's not here right now—"

"No, Lisa, *this* is Donna!"

"Oh!" She gasped. "Don, are you alright? You sound a little, er, frantic."

"Listen closely," Donna replied. "Is Sue there? Put me on speaker so you can both hear what I'm about to tell you."

With a concerned glance at Sue, Lisa obediently followed Donna's hurried instruction and set the receiver on the counter. "Done. You still there?"

"Hey, Donna!" Sue chimed in.

"Hey, Sue," Donna's voice echoed across the compact kitchen. "Good. Okay, listen up. Do *not* panic, but I have reason to believe that someone may be, um, coming to the apartment."

Sue shouted back. "Someone? *Who*, Donna?"

"Like a visitor? Pizza guy?" Lisa added.

"No, not a visitor!" Donna answered with urgency in her voice. "Like *men*—with *guns!*"

"Guns?" Both women exclaimed. Sue hurried cautiously toward the front window and peered her head around the edge to survey the parking lot.

Lisa trembled into the phone. "Donna, what on earth have you gotten us into?"

"They work for a woman named Angela—never mind. It's a lot to explain, but I'm going to get you out of this, you understand?"

Lisa nodded, too nervous to realize that Donna couldn't hear the gesture.

"I need you to take Starla, get in your car, and meet me at the Pelican building—"

"Oh my goodness!" Sue shouted from the window. "I think she's right! There's a couple black cars parked right outside."

"What?" Lisa hurried over to see for herself.

"Girls?" Donna's crackling voice boomed from the kitchen. "Did you hear me?"

Both women were preoccupied with inspecting the parked, dark vehicles at the edge of the lot.

"Sue? Lisa? You still there?"

"Still here, Don!" Lisa shouted back.

Donna's voice was tense and impatient. "Would you get back to the phone? I can barely hear you—this is important!"

Quickly, Lisa scrambled back to the phone, keeping low as she moved across the room.

"We heard you, Donna," she piped back. "Get Starla to Pelican."

Sue arrived at Lisa's side. "But they may be watching us!" She made a grand gesture toward the door and window.

"We may have a way to save Starla," Donna said finally. "And get rid of this—this *curse*. But I need you to bring her to us—to the lab—as soon as possible."

"Us?"

"Long story. I'll explain later. Can you do it?"

Creeping back to the window, Sue nearly screamed. "A third car just pulled up!"

"Sue, Lisa," said Donna through deep, steady breaths. "You're my best friends. I need you. I'm counting on you. You can do this."

Lisa inhaled sharply and nodded. "We've got it, Donna."

"Good," she replied. "See you soon. Be careful!" The line clicked as Donna hung up on the other end and Lisa replaced the receiver.

"Leese, I've got a bad feeling about this," Sue muttered from the window.

"No kidding," replied Lisa, returning her attention to the small, golden girl in the kitchen. She shook her head and mumbled: "What are we going to do with you?"

Sue hurried toward the kitchen again. "We need backup!" She was already moving toward the phone.

"Backup?"

"Hold on," said Sue. "I'm just gonna make one call—I promise, this will be worth it."

The dark-haired woman dialed the number and placed the phone to her ear, tapping her foot and biting her lip as the line rang. And rang.

And rang.


Outside at the curb, bathed in the rosy glow of Debonair's garish fluorescent signage, Officer Castillo sulked in the driver's seat of the squad car. He checked the time; it had been several minutes since Marcus and Angela set off on their walk. *What's taking so long?*

He flipped the radio on and, despite the fuzzy soundwaves competing with the thumping from the lively club, began to sift through stations. First, a poppy, synth-laden ballad. *Click.* Then a twangy country tune. *Click.* A few seconds of a familiar show tune. *Click.* A man crooning in Spanish along with a delicate guitar. *Yes.*

Rico took a deep breath and adjusted the volume, then sank back into the seat. It was a comforting, relaxing sound. *Just what we all need after the last few days—*

*Brrrring! Brrrring!*

It took a moment for the officer to realize that the tone was emanating from the carphone built into the dashboard—it was rarely used since their radios usually sufficed for any fieldwork.

*Brrrring!*

Castillo hesitated, turned down the radio volume, then leaned forward and picked up the receiver.

"H-hello? This is Castillo."

"Rico! Thank goodness!"

"Who is thi—*Sue?*" The officer puffed when he recognized his sister's voice.

A second voice chimed in: "And Lisa—I'm here, too!"

"What the heck do you think you guys are doing? Sue, I told you that this line was only for emergencies!"

Sue took a deep breath on the other end. "This *is* an emergency, Rico! We're in big trouble—they've got us surrounded!"

Rico was frazzled and shook his head as he tried to put the pieces together: "Trouble? *Who's* got you surrounded? What's going on—"

Before he could finish the thought, he caught sight of Marcus returning down the sidewalk, arms linked with Angela.

"Well, we're at Donna's," Sue began. "There's a bunch of black cars outside the apartment—Donna said they have *guns* and—!"

"Guns?" Castillo exclaimed. "Is Donna *sure*? Can you put her on?"

"She's, um," started Lisa. "She's not here right now. But she said they're here to take Starla—"

"Who's Starla?"

"The kid. Donna's sister's girl. It's a long story but she's sort of, um, turned to gold and we—"

"What?" Castillo nearly shouted. "If you don't start making sense in three seconds, I'm hanging up."

Sue took a deep breath and continued the story: "Donna got this weird power to turn things to gold; we didn't believe it either 'til the little girl ran in here and they accidentally touched and now she's standing in the kitchen like one of those da Vinci statues." The woman barely paused for a breath before continuing. "Don said some lady named Angela sent these guys to get her *or* the girl but now *we're* here and *she's* not and we could use a little help—"

Castillo raised his eyebrows and he ducked closer to the

phone's controls, speaking in a harsh whisper: "Did you say *Angela?*" Marcus and Angela were nearly at the car.

"Yes, that's what Donna told us," Sue chimed. "Aren't you listening?"

"I'm listening," the officer assured his sister.

Marcus and Angela reached the edge of the curb. The officer tapped on the window and Castillo slowly rolled it halfway open.

"Who are you on the phone with?" Marcus asked.

Castillo gave him the "*just a minute*" finger. The couple on the sidewalk took a step away.

"Okay," Castillo said into the receiver with a feigned smile. "Where did you say you are?"

"Donna's apartment!" Lisa nearly shouted. "But Don said we've gotta get the girl to the Pelican Innovations headquarters *ASAP*."

"Alright," replied Castillo with a nod. "I'll be on it as fast as I can."

Before either of the women could respond, Castillo hung up the phone and gave a wide grin to Marcus.

"What was that all about?" The approaching partner asked with concern. "We getting called into another case?"

Angela held his arm. "If you need to go, we can do this another time—"

Castillo shook his head rapidly. "Just a little drive-by," he spouted. "One-man job."

Marcus raised an eyebrow. "You sure?"

His partner nodded.

"He said he's got this," Angela assured Marcus in a soft voice, squeezing his hand. "What do you say we go somewhere a little more... private?" There was a sensuous sparkle in her eyes, cast in the pink neon light.

Officer Myles took a deep breath and turned to his partner. "Thanks, Rico."

"Don't mention it," Castillo gave a nervous smile back, casting a fleeting look at Angela.

"Come on," she nudged Marcus back down the sidewalk. "We can take a cab. I know just the place—best view in Miami."

As the two vanished down the dark side of the street, Castillo turned the key in the ignition and the engine roared to life. He flicked the volume back up on the radio and revved away through the breezy night.

# CHAPTER 25

In the shadow of dusk, the tower that housed Pelican Innovations still managed to look impressive. The glow from the rest of the coastal city lights intermingled with the nearly full-glass exterior of the relatively new building, creating a shimmering optical illusion as Donna craned her neck from the ground to glimpse its highest point.

She and Dr. Lansing huddled behind a patch of lush landscaping and a minimalist sculpture crafted of sliced steel I-beams painted a bright red.

"Why are we hiding?" Donna asked. "Don't you have a key or something?"

"It's like I told you," Roger shook his head and took a deep breath. "Angela and I didn't part on the best of terms—well, actually, she fired me—so all of my access cards and codes have been deactivated."

"Then how the heck are we supposed to get in there to get

the antidote?"

"You phoned your friends," he replied. "I phoned a friend, as well."

"Who?"

Roger shook his head. "That would spoil things."

"Are you serious? Can't you just tell me?" Donna glared at him.

"Oh, Miss Locke," Roger smiled. "Isn't it more fun when I keep you in suspense?"

Donna rolled her eyes and shook her head.

"She'll be here any minute now," he added to appease her.

While she focused her gaze on the entrance to the building once more, Donna quipped, "You are an *interesting* man, you know that?"

"Thank you," replied Roger in earnest. "And *you* are fascinating to me, Miss Locke."

"Yeah? Why's that?"

"Well—how do I say this?" He muttered to himself, then turned back to Donna. "After I developed the early iterations of the compound we tested on you, Angela told me we had to move to human trials—to accelerate our normal procedures and bypass some of the more ethical ways of testing."

"If you're trying to tell me you're sorry for all this," Donna interrupted, "it's okay. I don't hold it against you." She hung her shoulders. "I chose to join the study myself."

"I appreciate that, Donna, but that *isn't* what I'm trying to say." Dr. Lansing took a deep breath. "What I'm trying to say is that I couldn't bear to apply the compound to unwitting human subjects without testing it first. So, I used the most accessible person I could find—me."

Donna's attention was laser-focused on the man now. "Are you saying this happened to you, too? And that's how you discovered that water's what activates our powers?"

Roger inhaled sharply. He shook his head, clearly getting frustrated. "No, Donna." He took another long, deep breath. "I'm saying that the compound *didn't* work on me. There was no change, no power, no nothing—other than a brief feeling of nausea."

"So," said Donna, "what does that mean?"

The doctor leaned closer and locked eyes with Donna. "It means that I believe your blood is... um... *special*, Donna."

The woman's mouth was agape as she tried to process the doctor's words. "Special *how*—?"

At that moment, both Donna and the doctor whipped around at the sound of footsteps on the grass. A dark figure slinked through the shadows, moving toward them in a half-crouched position. Finally, the figure passed through a sliver of light and reached their side.

"Good! You made it," said Roger to the familiar face. Then, turning to Donna, added, "Miss Locke, you remember Debra, our receptionist?"

Debra flashed an exuberant smile. "Hello, Donna; good to see you again—" She stretched out her hand to shake, but immediately the doctor swatted it down before either woman could touch.

"Best not to tempt fate," he whispered.

"Oh, right," Debra sputtered. "Almost forgot about the whole *gold* thing you mentioned on the phone."

Donna nodded and gave her greeting, then the doctor pointed through the bushes toward the entrance to the Pelican building, where a trio of security guards stood at attention inside the glass atrium.

"Debra here can get us past the lobby," Roger explained then looked at his watch. "In just a moment, there will be a brief window of time where there's only *one* guard on duty as the others are swapped out for new ones starting their night shifts. While Debra creates a distraction, we'll sneak our way to the elevators, then she'll meet up with us afterward."

Listening intently, Donna nodded, "And then?"

"The next part is where things get most tricky," the doctor said, pausing for another long inhalation. "The two vials of what we're calling 'the antidote' are stored in the vault, which is on the seventeenth floor. The vault's embedded down a maze of hallways, but if you even step *foot* on the seventeenth floor without the proper access codes, you'll set off a silent alarm."

"I thought you said you don't have proper access codes?" Donna tensed.

"That's correct," Roger affirmed, then turned. "Debra, do you have what I asked for?"

Debra nodded eagerly then opened the flap of a large purse slung across her side. On the grass in front of her, she laid out a set of headphones, a flashlight, a bottle of water, a portable tape recorder and player, a duo of compact walkie-talkies, an audio cassette without its case, and a pair of cutting pliers.

As he verified the objects that Debra placed before him, Dr. Lansing picked up the pliers and continued, "As I said, the vault and the wing that leads to it have a silent alarm. If we cut the power, the alarm will eventually reset via a backup generator. We'll have a short window to get in *and* out before the generator kicks in and the alarm comes back online." He set the pliers beside him.

Donna interjected, "How short?"

"I'm getting to that," replied a flustered Roger. "But the vault itself is temperature-controlled, so too much heat will set off the alarms as they begin to come back online. Just in case, this is where you come in, Donna: there are heat sensors around the edges of the vault itself *and* each of the sealed corridors that lead into it. If you turn each of them to gold before the generator completes its cycle, that should freeze the sensors, in effect deactivating them, and buy us the time we need."

"I think I can do that," she answered. "As long as my special *power* doesn't run out before we need it." Donna held up her hands and wiggled her fingers.

"We've got you covered," the doctor said, gesturing toward the bottle of water on the grass. "Debra, would you do the honors?"

Compliantly, Debra nodded, grabbed the bottle, unscrewed the lid, and held it toward Donna's mouth. Confident that the blonde woman's hands were out of reach, Debra placed the water bottle to Donna's lips and helped her drink a few hurried gulps.

When she was finished, Donna wiped her mouth with the back of her arm. "So you never answered my question," she pointed out. "How much time do we have until the silent alarm kicks back in and—more importantly—how we will know if it *does* if it's silent?"

Roger delicately reached for the walkman and head-phones, connecting them via the auxiliary port as he spoke. "You'll have plenty of time. Approximately six minutes and six seconds, actually." He took the cassette tape and held it out for the women to see. "That happens to be the exact length of the first track on this tape: Michael Jackson's *Don't Stop 'til You Get Enough*."

Donna chuckled. "You're kidding me, right?"

"What?" Roger said defensively. "Don't you like Michael Jackson?"

She nodded. "'Course I do," the woman said. "This is all just so convoluted that I'm starting to think it might *actually* work."

"Why wouldn't it?" The doctor placed the tape into the deck. "Six minutes is plenty of time, thankfully. You should have no problem getting in, locating the vials, and getting out, especially if you've turned all of the heat sensors to gold—you'll just have to make sure you're out of the vault itself by the time the song ends. If that door is ajar or opened once the power comes back, we're toast. Unfortunately, I won't be able to make it up there from the breaker room, but I've written you instructions to open the vault's combination lock and locate the proper vials." He produced a folded piece of lined yellow paper and handed it to Debra, who placed it into a purse pocket with care.

As Debra gathered the items and placed them back into her purse, the trio turned back toward the building. Roger checked his watch.

"Any second now," he muttered.

From their vantage point behind the bushes, they watched closely as two of the security guards left their posts and disappeared into what they presumed was some sort of break room.

When they were out of sight, the doctor nodded. "Alright," he said quietly. "It's now or never!"

Silently, Roger, Debra, and Donna scurried across the front lawn, where they ducked behind a large sculpture. The doctor nodded to Debra, who straightened her shoulders and brushed off the front of her skirt. With a smile, she gave a 'thumbs up' to the others then headed toward the Pelican lobby. Donna held her breath.

*This had better work.*

The black cars were situated at the far end of the old apartment building's parking lot; Sue's car was parked at the foot of the stairs, close to the building.

Lisa peered around the edge of the window again. "How the heck are we going to get the girl to the car without them noticing?"

"They don't know we're here," Sue tried to assure her.

"But Donna said they've got *guns*, Susana!" Lisa raised her voice. "Are we just going to sit here and wait for your brother to run in here like Mad Max or something? We don't have time for that!"

Sue quickly paced around the living room a few times, then stopped and turned toward Starla. The golden girl's motionless figure was still adorned with the gaudy feather boa from earlier.

"I've got an idea!" The woman said with a smile. Sue rushed into the back room.

Lisa rolled her eyes as Sue returned a moment later with her arms full of clothing. She dumped the items into a pile in front of Starla—a jacket, tube socks, a maroon fedora, Donna's inline skates, and a few other loose items of clothing.

"Uh, Sue, what are you doing?"

Sifting through the clothes, Sue grabbed the jacket and began to slip it over Starla's immobilized arms. "If those guys see us lugging a golden statue out the front door, they'll be on us in an instant. Maybe a disguise will buy us some time."

Lisa shook her head. "You're crazy. This is crazy!"

"Just making this up as I go, Leese," she snapped. "Now, you gonna help me out or what?"

With a deep sigh, Lisa hurried to Sue's side and the two began to adorn the golden child in the trappings secured from Donna's closet. When the girl was covered in thick clothing to hide her gilded form, Sue tipped the statue on its side. "Hurry—get the skates on her feet."

By this time, Lisa decided not to argue with her friend; instead, she shook her head as she struggled to strap one of the wheel-lined blades onto the girl's foot. When that was done, she managed to get the second skate in place with less difficulty.

Sue pivoted the girl back into an upright position and the two women stood back to admire their handiwork.

"Not great, but it'll do," she said with a quick nod.

While Sue wheeled the girl toward the door, Lisa took one more furtive glance out the window. "Alright, they haven't moved yet. If we just act natural, I think we can make it to the car." She turned back to Sue. "You got the keys?"

She felt the small purse at her side to verify. "Yep." Sue took a deep breath and counted down with her fingers. "Three. Two. One!"

The women swung the door open. Lisa was shaking, but grabbed Starla's outstretched hand and began to pull the statue-like girl down the open-air landing toward the stairs. Warily, she slanted her eyes toward the black cars and thought she noticed one of the doors open.

"Act natural!" Sue whispered harshly through gritted teeth.

They had nearly made it to the stairs when they heard the sound of another car door clicking open. Again, the women tried to act like nothing was wrong.

"What now?" Lisa muttered as they arrived at the top step. They had not thought through how to get the girl down the stairs while she was on wheels.

"One step at a time," nodded Sue. "Careful she doesn't slip."

Lisa complied and took the first step down. She helped Sue lead the frozen girl so that the skates came to rest on the step. "Good," Lisa affirmed. "Now the next."

The women carried on in this manner, making slow but steady progress toward the ground floor. As they rounded the halfway point where the staircase bent the opposite direction, Sue stole another glance at the black cars at the far end of the lot. She could see several large figures in black standing outside the vehicles, making surreptitious steps toward the building—and the women.

Lisa's voice quavered. "Where the heck is your brother?"

"He'll get here. Alright, keep your eyes on the girl, Leese," Sue muttered, mostly for her own sake. "Car's right there— we can make it." The little blue sedan was parked in the second spot, right at the foot of the stairs, and they had only a few steps to go.

Lisa looked up. Her eyes widened as she saw one of the men—he was holding a handgun that caught the light of a streetlamp. "Uh, Sue?"

Sue saw it, too. "Um," she scrambled for what to do as they cleared the second-to-last step. "Alright, dear, that's good!" She spoke loudly. "Just loosen up, dear, that's it—one more step!"

At first, Lisa was confused, but then she realized what Sue was trying to do: convince the guards that all was well. It must've helped, as the man who was nearest to the apartment building slowed his steps.

Starla's skate-strapped feet touched the pavement and the

women rolled her quickly toward the car. While Sue fumbled around in her purse looking for the keys, Lisa continued the loud rambling chatter: "Oh, good job, dear. Um—your skin is so nice, it's glowing—sparkling, even—what lotion do you use—?"

The men resumed their approach. They weren't far from the car now.

"Just find the freakin' keys, Susana!" Lisa whispered.

Finally, Sue removed a jangling fistful of keys and jammed one into the driver's side door lock. The door clicked open, then Sue proceeded to press the button inside to unlock the remaining doors.

"Help me out with this," Lisa demanded as she attempted to stuff the golden girl into the back seat. Sue hurried around, watching the men slowly raise their weapons. With a large push, the two women lodged the solid gold Starla into the car and slammed the door shut. The women leaped into the driver and passenger seats and closed the doors as Sue fired up the engine.

Sue pivoted to look out the back window. Over the bundled silhouette of Starla in the backseat, the woman saw one of the men standing directly behind the vehicle. His gun was pointed right at her!

"Where's Rico?"

"No time to wait around for him," Sue snapped. Then, thinking fast, she slammed the car into *reverse* and punched the gas pedal. The crumby little car flew backward—right toward the thug with the gun.

Lisa screamed as they heard a loud *thump* under the car. The two women locked eyes with one another in shock, then turned to look out their respective windows almost in unison. A cadre of the other men with guns planted their feet and pointed their weapons toward the car. One fired off a bullet that splintered a side window, eliciting another shriek from Lisa.

"Go!" She cried, leaning away from the broken window.

Sue snatched the transmission shift lever and threw the car into *drive*. With a heavy foot on the gas, the car lurched forward—with a second *thump* as they doubled back on the same course—and screeched across the parking lot, leaving tread marks on the asphalt.

In the rearview mirror, Sue watched as the men hurried back to their black cars.

"What the heck were you thinking?" Lisa shouted over the breeze through the shattered window. "You could've got us killed!"

"I think I just saved us," Sue managed a chuckle of surprise. "But hang on," she said, gripping the steering wheel tightly. "We're not out of this yet."

As they skidded out of the parking lot and onto the highway, Lisa looked back over the passenger seat and saw pairs of lights wheel out behind them. The men were hot on their tail.

Lisa felt light-headed and gripped the side of the car. "God help us all!"

# CHAPTER 26

Donna and Dr. Lansing waited anxiously behind the metal sculpture, watching through the glass atrium as Debra walked confidently toward the remaining, lone security guard. The secretary used exaggerated hand motions as she communicated with him.

"Wait for it," whispered Roger, holding up a hand.

Donna studied the entrance. "Doctor, what about the cameras?" She pointed to a set of shiny new video cameras mounted at strategic points above the doors.

"Don't worry," he dismissed her. "They were just installed. They haven't got these cameras working yet." He gulped and whispered under his breath: "At least I *think* so."

This did little to calm Donna's fears, but she decided to return her attention to the task at hand and trust that the doctor knew what he was talking about.

Through the glass, the security guard gestured toward the

unoccupied front desk, where Debra picked up the sign-in clipboard. With expert poise, she managed to situate herself so that the guard now stood with his back to the front door—and the route to the elevators.

"Now!" The doctor had barely got the word out before he was moving across the large pavers toward the front door. Donna followed closely behind. As Roger reached the door, he carefully, quietly pulled it open and ushered Donna inside. He could hear the mumblings of Debra's conversation with the guard, but a rippling water fountain in the center of the atrium muffled the words and the intruders' steps.

The doctor surreptitiously gestured toward the elevators past the reception desk—out of the guard's line of sight. Donna and Roger moved cautiously through the vast room, ducking behind large planters at every opportunity to stay out of sight. On one occasion, Roger noticed Debra's expression shift to one of concern, but she quickly brushed it off and finished filling out the clipboard.

Over the security guard's shoulder, Debra could see Roger and Donna slinking the final stretch to the elevators, where they'd soon be out of sight. With a flirtatious smile, she cocked her head, thanked the guard, and set the clipboard back on the desk before walking confidently—but not *too* quickly—to join the others at the elevator.

Debra made a final glance over her shoulder to make sure the guard didn't follow, then arrived at the elevator. She pressed the button as Donna and Roger emerged from behind a large potted shrub. The doors to the elevator slid open and the trio piled in. Roger pressed a button to send them down to a lower level.

As soon as the doors shut, all three exhaled.

"Everything okay?" Roger inquired of Debra.

The receptionist shook her head slightly. "Not exactly," Debra muttered, her face angled down. "I just discovered something."

"What is it?" Donna's brows furrowed.

"It's Miss Hyde," said Debra. "Angela. She's here!"

Both of her listeners held their mouths agape.

Dr. Lansing leaned closer. "What?

She nodded. "The guard told me she arrived a few minutes before I did," Debra explained. "Said she's preparing for the board meeting tomorrow, which is also what I told him *I* was doing here so late at night.

"Are you sure?"

"I saw her name on the clipboard," Debra verified. "And there was someone else," she added. "They said she had someone with her—according to the sign-in it's someone named Marcus—Marcus Myles, I think it was."

Donna's eyes enlarged with concern. "They're *both* here?"

"We'll be fine," assured the doctor. "As long as she doesn't know *we're* here, all will go according to the plan."

Before Donna could respond, the elevator doors swung open with a chime. The space in front of them was dark. The whole area appeared unfinished, with wires, cords, and conduits running along the walls and ceiling.

"This is my stop," Roger said, holding up the cutting pliers as he stepped through the doors. He gave the pliers an oblig-atory *click-click*. Debra handed him one of the walkie-talkies from her large bag and took the other in her hand.

"They're already set to channel three," noted the secretary as they switched on the devices.

"Excellent," the doctor replied, verified the channel, then turned to the women. "Take the elevator to Level 17, but don't step past the first corridor until I say so." He clicked the button on the walkie, emitting a bleep from its twin.

Roger turned away as the doors started to close, but Donna thrust her arm between them to stop it. "Doctor!" She exclaimed.

He turned. "Yes, Miss Locke?"

Donna took a deep breath. "I just want to say: thank you."

Roger smiled. "It's the least I can do," he nodded. "Remember, Donna: whether you can turn things to gold with a touch or not, you're special."

The woman acknowledged this with a slight nod then backed away to let the doors close once more. Quietly, Debra pressed the button for the seventeenth floor and the women felt the rotors begin to whisk them quickly upward. As they waited to arrive, Donna tapped her foot nervously and took a long, deep breath.


Marcus stood beside Angela as the elevator rose.

"Almost there," Angela smiled as she watched the digital floor number indicator.

Marcus tried not to show his discomfort. "You sure we're allowed up here?" The nervous officer clenched his fist to keep from shaking.

Angela chuckled. "Of course. You can relax."

The elevator dinged and the doors opened. As they stepped out into a dark space and the door closed behind them, Angela felt for a set of switches on the wall. Marcus heard a faint hum and focused on what he had perceived as a wall. Instead, he realized that it was a tall window—nearly two stories until it met the cavernous ceiling—upon which a curtain now withdrew by some unseen, humming mechanism. Another click and hum prompted a faint, light soundtrack of saxophone to play from a hidden speaker system.

The room was gradually filled with moonlight, making the two figures visible once more. Marcus made a quick visual sweep of the room—an adjoining space was lined with bookshelves and featured a secretary's desk guarding the way to a closed wooden door. He nodded toward it. "That your office?"

"Not yet," Angela smirked. "But someday." Angela beckoned for Marcus to follow her to the now-revealed window, which he did with a nod.

"What did I tell you?" She said with a sweeping gesture. "Best view in town."

Marcus cast a glance downward as he stepped to place his hand on the glass. From this penthouse window at the very top of Pelican headquarters, the young officer could see for miles—the bay and the entire city of Miami, stretched out like a miniature playset with specks of glittering light dotting the scene. "Really makes you realize how small we are," he said, trying to pinpoint the exact location of the police station.

"How small we are," Angela affirmed. "But how high we can climb with enough determination, drive, and—" She gave Marcus a sultry look, "—vigor."

Marcus swallowed to clear a lump in his throat, hoping Angela wouldn't notice in the dim moonlight. She moved closer to him, placing a hand over his on the glass in synchronization with the faint, romantic music.

Without a word, the two moved their hands from the window and interlocked their fingers. "Dance with me," Angela said, more a command than a question. The young officer nodded and forced a smile, taking the woman's other hand in his own. The two swayed across the polished floor as the starry night cast a sparkle—nature's very own mirrorball.

"There's no place I'd rather be right now," whispered Angela into Marcus' ear. "Here. With you. High above the Magic City."

Marcus nodded and answered back, "I feel the same way." He almost believed his own words.

The pair shuffled their steps around the room, circling and swaying.

Marcus felt a shift in Angela's pulse. "You're tense. Everything alright?"

"Tomorrow's the biggest day of my career," Angela continued.

"Oh?"

"There's a project we've been working on for years," she explained, her arms now draped loosely around Marcus' neck. "Tomorrow I present our, er, findings to the board—they're going to be shocked, frankly."

Marcus raised an eyebrow. "What's the project?"

"It's a bit hard to explain," Angela muttered. "We set out to create a substance that would change the landscape of war and defense—a compound that would eliminate the need for things like guns, weapons, bulletproof vests—instead reinforcing the human body itself."

"So you've created such a substance?"

Angela let out a short sigh. "Not exactly. What we've created is much more powerful."

"I'd love to hear about it—"

A large jolting sound cut Marcus off. The music ended abruptly and the room immediately felt warmer as the air conditioning stopped blowing.

The officer looked around the dark room. "Uh, what just happened?"

"Power's out," Angela muttered, her pulse suddenly heightening.

"That happen often?"

Angela shook her head. "There's a backup generator, but it takes a few minutes to kick in." She seemed pensive, deep in thought, and added under her breath, "Something's not right."

As the two ambled through the dark toward a nearby

stairwell door, hands stretched out in front of them, Marcus took short breaths. Something about the way Angela had reacted made him apprehensive to follow. But he couldn't give up now—the case depended on it. He had to stay close.

A few floors below—only minutes earlier—Donna and Debra stepped off the elevator into a compact holding space. The doctor had given clear and specific instructions for them not to pass the first door before them until the power was shut off, so the two used the time to ready themselves for the time-sensitive mission ahead.

Debra removed the headphones and walkman from her bag. "You'll need to be the one to wear these," she said. "I can't focus when there's loud music playing."

Donna agreed. She was about to reach for the device when she remembered what would happen if she touched it. With a chuckle, she retracted her hands. "Guess I'm going to need a little help," she said. "Just the thought of making... *that happen* to another person makes me sick."

"Of course. What do you say we keep a few feet between us at all times—just for good measure?"

The blonde woman nodded, then Debra clipped the chunky, battery-operated tape player onto Donna's waistband. She removed the cassette tape from its case and slid it into the player, closing the hatch with a satisfying *click*.

"Thank you for helping me and my girl, Debra," Donna spoke earnestly. "After all I've been through this past week—

well, it's been tough. You know, it's crazy: when I first found out she was going to live with me, I was terrified. But now? I just want to get my Starla back."

The secretary untangled the headphones and placed them over Donna's ears. They sat lightly, so that the woman would still hear Debra's voice as long as the music wasn't playing too loudly.

"That's nice." Debra forced one of her exaggerated smiles. "No offense, Donna, but I'm not doing this for you. I'm doing this because I think Angela is a terrible person and I don't want to give her the satisfaction of winning." She nodded, then added, "But don't worry: we're going to get you and your girl all better really soon."

Finally, Donna was ready. Whenever the doctor gave the cue, Debra would press the play button for her to start the tape to keep Donna's hands off the player. But for now: they waited.

"Just shout to me when we're getting close to the end of the song," the secretary instructed as she unfolded the yellow piece of paper upon which Roger had transcribed the combinations for the series of doors and corridors that led up to the vault itself.

"Got it," Donna replied.

The walkie-talkie crackled. "Everybody ready? Over." It was Roger's voice.

Debra held the button and replied, "Totally. Over—I mean: Roger that, Roger."

They couldn't see him, but Donna was almost certain the

doctor was rolling his eyes on the other end of the line. His voice came through a second later following a sigh: "Here goes nothing. Over."

Both women took a deep breath and moved closer to the first door. Debra returned the walkie to the bag, exchanging it for a flashlight, and then placed an outstretched finger over the walkman at Donna's side.

"Remember," Debra said. "I'll crack the combos while you take care of the heat sensors—just in case we need a few extra seconds on the way out."

Donna nodded. A second later, they heard a loud thud and the lights turned out. All at once, Debra clicked the play button to start the tape then whipped around to face the combination lock on the first door. Using the flashlight to illuminate Roger's instructions, Debra began following the steps.

Donna breathed deeply as the music faded in, that iconic, slapping bass building a rhythmic anticipation. At the exact moment Debra cracked the first code, Donna heard Michael Jackson's signature squeal of delight and glee that ushered in the infectious melody of the track. The door swung open and the two rushed forward, strings swelling and swirling in Donna's ears. The countdown had begun.

# CHAPTER 27

The combinations for the airlocks leading to the deepest heart of the vault were lengthy; the building's creators had opted for the more tactile security measure as backup to allow protected access even on occasions where the power was out. As they proceeded into the first section of the corridor, Debra waved the flashlight up along the seam where the walls met the low-hanging ceiling.

"The heat sensors," the secretary nearly yelled, exaggerating her mouth movements so that Donna could interpret over the music in her ears.

Donna understood. She counted four sensors in this room—one near each corner. As Debra hurried to the next locked door to begin rotating the combination spinner, Donna poised herself under one of the sensors and reached her hand up toward it. She was just an inch or two shy of it when standing tiptoe.

Checking to make sure the tape player was secure, Donna returned her attention to the sensor above her, then wiggled her fingers and arched her legs. She kicked off, a light jump. Her bare fingers tingled a bit as they touched the edge of the sensor. In the dim spill of the flashlight's glow, Donna's feet planted back on the floor and she watched as the heat sensor turned to gold.

*One down*, she thought, as Mr. Jackson moved through the first verse in her ears.

Donna repeated her strategy on the opposite sensor, then on the pair closest to the door by Debra. The secretary had only a couple of numbers left to cycle through. Within a few seconds, the combo clicked and the second door swung open into a nearly-identical corridor.

*Keep going*— The words in Donna's head urged. *Can't stop*—

The two women repeated the process with relative ease as the tape played on, a musical ticking clock with still a few minutes to go.

The blonde woman took a deep breath as she gilded another sensor. *Plenty of time*, Donna thought to try and encourage herself. But she was shaking. If they didn't get those vials, she *and* Starla would be stuck like this—quite possibly forever.


*Screeeeeeech!*

"Maybe this will lose 'em!" Sue's car skidded around a corner at the last minute, and she puffed through quick breaths. "Did it work?"

Lisa bent back to look past the golden girl in the backseat and out the rear window. A second later, the three ominous pairs of headlights materialized, making the same turn. "Unfortunately, no." The red-haired woman realigned herself back into the passenger seat and grabbed the side of the car as Sue took another sharp turn, narrowly missing a mailbox. "Careful, Sue! We're transporting precious cargo, remember?"

The driver didn't reply. Instead, she sunk her foot onto the gas pedal, nearly pushing it to the floor.

Soon they were almost out of the neighborhood. In the rearview mirror, Sue noticed that only one car was still on their tail. "Guess we lost their buddies?"

Lisa screamed and pointed out the front window. As Sue's attention readjusted from the mirror to the view before her, she saw the flashing red lights that signaled the arrival of a passing train ahead. The flimsy gates were closing slowly. The car wasn't far from the tracks. They could make it, Sue presumed. She checked the rearview mirror once more. Still one car tailing.

"Sue! What are you doing?"

The driver revved the engine of the little car and soared toward the gates, now halfway down. "Donna said to keep Starla safe," she grunted, biting her lip. "That's what we're going to do."

The flashing lights illuminated the women in red as the car jumped a little, its tires hitting the first edge of the track with a jarring jolt. But the vehicle kept moving at breakneck speed, ignoring the horn from the oncoming train. In milliseconds, the light blue car reached the other side, the final drop of the gate barely scraping the trunk as they passed through.

Lisa's eyes remained wide as she watched the black vehicle—a dark sportscar—attempt to crash through the gates to follow them. "What!" She screamed. Before the black car could make it across the tracks, an enormous locomotive appeared and pummeled it, undeterred. Lisa looked away as Sue swerved onto a road that ran parallel to the tracks.

"Guess that takes care of them," muttered Sue, nodding to herself through deep breaths.

"What about the others?" Lisa pleaded. "There were two more, right?"

Almost on cue, two pairs of headlights appeared behind them, nearly blinding the women as they peered through the back window. The duo of dark cars revved their engines—a cruel and taunting roar.

"Where's your brother when you need him?" Lisa shook her head.

"He'll catch up to us," Sue nodded. "I know he will."

Sue navigated the car in and out of lanes, crisscrossing around city blocks that were mostly empty at this hour—the real traffic would start once they got off the mainland and onto the island. They nearly lost the pair of black cars on a couple of occasions, but their drivers seemed ultra-familiar with the layout of the downtown area and unfazed by Sue's tactics.

"I think they're gaining on us, Sue!"

"Would you be quiet and gimme a sec to think?" The dark-haired woman tapped one of her clenched fingers on the steering wheel as she dipped the car down another sidestreet. "The causeway's just up ahead. Maybe we can lose 'em."

The tiny car zipped under an overpass and spat out the other side, ascending the ramp to the long bridge that ran across the bay and over to the island.

"Now," said Sue with a smile. "Let's see what this baby can do!" With her fingers gripping the wheel tight and only a few cars dispersed across the bridge ahead of them, Sue slammed her foot on the gas, pushing it even harder than before. The engine roared, accelerating quickly across the relatively straight road.

Sue smiled as she wove in and out of the light traffic, her adrenaline soaring as she glanced at their followers in the side mirror. To her delight and relief, they were gaining a significant lead on the black cars.

"Uh, Sue!" Lisa tapped her shoulder and pointed ahead. "Slow down! Cop ahead!"

For a moment, Sue considered the options. "If those guys back there catch us, we're dead. I'd rather take my chances."

"But Sue—"

"Relax, Leese," said Sue as they drew nearer. "I got a good feeling about this."

Sue's little blue sedan barreled across the causeway with the two black cars in tow. Approaching the cop car, Sue laid her hand squarely on the horn then pressed it in rapid succession for a few seconds as they whizzed past. Immediately, the tell-tale blue and red lights appeared atop the vehicle. The squad car veered out of its spot in the shoulder and took up the chase behind the two black cars just as they roared by.

"Wait," said Lisa, looking back again. "Is that—?"

"Officer Enrico Castillo," Sue grinned. "I'd recognize my brother anywhere."

Lisa's breaths of relief were short-lived, for a moment later she heard a loud *crack!* accompanied by the *plink!* of a metallic ricochet off the side of the car. Her mouth agape, the red-haired woman quickly craned her neck over the seat once more. *Crack-plink!*

Lisa ducked instinctively. "They're shooting at us, Sue!"

Sue clenched the steering wheel tighter and tried not to look back. "I can hear it," she muttered through deep breaths. "Just hang on! We're almost to the island."

Donna and Debra entered the next airlock with several chambers already behind them. Donna couldn't recall how many were left, but she hoped they were nearing the vault itself; the cassette tape filtering through the loosely-fitting headphones had maybe a minute-and-a-half—at most—left on its opening track.

This room had four of the heat sensors just like the last. While Debra hurried away, rotating through the digits for the next door's combination lock, Donna poised herself under the first sensor. With a quick crouch to wind up, she jumped and barely scraped the device with the tip of her finger. It turned to gold, glittering in the edge of the flash-light beams. Her headphones jiggled a bit, and Donna tried to adjust the pair with her forearm without touching them with her fingers.

*Good enough. Keep*—she gritted her teeth—*on*—

The voice crooned over the swelling, repetitive hook in Donna's ears.

Donna hurried to the next sensor, wound up for the leap, and pushed off from the ground with her fingers outstretched. To Donna, it seemed like it happened in slow motion. The heat sensor turned to gold as she fell back the few inches to the floor. The woman felt the headphones slipping off her head—yanked by the cassette player falling loose from her waist—and she reached out instinctively to grab them before they hit the ground. Donna hardly realized what she had done until she watched as the pair of foamy earmuff-like speakers became solid, malleable gold, along with their auxiliary cord. The tape player itself detached from the cord just before the gilding was complete, leaving only the speakerless device to continue spinning its wheels in silence while Donna held the shimmering remnants of the doctor's strategy.

Debra turned when she heard the sound of the tape recorder hitting the floor. She gaped at the scene. "Donna! What happened?"

"I-I don't know," she scrambled. "It slipped and I didn't think—"

"The song!" Debra reminded her, scooping up the fallen tape deck. "That was the only way we could tell the time remaining until the alarm kicks back on. Do you remember how much was left?"

"Um, a minute—or two? I can't remember."

"Pick up where it left off," she said quickly. "You know the song, right?"

Donna nodded as she closed her eyes to try and remember what came next. "Yeah, the entire final minute is sort of an infinite loop until it fades out and—"

"Sing it while we finish!" Debra ordered and pivoted back to finish what remained of the combination.

With a deep breath, the blonde woman began to mumble the chorus as Debra clicked the digits into place: "Keep up… dah dah dum, won't stop," she sang a little louder as she readied herself to jump toward the next heat sensor. "Do *not* stop."

# CHAPTER 28

"Keep up, uh, bet you won't stop," Donna fumbled through the words to the song. "Do not stop—"

Debra exhaled sharply. "A little quieter," she snapped. "Remember, I can't focus with music playing."

"Sorry," the blonde woman said, then lowered her voice as she continued. "Keep up. Better not stop—"

"Those aren't even the wo—oh, never mind!" She shook her head. "Just be quiet—and keep track of the time we have left, okay?"

Donna nodded and leaped toward the final heat sensor. *Keep going.* She touched it and it instantly became gold.

"Phew, that was a tough one," Debra exclaimed as she finally clicked the last piece of the combination into place. The door unlocked and she swung it open, revealing not another hallway but a larger, wider room lined with locked, sealed cabinets. "The vault," the secretary said with a smile.

"How much time left?"

"Uh," Donna scrambled. "A few more 'don't stops' before the instrumental part, I think?"

Debra ignored her answer as she studied the yellow paper from Dr. Lansing, looking up to compare his notes with the layout of the room. On the far side of the vault, the secretary noted a metallic, steel set of double doors. "I think the vials are in that fridge," she said, shining the light toward it.

"—'til we get it right," Donna sang softly and nodded.

"It's 'enough' not 'right'!" Debra rolled her eyes. "Let's get those vials and get out of here—fast."

With the vault door hanging open behind them, the two women slinked quickly across the room. Standing before the large refrigerator, Debra consulted the doctor's notes to type a four-digit code into the panel on the door. When she finished, Debra hit the *enter* key. But there was no click. No beep. Nothing.

At her side, Donna gave a look of grave concern. "What's wrong?"

Debra quickly glanced behind the fridge, then turned to Donna with eyes wide. "Good news is: the power's still out. Bad news is: we need it for the keypad to work."

"Can you make it work without it?"

"No time," Debra said, shaking her head furiously. "We need to be back in that corridor by the time the power comes back or we'll trip the alarm that's tied to the vault's door."

As defeat began to set in, Donna turned and began to look around the room. She couldn't give up. *Can't stop. Not now.*

*There has to be another way.*

Donna took a deep breath. She felt her fingers tingle again.

*Of course.* She glanced at the heavy door. "I've got an idea," Donna said, moving toward the fridge. "Gold is more malleable than steel right?"

Debra stepped back. "Uh, yeah, but—"

Before she could finish, Donna's fingers met the cold door. She quickly pulled away as a wave of gold swept out from the place she touched, enveloping the keypad, the door, and its hinges but stopping right as it met their hidden outermost edges. With care, Donna repeated this act for the second door of the fridge, only allowing her hand to meet the metal for a split second.

"Now what?" Debra asked when Donna stepped away from the gilded duo of doors.

Donna pointed to the doors; her instructions were simple. "Pull *hard!*"


*Crack-crack-ow!* As a pair of bullets fired from ahead of him, Castillo swerved around a civilian's beat-up coupe that was moving well below the speed limit. The young officer floored the gas pedal as soon as he had the pair of black cars in his sightlines again. There was something unusually familiar about one of them that he couldn't quite place. He noticed a large scrape along the side of the vehicle.

"Wait a minute," Castillo mumbled as he neared the pair. "No way!" It had to be true: one of the remaining black cars was the same vehicle from the bridge chase a few nights prior—the one from the small island parallel to the causeway upon which they now darted in and out of traffic. *The driver who tried to push us off the bridge!*

Castillo shook his head in disbelief as he pressed on, barreling closer to the mustachioed offender and his side-scraped black sedan. Ahead of the two black cars, Officer Castillo could see his sister Sue's small blue car, barely maintaining its lead as a few more gunshots fired off in its direction.

"First, you try to knock me off the bridge," the officer mumbled under his breath. "Now you shoot at my sister?" The cop car throttled toward the black sedan with surprising speed. Rico rolled down the windows, trying to ignore the deafening roar of three engines as the cars neared one another. Little by little, the squad car inched into the space between the two black cars.

Precariously riding halfway between lanes, Castillo glanced out the passenger side window. Not far beyond was the cool, glistening bay—its waters rippling with moonlight. But between the officer and the causeway railing: the scraped black sedan. Its driver held a gun out the window and fired toward Rico.

He ducked, then shouted through the open window. "*Nobody* shoots at my sister!"

Before the other driver could react, Castillo yanked his steering wheel clockwise, ramming the sides of the two cars into one another. Keeping his foot firm and steady on the gas pedal, the officer's car pushed the other—slowly—toward the thin railing: the only thing separating the sedan from the water below.

As the driver of the second black car realized what Castillo was doing, he and his passenger began firing at the cop car. With one final ram while ducking as low as he could, Castillo felt the sudden lack of resistance as the sedan—and its driver—tumbled toward the cold, dark, unforgiving waters of Biscayne Bay.

This allowed Castillo to widen the gap between him and his remaining assailant. Rico narrowly evaded a number of whizzing bullets. His side windows were gone by now, shattered into infinite pieces across the asphalt behind them. A new shot generated a rippling spider-web fracture across the front windshield, obscuring Castillo's view of the road and his sister's car. To his relief, he watched through a clear shard as the blue car veered toward the foot of the causeway and swerved down a narrow road.

*They're on the island,* he nodded. *But this isn't over yet.*

The cop car and the gunmen's vehicle were neck-in-neck, nearing the end of the causeway. The determined officer slammed on his brakes, forcing the black car to zoom past him. Then, when enough space had formed between the two vehicles, Castillo sunk his foot onto the gas pedal and kept on the car's tail. The man ahead in the passenger seat aimed a gun back at Rico and began firing at the squad car. Castillo swerved a bit, but continued to accelerate, reaching for his own sidearm.

The officer squinted, aimed low, and fired. *Crack-crack!* Two shots. One missed, while the other punctured the rear right tire. The driver of the black car gripped the steering wheel tight and pulled hard to avoid veering off the bridge like his predecessor. To Castillo's dismay, the vehicle continued forward at breakneck speed, somehow compensating for the crumpling back tire.

*Dangit. Worked before.*

He tried for the other tire, but the dark vehicle was gaining speed and maintaining an unpredictable side-to-side motion.

They wouldn't be able to drive like that for long, though, the officer knew. But they didn't need long; they were both leaving the causeway, following the same route as Sue's blue car, and now there was only a straight, short stretch to the southernmost tip of the island before they arrived at Pelican's headquarters.

In the cool night, Rico could now see the tower glittering in the distance, its glass-covered frame scintillating with reflections of the colorful city life below.

*Almost there. We can make it. We* have *to make it.*

Marcus held Angela's hand as they felt their way through a dark hall. He hoped the woman couldn't sense his elevated pulse—that she wouldn't see through the ruse of his feigned interest in her. Those things seemed far from the woman's mind, Marcus concluded, as Angela released his hand, fumbled with a set of keys, inserted one into the shadowy door, and pushed through into another dark chamber.

"I suppose there couldn't be any flashlights lying around, could there?" The officer quipped quietly. The only light in the room came through a small window at the far wall.

"Power should be back any minute now," Angela assured him. She shuffled her way across the room, navigating around the bulky shadows of what appeared to be desks and monitors of some sort. The room was warmer than the hall, leading Marcus to infer that this space housed important electronics rendered inert by the power outage.

Marcus froze, hearing a deep *thump* from somewhere within the walls. Then a dozen clicks and beeps sounded off in near-unison as a dim overhead light flickered on. The officer covered his eyes to adjust to the light, then surveyed the newly-lit room through his fingers.

Angela gave a sigh of relief. "See?"

The space was filled with desks, upon which sat bulky computers. One wall of the room was entirely devoted to small television screens, which began to cycle from black to static to images of what appeared to be live footage from around the building.

One of the last pieces of technology to boot up was a panel on the wall which consisted of a small rectangular interface and a single large siren-like bulb in a plexiglass casing. Immediately, this began to flash red.

"I knew it," Angela muttered, hurrying toward the wall of screens.

Marcus tailed closely. "What is it?"

"Silent alarm's been tripped," she pointed toward the red flash. "There's someone unauthorized in the vault. And I'll bet I know who." Angela mumbled with obvious irritation, bouncing her attention between a few of the security screens as if looking for something specific. "They finally got these cameras up and running," she added.

Angela's gaze fell on one screen which seemed to show a man waiting for an elevator. She leaned in closer. "Roger. I knew it." She nodded. "But if you're on the lower levels—" she spoke as if the doctor could hear her, then continued scanning across the vast wall, "—then who's in the vault?"

Both Angela and Marcus saw the small boxy screen at the same time. The grainy black and white footage showed two women—one struggling to yank and bend a large metallic door while the other stood close by. Marcus recognized the second woman immediately and his heart sank: *Donna!*

"Oh, look," said Angela with a devious smirk. "It's your little ex-girlfriend."

Strangely, Marcus noted, Angela didn't seem particularly surprised. *What does she know?*

Angela studied the image for a moment longer, then pivoted and marched toward the door.

"Where are you going?" The nervous officer called out, starting after her.

"She intends to steal something that belongs to me," Angela said with her brow arched. "I'm not going to let that happen." The woman nodded toward the door as she reached it. "Are you coming?"

With a deep breath, Marcus agreed and followed quickly as the two hurried back into the hall. Angela sauntered with determination toward the elevator and slammed the button with her finger. Marcus gulped as they waited, Angela tapping the toe of her shoe on the venous tile floor.

*Not good,* Marcus thought. *Donna—you better have a good reason for what you're doing here.* The elevator doors chimed and swung open.

# CHAPTER 29

Donna watched as Debra pulled hard on the golden refrigerator doors. The lock and keypad were situated in such a way as to link both of the dual doors together, but the gold was starting to bend and budge.

"You can do this," Donna urged from a few feet away. She didn't dare touch the fridge any longer and risk transforming the secretary or the vials behind the doors into gold, too. "I think you're making progress." She wasn't so sure, but it was a nice sentiment.

Suddenly, the women heard a loud thumping noise within the walls. The lights flickered on above them, casting a bluish-purple glow over the room. Donna whipped around in horror as she watched the vault door shut by some mechanical automation.

"Oh, no," Debra said, shaking her head. "Power's back!"

"Did we trip the alarm?" Donna's eyes were wide as she

began to pace around the now-illuminated space.

"I don't know!" The secretary snapped, still trying to yank the doors open. "But you turned the keypad to gold and this isn't working—gold isn't *that* malleable!"

Donna became defensive. "How was I supposed to know that?"

"I tried to tell you!"

"Sorry! I really didn't think that through—"

Both women tensed. Donna began to wiggle her fingers to stretch them out, as she didn't think it wise to clench them. *We have to get this open. For Starla.* As she began to pace the room, something caught her eye. Donna pointed and shouted: "Try that!"

Debra's eyes followed the gesture to a fire extinguisher mounted on the wall. The woman shook her head but realized there was no other viable option at the moment. With a quick puff, Debra hurried to grab it, unlatching it from its nesting place, then ran at the fridge door. "Hope this works!" She shouted. A moment later the heavy extinguisher met the solid gold keypad latch with a *cling!*

To the surprise of both women, the latch ripped straight off the fridge doors, leaving only golden screw holes to show where it had once been mounted.

"Did that do it?" Donna moved closer.

Debra set down the extinguisher and then grabbed one of the doors. "I think so," she said as she managed to pry it open slowly.

A cool, breathy mist emanated from within the fridge as

the door was opened. Inside, Donna could see rows and rows of vials, all identically packaged and stored with only a label to differentiate each from the ones beside it.

Donna had a glimmer of hope.

"Which ones are the antidote?"

Debra scrambled for the yellow paper again and read its instructions, then ran her finger along one of the wire shelves. A series of small nameplates separated batches by row and group.

Instinctively, Donna looked back toward the vault door. The woman thought she'd heard something—some move-ment—beyond it, but she convinced herself it was just her imagination.

As Donna turned back to the half-open fridge, Debra shouted: "Found 'em!" The secretary carefully removed two matching glass vials from an upper shelf. The liquid inside was clear and viscous as she held them up for Donna to see for herself.

"One for me," Donna affirmed. "And one for Starla."

Suddenly, they heard a deep latch-click behind them. The two women whipped around to watch as the door to the vault inched open. In the light of the corridor beyond, Donna immediately recognized the outlines of three figures: Marcus and Angela, with Dr. Lansing trembling at her side.

Donna exclaimed, "Marcus?"

"Donna—" he nodded.

"Doctor!" Debra's eyes were wide, as if she was caught red-handed wielding the vials.

Angela nearly gasped. "Debra! I didn't expect to find *you* working with these pathetic interlopers." The woman nudged Roger forward into the vault. Marcus remained at her side as they stepped over the threshold.

"Oh, ladies," the doctor tried to avert his eyes—a look of shame and defeat. "I'm so sorry. They intercepted me before I could warn you—"

"Quiet, Roger!" Angela snapped, then turned toward the pair of women who stood near the fridge. With a commanding and inquisitive posture, the woman inspected the intruders. "What *are* you looking for up here, anyway? Perhaps a certain compound connected to your new... powers?"

Donna tried not to let her gaze drift to Debra's hands, which were poised and trembling behind her back—a vial in each. Instead, the blonde woman's attention moved to her preternatural ability.

"Not going to tell me?" Angela sauntered toward them slowly. Marcus kept close.

*I could use it—I could touch her and this would all be over.* Donna actually considered it for a moment. *But if we have both of the vials of the antidote—the only in existence—transforming her to gold would be no less than a death sentence.*

"I know you're hiding something." A step closer. Angela reached toward her side.

Donna bit her lip. *No. I can't—I could never take a life like that—not on purpose. Not after what happened to Starla...*

As Angela finally stood before Donna, within arm's reach, the intimidating woman swiftly produced a compact blade from within the folds of her red dress. Debra shrieked, almost releasing her grip on the precious items she held behind her back. Donna immediately reconsidered her thoughts: *Self-defense? Now that's another story. Isn't it?*

Before she could make up her mind, Donna heard a click. Marcus whipped out a small handgun and held it up, pointing at Angela.

"M-Marcus!" She stammered. "What on earth—?"

"Don't touch her," he said through gritted teeth, gripping the gun with both hands. "Don't lay a finger on Donna—or the other one."

The secretary forced a labored smile. "Th-thank you—it's Debra," she muttered sheepishly.

"Or what?" Angela's fear turned quickly to amusement. As she noticed Debra's obscured hands, she inched toward her, still holding out the knife. When she was near enough, she pointed the knife toward the secretary. "Well? Show us what you've got."

With trepidation, the woman moved her hands from behind her back, revealing the twin vials to Angela and the other onlookers. Quickly, Angela snatched one of the vials from her hand, then pointed the knife at the other. Debra reluctantly handed it over, with Angela holding it and the compact knife in the same grip.

"Let's see," Angela mumbled as she read the label to herself. She let out a disingenuous chuckle. "You aren't trying to create more of your power after all—you're trying to erase it." Angela stared Donna down, as if waiting for her verification of the claims, then stepped closer and added in a taunting whisper, "Oh, I see. Something happen to your little girl, hmm?"

Marcus tightened his grip on the gun but held his ground.

Donna swallowed. "Please! You have no idea what we've been through—"

"So it's true," Angela smiled. "She's all the evidence I need to stick the landing with the board tomorrow. With any luck, we've already got her." As she delighted in Donna's look of horror, Angela's eyes drifted to one of the vials. Then, in a sudden, unexpected motion, the towering woman threw the vial to the ground, where it shattered just a few feet away from them.

*No!*

Donna held her mouth agape, instinctively reaching out toward the spilled liquid.

"The antidote!" Debra shouted, lurching forward slightly before stepping back at her recollection of the weapon in Angela's hand. Debra adjusted her large bag so that it sat less intrusively at her side. Some of its contents pressed uncomfortably against her body, so the secretary stuck her hand in to rearrange.

Donna couldn't speak. It was too late now. There was no way they could recover the lost contents of the vial.

"Angie, you're a wicked, wicked *witch!*" Dr. Lansing exclaimed from behind Marcus.

Angela twirled the remaining vial as she gripped her blade with the other hand. "I'm just a woman trying to make it a man's world." She shook her head, then stepped away from Donna. "Sometimes we have to make choices—*hard* choices—so that we aren't left in the dust."

"How could you?" Donna shook her head in disbelief. She eyed the second vial. "Please, Angela! Let me have the antidote!"

"You have a choice to make, Miss Locke," Angela taunted, moving toward Marcus and his gun as she spoke. "Option A: Cure yourself of the power to turn anything you touch to gold—why anyone would give that up is beyond me. Or there's Option B: Save your little girl." She pivoted next to Marcus and faced Donna once more. "You've turned her to gold, haven't you?"

Donna didn't answer. A single tear formed at the corner of her eye and started to snake down the side of her nose.

Seeing Donna's dilemma, Marcus made a swift movement and brought the barrel of his firearm to Angela's neck.

"You shoot me and I'll drop the other one, too," Angela said hastily, flourishing the second vial of the antidote.

Marcus took a deep breath, then recalculated his next move. "You used me to get close to Donna?"

Angela played dumb. "Who, me? I'm just an incompetent businesswoman. I would never." She cackled. "And *you're* one to talk, Marcus! What is it you've used *me* for?"

He didn't like when people called his bluff. Marcus took a deep breath, then lowered the gun for a brief moment as he fished for something in his pocket. Angela raised a curious eyebrow as she waited, then watched as the officer withdrew a small fragment of paper and held it up.

"Did you write this?" Marcus shoved it toward her.

It was a small, hand-scribbled note, written on a half-ripped piece of paper. A fraction of the Pelican logo adorned one corner. The note read:

*Sure about S.G.? Awaiting update.*

It was the slip of paper that Rico had swiped from Vander Newport's dresser. Angela studied it with a look that indicated to Marcus that she had never seen it before. Either that or she was really good at faking it.

"Did you? Did you write it?" He pressed it closer.

"What's S.G.?" Angela said, with a genuine lack of comprehension. "Is that a person?"

"That's not what I asked." Marcus held his gun up beside the note. "*Someone* inside Pelican wrote this."

Angela, flustered, spouted back, "I don't understand—"

"*Vander Newport*," Marcus clarified. "You were working with him, weren't you? Someone from Pelican wrote this. It was found in his things."

The woman, her hands held up with the knife and vial, finally began to crack. "Alright," she nodded. "Yes, I was working with Vander. I already told you he was a family friend. I knew we were on to something with this experiment—and I was right, it seems—but the funds from Pelican were drying up. Roger here provided the brains; Vander provided the capital we needed to keep going."

"Capital?" Marcus puffed with amusement. "You mean his profits from upselling smuggled drugs?"

"Who was I to question the generosity of a friend?" Angela said defensively. "Wouldn't you do the same?"

Marcus didn't entertain the thought. "But you knew," he leaned in. "Didn't you?"

The woman looked away, the tell-tale sign of someone mulling over a new lie, then turned back to the officer. "I had an inkling, yes."

Roger spoke up: "So forcing me to bypass numerous ethical standards and reviews wasn't your only transgression against the law."

"I did what I had to, Roger," she snapped. "Why should I be the one to blame that *you* hung on my every word?"

Marcus returned his attention to the slip of paper, which he thrust toward Angela once more. "So did you—or did you *not*—write these words?"

Angela shook her head, puzzled. "No, Marcus, I didn't— that's not my handwriting—I'm sorry—"

Roger, Debra, and Donna weren't sure what was happening, or why the officer thought that *this* was the moment to interrogate the woman threatening them with a knife and who held the promise of destroying any chance of a cure to the detrimental effects of Pelican's experiment.

With a deep sigh, Marcus moved toward Donna and showed her the note, lowering his gun slightly.

"Marcus, what is this?"

"S.G.: I think it's about your sister," he said softly. "You

were right—someone's after her. Someone inside Pelican—
higher up, maybe. I'll find them—don't worry."

Donna, already rattled by the night's series of shock-in-
ducing events, quavered and nodded. "Thank you, Marcus."
She averted her gaze, then, with fresh tears forming, looked
him in the eyes. The rest of the room seemed to disappear
for the briefest moment. "Marcus, I need you to know that
I'm sorry," she whispered. "I shouldn't have let you go. I-I—"
She stammered and stumbled over her words. "I love you,
Marcus."

He nodded and gave a gentle, comforting smile back. "I
love you, too, Donna Locke."

Out of the corner of her eye, Donna saw Angela take a
step forward—toward Marcus. The young officer seemed
entranced by Donna's vulnerability and beauty and made an
instinctive move to reach for her hand. She started to extend
her fingers toward him, but caught herself, sensing the faint
tingle that reminded her of her powers.

Before either of the pair could realize what was happening, Marcus felt a sharp force at his back—a firm thrust from
Angela. He lost his balance and stumbled toward Donna.
She reached out her hand to break his fall, to steady him.
That was the moment in which she knew she'd made a grave
mistake. Her fingers touched his chest—it was an accident.
Donna recoiled, but it was too late. She watched as Marcus'
clothing and his smooth skin became hard, solid gold—a
statue—immobile, there in the middle of the wide vault. His
gun clattered to the floor just before the gilding extended to

his fingers.

Donna gasped. "Marcus—!" It was all she could muster as she took a few slow steps away from him. The golden man was suspended, frozen. Just like Starla.

Finally, Donna's focus expanded to the rest of the room and her eyes met Angela's. She had deliberately shoved the man Donna loved right into her cursed hands.

"May I present Option C," Angela scowled. "Use the last of this compound to save the man you love."

Donna couldn't speak. Her mind was racing—part shock, part fury.

Angela stepped backward slowly. "No answer? Perhaps I can narrow it down for you. Heads up, Roger." In a dizzying blur of motion, the woman tossed the vial toward the doctor, who fumbled forward to catch it, while Angela took another step back toward the wall. Roger dove and grasped the glass vial just before it reached the floor while Angela opened a hidden compartment in the wall and quickly withdrew something resembling a compact gas mask. "I've got everything I need now," she smirked. "He's mine. Good luck, Goldie."

Inside the compartment in the wall was a glowing keypad. Angela placed the mask over her face, pressed a large square button, and, immediately, the sound of rushing air filled the room. It was at this moment that Donna noticed a series of vents lining the bottoms of the vault's walls, through which a cloudy, gaseous substance materialized.

"I'd get out of here if I were you," Angela suggested in a mask-muffled taunt.

Dr. Lansing's eyes grew wide. "We have to go! This gas will knock us out for hours." He took a deep breath and sealed his lips.

Debra hurried toward him while Donna turned back to Marcus, seemingly in denial about his untimely transformation. "I can't leave him—not again."

"Miss Locke, please!" The doctor urged, already stepping toward the vault door with the secretary in tow.

Donna placed her hands toward Marcus but stopped short of touching him. *Marcus, I'm so sorry. I promise I'll fix this—I promise I'll find a way.*

"Donna!" Debra shouted over the misting gas that was now grabbing at their ankles.

*Angela! She's gonna pay for this,* Donna vowed. But as the woman took another look around the room, she could no longer see Angela—the mist had grown thick. With a quick breath, Donna relented and finally ran to join the doctor and Debra.

The ensuing journey through the corridors to the elevator was a blur filled with flashing red alarm lights. Angela had vanished. A foggy film covered Donna's puffy eyes, but she dared not wipe them with her hands. She attempted to clear her vision using her forearm, but this only exacerbated the issue.

Finally, the elevator arrived. The trio piled in, the siren-lights blinking harshly but quietly. Donna collapsed to the floor in a crumpled heap, resting her arms on folded knees, and, at last, began to sob. Though they desired so badly to comfort her, neither Roger nor Debra dared risk the effects of the deadly golden touch.

"I'm so sorry, Donna," was all Roger could muster as he stooped to her level.

When they arrived at the ground floor, the elevator doors swooshed open. Here the alarm now produced a grating beep that pierced the ears of the weary three. They hurried toward the glass doors. A pair of security guards tried to intercept them but relented when a police officer waved them off, having just pulled up to the entrance. Donna looked up long enough to recognize his familiar face.

"Rico!" She exclaimed, then began to cry again and buried her face in the crux of her arm. Castillo moved to embrace her, but the doctor motioned for him to keep his distance.

"What happened?" The officer asked Roger and Debra, dumbfounded.

Roger tried to briefly explain their secretive mission and the unbelievable circumstances that surrounded Donna's powers. "But we've got the antidote," he concluded, holding up the glass vial. "This can begin to make things right."

Debra stepped forward and fished into her bag. "And we've got *this*," she said, holding out the cassette tape record-er. "It might be helpful, officer. Got the whole thing on tape." The secretary gave a half-smile, proud of her own ingenuity. She ejected the tape.

Castillo thanked her and received the tape gratefully. At that moment, a pair of voices called out behind him, running up the driveway to the building.

"Don! Donna! Are you okay?"

Donna looked up with a teary gaze; it was Sue and Lisa.

She cracked a soft smile, but her expression quickly became somber. "Sue. Lisa. Where's Starla?"

"Don't worry," said Lisa. "She's safe—she's in the car." Lisa pointed to Sue's little blue car, one side covered in bullet holes and most of its windows shattered.

Donna hurried toward the beat-up vehicle and leaned her head into the backseat. She took a deep breath. There was Starla, draped across the cushions. Her golden girl.

Dr. Lansing appeared quietly behind Donna. "Have you made your decision, Miss Locke? How you'll use the last of the antidote?"

Donna turned to him. "You're sure it's the last?"

"The formula is the property of Pelican now and the ingredients are too rare and too expensive to acquire on my own. It could take months—*years*, even—for me to recreate, unfortunately—and a fully-equipped lab. So, *yes*," he nodded. "I'm afraid this is the last of it. For now."

*Starla. My Starla.* Even in gold, the girl's face was sweet and kind. Precious. Innocent. *But how can I live with this and risk ruining more innocent lives—even if it's by accident?* Donna examined her hands—those extremities which held the power of life and death.

"What do you say we get you home?" The doctor suggested. "Give you a little more time to think."

Donna agreed. While Castillo made a call for a squad to investigate the night's events, the rest of the party piled into the pair of heavily-battered vehicles. Donna took Sue's front passenger seat as they finally drove off, the weary woman watching the blaring lights and alarms of Pelican Innovations disappear in the rearview.

*Marcus,* she thought. *Will I ever see you again—will we ever touch again?* She craned her neck to look once more on Starla's sparkling, motionless face in the back seat. Soon they'd be back home. Safe, but not the same. Donna's eyelids began to droop as the car whisked through the humid night.

# CHAPTER 30

All Donna saw was red. Dark red. Vivid light shining its way through her closed eyelids. She opened her eyes, then closed them again quickly, faced with garish, oppressive sunlight beaming through the front window. Slowly, she adjusted to the late morning light and leaned herself up onto the arm of her pink couch, yawning expansively.

For a moment, the woman just sat there, her blonde hair a tangled mess. She didn't remember much about the day and night before—how she got here; how she'd changed clothes. But there were two images that couldn't escape from her memory no matter how hard she tried to shake them: *Marcus and Starla.* The uncanny touch that scarred her thoughts permanently. Both accidents. Unavoidable. Out of her control. She would do anything in her power to stop that from happening ever again.

She remembered the singular vial of antidote. The last

thing that occurred before she drifted off to sleep. Now it was coming back to her: the choice between saving Starla and curing herself for good—the latter of which might, in essence, proactively prevent another horrific repeat of the fate of her niece and her love. It was the hardest choice she'd ever made.

As she sat on the rosy couch, the light danced around her sun-kissed legs. Donna softly danced her hands and fingers through the glowing, ethereal beams. Something was different. *The tingling.* She twirled her hand. *It's gone.*

Donna sunk her head then breathed deeply. Examining the coffee table before her, she scanned it until her eyes landed on the television remote. Slowly, she reached out for it, extending her delicate fingers until they hovered just above it. Then, with another deep inhale, Donna lowered her fingers to rest on the grayish remote.

*Nothing.* No gold. No tingling. No queasy feeling. Donna exhaled.

Suddenly, a playful voice called out from the back room: "Good morning, Aunt Donna!"

*Starla?* Donna started. *This has to be a dream.*

Hesitantly, the woman bent around over the low back of the couch. She glanced down the hall but saw no one. She heard sock-covered footsteps that sounded small and dainty. Then, suddenly, a smiling, freckled face appeared, jumping up from behind the sofa—an extreme close-up full of misty, oily child breath. Donna had never been so happy to experience such sensations in her life. It was Starla—living, breathing Starla.

For the first time in days, Donna smiled with her whole body, a loose, free feeling coming over her as the girl rounded the furniture and leaped onto her half-prone aunt. Donna exploded with laughter, then shoved a pair of tickling hands under the girl's armpits. As the child giggled with delight, Donna started to cough. Her throat felt dry. No—she was thirsty.

*Of course.*

"Just a minute, kiddo," Donna said as she rose and moved toward the kitchen. As she opened the cabinet full of glasses, she paused and realized there would come a day when she'd have to explain to the girl what happened. *Someday. Not today. Today is for us—to be together as a family again.* She reached into the cabinet.

A loud knock on the front door startled Donna. She carefully placed the empty glass on the counter and moved to the door. "Who's there?" She squinted through the peephole and motioned for Starla to move away from the window.

"Metro-Dade police," replied a deep, somber voice.

Frightened, Donna unlatched the lock and cracked open the door. To her relief, the guest was smiling. It was Castillo, accompanied by two others: Lisa and Sue.

"Sorry, Donna, I had to," Rico joked.

Donna shook her head and threw her arms around the officer. "Thanks for coming," she whispered then let go and stepped back to embrace her girlfriends. They waved at Starla through the crack in the door and the girl ran to hug each of the women in turn.

When the girl had scurried back inside, Castillo became serious. "I've got some bad news, Donna," he said.

She covered her mouth. Donna knew what was coming, but she had to hear him say it.

"There's been no sign of Marcus since last night," he said quietly, his head low. "Our people got there and searched the place—even got access to that vault—but they couldn't find him. He's gone."

Donna shook her head. "And Angela?"

"Gone, too." Sue chimed.

"That doesn't make sense," Donna muttered. "She needed one of us for some *board meeting*—to prove that their experiments worked. I just—" She sniveled and wiped a trickle of tears from her cheek. "I need to find him."

"I promise you," Castillo continued. "I want to find him, too. He was my partner. We'll do everything we can." A thought seemed to come to him, and the officer reached for his pocket. "Oh, almost forgot." He withdrew a small cassette tape: a Michael Jackson album. "Your secretary friend got everything on tape. We analyzed it right away and had the evidence we needed to search the home of a wealthy businessman called Vander Newport. Turns out, our suspicions were true: Angela reaped the benefits of a smuggling supply chain with Newport—and his butler—at the center of it all. Our search turned up supply logs, manifests, a missing vehicle, and a few contraband samples."

"They got him!" Lisa interjected.

Donna cocked her head. "Already?"

"He's behind bars and the trial's next week," Castillo nodded.

"What about Roger—Dr. Lansing, I mean?" Donna's face expressed genuine concern and care for the man who had turned out to be quite kind to her.

"Don't worry," the officer said. "Miss Hyde's near-confession of forcing and coercing the doctor to violate numerous ethical standards was caught on tape, too. He'll have a hearing, but it's likely he'll be cleared of anything serious."

Donna felt her shoulders loosen ever so slightly.

"Here," Castillo concluded. "Take the tape. We've got our own copy, but I figure you'd appreciate hearing the other voice on there."

The woman thanked him and received the gift, then exchanged another round of long hugs.

"You gonna make it, Don?" Sue asked, concerned. "What with the golden touch and everything?"

Lisa leaned in: "And what about Starla? Does she, ya know, *know* what happened?"

"Not yet. But I'll tell her—soon," Donna said, inspecting the tape in her hands. "I guess I'll just have to take this one day at a time—to be more careful. I'll learn to master it. That's what people with superpowers do, right?" Donna smirked.

"Just take care of our girl, okay?" Lisa added, nodding toward Starla who played inside the apartment.

"That's the only thing that matters to me right now," Donna answered confidently. Then, softer, added, "That and finding Marcus."

"Keep your chin up, Don," urged Sue.

Donna smiled and thanked them again. They turned and disappeared down the open-air walkway. As Donna closed the door, she heard another voice call out.

"Miss Locke!"

Cautiously, Donna peered around the threshold. She relaxed when she saw that it was Dr. Lansing.

"Good morning, Miss Locke!" He greeted her eagerly with an outstretched hand, then started to pull it away.

"It's okay," Donna assured him, extending her own toward it.

To quell the doctor's fears, Donna held out the cassette tape in her other hand to show the man that it had retained its normal qualities. "Not gold." Satisfied, Roger cautiously shook Donna's hand.

"You must be quite parched," the doctor noted.

"A small sacrifice to be able to hug my girl again," Donna exhaled deeply, then motioned for him to peer inside the doorway to see Starla. The little girl waved; her freckled smile was contagious. "Thank you again for the sacrifices you made," Donna continued. "I know it wasn't an easy choice to make. Helping me, I mean."

Dr. Lansing inhaled sharply. "While it's true that I'm out of a job, I have to say it was worth it. I wouldn't want to work for that company anymore anyway. There's some shady business going on."

"You mean Pelican is still going to keep operating?" The

thought made Donna stagger. "As if nothing ever happened?"

"Pelican's got money," the doctor said in a defeated tone. "Though, not in the places it should be going. They'll keep this story quiet just like the last one. And the one before that. They're not going anywhere, unfortunately."

A cool breeze ruffled the palms just outside the apartment—signs of life on that particular spring morning.

"Doctor," Donna began, her face creased in thought. "Last night, you said that I was, um, *special*—that all of this happened because my blood was *different*. What did you mean by that?"

Roger appeared uncomfortable with the inquiry and stumbled over his words. "I-uh," he started. "I'm not sure exactly, to be honest, other than that the experiment yielded far different results with you than any other patient." Donna tried to make sense of it as he continued. "I'd have to do some more in-depth testing. Perhaps once I get back on my feet we can get you into the lab—well, once I find a new one—and I'll see what I can do."

"S-sure," Donna nodded.

"Well, Miss Locke," Roger said more confidently. "I just wanted to drop by to make sure Starla was healing well and to tell you in person that I will give my everything to try and replicate an antidote. We'll fix you and your precious Marcus. We'll find a way, Donna. Some day soon."

"Thank you for everything, Roger." She smiled.

The two bid farewell and Donna returned to Starla inside the apartment.

"Why are all these people here so early?" Starla wondered aloud, half-occupied with a set of plastic figurines on the floor.

"Just friends checking in," Donna answered, looking down at the tape Castillo had given her. "That's what friends do." Clutching the tape close to her chest, Donna moved toward a hall closet. "What do you say I make us some breakfast soon?"

"Eggs! No pepper!" Starla hollered.

Donna chuckled as she rifled through a basket of items until she found a walkman with headphones plugged in. "No pepper—you got it," she replied. "Just give me a minute and I'll get it going."

Cassette tape and player in hand, the woman went into the bathroom and shut the door, then sat on the closed lid of her golden toilet. Donna carefully placed the tape in the deck, shut its plastic door, and slung the headphones over her ears. As she hit *play*, she heard loud crunching sounds and static. Then the voices began.

"Did you write it?" It was Marcus.

Angela's voice replied: "What's S.G.? Is that a person?"

"That's not what I asked. *Someone* inside Pelican wrote this."

"I don't understand—"

"*Vander Newport.* You were working with him, weren't you? Someone from Pelican wrote this. It was found in his things."

Donna recalled the moment, fast-forwarded the tape a bit, then hit play.

Her own voice spoke through the headphones now: "Marcus, what is this?"

"S.G.," Marcus answered, referring to the slip of paper. "I think it's about your sister. You were right—someone's after her. Someone inside Pelican—higher up, maybe. I'll find them—don't worry."

"Thank you, Marcus. Marcus, I need you to know that I'm sorry. I shouldn't have let you go. I-I—" The anticipation of the coming moments caused Donna to instinctively tense as tears welled up in her eyes. "I love you, Marcus."

Then, his deep, comforting voice: "I love you, too, Donna Locke."

There was a brief scuffle, then a strange warping sound in the static before Donna heard herself shriek: "Marcus—!" Donna slammed the button on the player to stop the tape. She took deep breaths and allowed her tears to flow. She could see the moment in her mind. The kindness in his eyes. Their connection...

Donna yanked off the headphones and returned to the other room, wiping her face with the sleeve of her shirt. "Alright," she said when she saw Starla. "Who's ready for some eggs?"

Donna began the preparations for breakfast. The pan sizzled as she cracked a few eggs and tossed the shells into the trash. While the meal was heating up, Donna reached for the phone and dialed the number for the hospital.

Someone picked up after a couple of rings.

"Hi, my name is Donna Locke and I'm just calling to check in on my sister—Sondra Gordon."

The woman on the other end told her to wait a minute.

When she returned, Donna could sense a seriousness in her tone. "No change in her condition, unfortunately."

"Oh," Donna lowered her voice.

"Miss Locke, sometimes these types of things can last for some time." The woman said softly. "I don't mean to be a downer, but we're giving her the best care possible. You should prepare for the long haul."

"Alright," was all Donna could think to say.

The receptionist added her usual spiel: "We'll let you know if anything—"

"—if anything changes with her status—I remember." Donna thanked the woman and hung up. She took a deep breath, then served up the eggs onto two plates. "Ready!"

Starla hurried over to the counter and inspected her plate. "No pepper?"

"No pepper," Donna affirmed with a smirk. "Just the way you like it, kiddo."

As the two began to eat, Starla threw her fork down and pushed off from the counter. "Oh! Aunt Donna, I forgot I had something to show you!" The girl ran across the room toward her backpack and began fishing through it.

A moment later, the girl returned waving a sheet of paper and used some of the few magnets Donna had on her refrigerator to pin it up for the woman to see. It was a rudimentary crayon drawing depicting three characters—slightly more refined than stick figures.

Starla stood next to it proudly and began to point at the figures: "That's me, that's my mom," then, at last, "and that's you, Aunt Donna. It's me and the people I care about most—our little family."

Donna fought back another wave of tears, inhaling slowly. She forced a half-smile. "That's very special, Starla," Donna said softly. "I love it." The woman crouched to Starla's level and extended her arms: "Come here, kiddo."

There in the middle of the kitchen, Starla leaped eagerly into Donna's arms, where the woman squeezed the girl tight. Donna ran her fingers through the girl's thick, reddish hair and closed her eyes. She didn't want to ever let go.

As Donna opened her eyes, she inspected the drawing once more over the girl's shoulder. The round faces. The crayon lines scribbled this way and that to add texture. The girl's initials in the bottom corner. Donna suddenly tightened her grip on the girl.

*The initials!*

At the edge of the paper, Starla had drawn the outline of a five-pointed star and, inside it, her initials: S.G.

*Starla Gordon.*

Whoever it was that had written the note about which Marcus had told Donna—maybe they weren't after Sondra at all. *They were looking for Starla!*

*No.* Donna tried to push the thought from her mind, but it lingered. *Someone is watching one of them—my family. And if Angela didn't know about it, then who was it? What do they want?*

As Donna released Starla from her embrace, the two looked at the drawing again.

"We can make it like our own art gallery," Starla suggested.

"One drawing hardly makes this a gallery," Donna shot back.

Starla didn't reply. Instead, she hurried off toward the living room again. She returned holding two small, squarish items in her hands: a pair of Polaroid pictures. The girl grabbed a magnet for each and placed them next to the drawing.

The girl looked on in pride. "*Now* it's a gallery!"

Donna pulled the girl close again. "Yes," she replied softly. "Yes, it is."

In the dancing morning light of the kitchen, their gazes rested on the photos. The first was Starla, frozen in a moment of joyful laughter; the other was the first picture of the pair together: Donna and Starla—an unlikely duo. Far from normal, but truly and undeniably the thing for which Donna had long yearned—something worth caring for, living for.

A family.

The story continues in
*The Dream Team*
*A Magic City Wonders Novel*
(Coming in 2023)


If you enjoyed *Goldie*,
would you be so kind as to leave
a review for it on Amazon or your
preferred book vendor's website?
Every review helps my books
get found by new readers!

Thank you for reading,
- Taylor

## ABOUT THE AUTHOR

Taylor Thomas Smythe is a native of West Palm Beach, Florida, which has been a source of inspiration for a variety of his creative works. In 2019, Taylor released the first installment in his acclaimed *Kingdom of Florida* middle-grade fantasy series, which was a silver-medal winner in the Florida Authors and Publishers Association President's Book Awards and a finalist in the National Indie Excellence Awards. The seventh and final book in the series was released in 2021. Taylor enjoys creative writing of all kinds and topics, but he especially likes to write stories about imaginative places and secret, magical worlds.

*Visit* ttsmythe.com *for more from Taylor Thomas Smythe.*

CPSIA information can be obtained
at www.ICGtesting.com
Printed in the USA
JSHW020954121122
32234JS00006B/23/J